The Wildflower of Assam

GAYATRI SARKAR

Book Cover by - Tsign Studio

First edition 2025

Author Website : www.gayatrisarkar.com.au

Samb Sadashiv!

Author's Notes

I ndia's history is layered. It is not just the British rule, the unfair partition of the country, and the consequent sufferings. It is also about the delayed realisation of unity, the power each of us holds, and the need to let women lead in whatever capacity they could. Behind every riot, clash, and conflict lies a silent buildup of societal pressure, long-standing marginalisation, inconsistent government support, and, most importantly, unspoken suffering. In most riots, women and children formed the majority of victims. Men, with greater physical strength, often managed to escape. While women, perceived as weaker, were targeted first. The act of raping women and girls was treated as a display of dominance, especially when women of the enemy's community were attacked.

The Wildflower of Assam portrays these struggles, the suffering of women in a world ruled by men, where decisions were made for them and their voices were silenced. Rape was not the only injustice they endured; they faced disrespect, constant ill-treatment, polygamy, character as-

sassination, lack of freedom, and relentless judgement –
even from other women. Many of these realities remain
unchanged today.

Set against the societal tensions and political upheavals of
mid–1900s Assam, this story is not about assigning blame
but about bearing witness. It seeks to show life as it was and
how people navigated those storms. Above all, it is a tribute
to the quiet strength of women whose existence was often
taken for granted — and a reminder that feminism is not
opposition, but an opportunity for women to learn, choose,
and lead.

To every woman who has bloomed despite being buried —
this story is yours.

Gayatri Sarkar

AGHA

EARLY 1979

I t is a day in summer, and the big rocks on the riverbank are warm enough to sit on. Tree leaves are dry. The bark is shrunk. The sky is clear, and the wind is still. Kopili is more beautiful than anything else in Matiparbat. How much I admire this river only *Allah* can tell! It is my stress reliever. Only here do I breathe the air of freedom. Whenever I am in a bad mood, I come to Kopili. Why is she so peaceful? I ask myself. Because she has no family. Because she has no one around. Because she is alone. Because she is doing what she likes. She is free.

I should go home as the sun has descended, but the river is intriguing. And back home, the room is too small for six people. I hate evenings when everyone is home. I keep my head down, do household chores, and sleep. A thought about the dinner strikes me, and I drag myself back to this view. I am pretty sure that dinner would be rice and left-over curry. I have seen this in the movies where rich people have kitchens stuffed with fruits, chicken curry, duck curry, *roti*, and whatnot. I have considered breaking into the kitchen of that huge bungalow on the way to Kopili from my home and eating all the food there. But that is something I am not comfortable doing, as it is not a permanent solution. I don't like dinner or lunch-I can't break into someone else's house twice each day. I have pushed up the sleeves of my kurta as I am sweating. My *burqa* and loose hair trouble me in the summer. There are birds, trees and mountains in front, and a half-broken wooden bridge on the right. I see no human; all must be at work or at home. Sitting in their houses by the side of a fan.

I pick up a half-dried *Kopou Phool* and start walking toward home. People walked over it. And it has no life left. No one saves it from dropping from the branch. No one loves it. It is one of many-I feel as if I am like this flower.

I sometimes curse Baba for not earning enough money and Ma for giving birth to four children, me, and Rani. Two girls. Sajid and Rashid. Two boys. My school friend Masha has no siblings. Even though it is hot, I cover my face with a *burqa* and feel the heat on my face; my lips are dry and cracked. Masha has a small box containing butter, and she applies it to her lips when her lips are cracked. I don't have a small box; I don't have the butter.

I am walking over the bridge now and looking at the water. I think I should wash my hair tomorrow morning.

After walking for over thirteen minutes, I reach a narrow road which has small houses on either side. All these mud-houses have just one room. Sometimes, the walls are coloured white from the outside; Sometimes they are not. All the doors are coloured green. There is a narrow gutter filled with black wastewater that runs in front of them.

There are shared toilets and bathrooms behind, and very few families have their own bathrooms. Sometimes people hang wet clothes on the rope that runs from the first house in the lane to the last and is exactly above the gutter overhead. The lane is so narrow that I can see what's going on in all the houses. Somewhere a baby is crying, or a man is beating his wife, or a woman is mopping the floor, or a girl is cooking. I don't like to witness their lives. I walk down this road for over fifteen minutes, passing almost fifty houses to reach my home. The door is closed. Very few families here close their doors during the daytime. Our door is always closed as Ma believes we should have our privacy-though I don't understand how a house that can be measured in five steps from one end to the other with six people living in it would offer privacy. I remove my *chappals* and keep them in the wooden box outside. I push the door open and can smell curry and see a fresh roti kept next to the stove. I enjoy eating roti until I realize that someone is standing outside the half-closed door and staring at me.

Chandan is our neighbour, five years older than me. He is ugly, dark, has a big nose, and his nose is covered with big and small pimples. His eyes are almost red, and his front teeth are long and have gaps between them. He is staring at me, but I don't like that. So, I closed the door in his face. He belongs to the richest family in our locality. His family has a two-room house and own bathroom. They also have a bed and a big soft chair. Chandan is the only son of his parents. He has money, so people like him. He likes me. I do not like him.

He always stares at me. He gave me a shiny blue envelope last year. I do not know why. I was coming home from school; He was on his bicycle. He handed me the envelope, and I took it without saying or asking anything. I checked inside: empty. I liked the colour. Masha said that he gave me the envelope because its colour matches my eyes, but I do not believe her. The only thing that I did was to wonder how Chandan knew whether it was me or someone else under the *burqa*. While I pondered Chandan and his persistent stares, Ma pushed open the door.

'Why are you late, Agha?'

'Masha was not well, so I went to drop her off at her home.' Ma believes me. She always accepts my lies. She keeps the bowl of fresh curry beside the stove. She borrowed it from Chandan's house.

'Ya *Allah*! Did you eat the roti, Agha?'

'Yes, Ma.' She says nothing and I do not feel bad for eating the only roti we had. We eat food when Abu comes home. He works in a paddy field. Ma has made some rice – we share the curry she has borrowed with it. I eat a little, as my tummy is already full.

'No roti?' Baba asks in his stern voice.

'No, there is no wheat flour,' Ma answers.

'But you said this morning that we have flour for one roti,' Baba continues interrogating. *So much fuss over one roti*, I think.

'I was mistaken; there was none,' Ma says. But Ma's big and round eyes say exactly the opposite.

'Did you give it to your lover? YOU RANDI!' Baba screams and slaps Ma with his right hand. He continues eating his dinner with the same hand. Ma puts her left hand on her cheek in shock. It was a hard slap. However, she finishes her dinner as it is a sin to throw food or to get up when eating. It is *Allah's* disrespect. I doubt Ma is intelligent enough to handle Baba and his rage. After almost seventeen years of marriage, she still gets beatings from him.

When everyone is done having dinner, I wash the plates outside our house. The narrow road between two parallel lanes of houses is also used for washing dishes and clothes. Chandan's house is in front of ours. He is sitting there on a chair and looking at me. I go inside and keep the dishes in the small cabinet, which hangs on the wall on the left side. It is just enough to hold our kitchenette.

There is a flat platform a little below the ceiling where we keep our school bags, three bed sheets, one pillow, and three blankets. Ma, I, and Rani share one blanket. Baba has a separate sleeping arrangement near the stove, which sits in front of our house entrance. Sajid and Rashid sleep beside Baba. After we all sleep next to each other, there remains no extra space even to keep a cup. We keep everything on the wooden shelf above. Rani and I have three pairs of clothes each, one school uniform and two to wear at home. Sometimes I wear Rani's clothes when I go out with Masha, but they are as bad as mine. I make sure that she does not wear my clothes. I am not sure how much clothing Sajid and Rashid have. But not over two pairs each. Both are taller than me even though they are two years younger to me and Rani. Rani is almost as tall as I am. But she has some hearing issues, so Baba and Rashid do not talk with her much. We must be loud to talk to her. She also replies in a loud voice back. I find that chaotic. So, I rarely start a conversation with her. Ma and Sajid do. I feel sorry for her, but the immediate thought is my hunger, and I forget about everyone else around me. Deep down I imagine times when no one is around, and I am alone in a big house that has a kitchen stuffed with all kinds of food.

I sleep next to the wall, with Rani on my left. Ma sleeps on Rani's side. Then Sajid and then Rashid. When I sleep, I always face the wall. I lick it. I like smelling the wet soil. I like the flavour of clay–and smelling wet clay is out of this world. I do this daily, and this habit has created a big patch on the wall. I am not sure if anyone has ever noticed. Everyone falls asleep quickly, except Ma. I am not sure what she thinks. I have heard her crying sometimes, but I never ask her what goes on in her head. In the very next moment, I focus on my hunger, my problems. Ma's crying becomes secondary and is gone in a fraction of a second.

We bathe in a shared bathroom at the back of our house in the early morning. There is no roof, and the door is half-broken. So, we take a bath at dawn when the world is asleep. Later, Ma washes our clothes. Meanwhile, Baba, Rashid and Sajid wake up and take a bath. My job is to fold blankets when everyone is up and keep them on the upper shelf. I am sixteen years old, and next year I will go to the tenth standard. I don't want to continue studying, and here in Matiparbat, I have seen women working only on farms. I don't want to work on farms. I want to be a makeup artist.

Once, I went with Ma to a big house made of cement. A wedding was about to take place, and Ma was called in for cleaning. We started with the bride's room. I was supposed to help, but I was ashamed to mop the floor. I don't want to be a cleaner; I want to be a lady who does the makeup of a bride. I ignored Ma's pleading to help her and sat on the bench with a cushion, staring at other women and hearing their talk. They were wearing new, shiny clothes—exactly the kind of clothes rich people wear; even their *burqa*s were shiny. They were wearing diamond jewelry. The makeup girl cleaned the bride's face with a wet towel. Then, she applied some cream over it. Then powder. Then, a stroke of a brush on her left and right cheeks. That made both her cheeks look red. She then applied some *Kajal*, starting from the outer side of her eye and moving towards the inner side. The bride looked beautiful. Her face was transformed. A woman walked towards me and asked me to sit on the floor. I got up from my place and walked to the other end of the bench and sat there. When Ma started mopping the floor, I did not pay attention to her. I did not want other ladies to know that she was my Ma. I don't like to be perceived as poor. But poverty is on my face, in my clothes, in my hair, and in my dirty *burqa*. Ma did not look at me; she continued her work. When she finished cleaning, she was handed two rupees by the bride's mother. Ma was disappointed. She expected at least five rupees, but she said nothing to the bride's mother. Ma picked up our *burqa*s kept on the floor in the corner, handed mine to me, and we both left from there. Ma did not speak with me on our way home, and I didn't speak with her. I knew she loved her small house, her cleaning job, and her poverty. She has the mentality of the poor.

MAHESH

12 March 1979

*T*hey all say life is not fair. And I cannot agree more.

   After Father's demise, I felt a little lonely. Taking care of Mother has been a tough job altogether. Father would understand her far more than I do. I never heard him complaining about her. She cries about the broken tile in the bathroom or the neighbours making noise or Father throwing his clothes and belongings all over the house when he has been dead for over ten years. But now, with time, I have learned the art of patience. She is alone at home all day, and as her son, I do care for her.

   I am at a stage in my life when I should get married. More than a life partner, I need a friend. Someone with whom I can share my feelings about everything going on inside and outside the house. Mother wants me to get married, but I am not sure if the chaos at home will reduce after my marriage or increase.

The shop is doing well. Father made an excellent decision to buy a shop near the university. I am earning more than I ever expected to earn. But these days, the university is not only about education. Word is that the Group has elected new Leaders. Good for them, good for everyone in Assam. Mother says call them students-as they are the students from the University who have formed this group to raise their voice against the people who enter Bharat illegally. She also asks me to refer to the Centre as Government. I call them the Group and the Centre, as Father used to call them. In fact, Mother is acquiring my vocabulary. She used to address Bhaijan by his name; now she calls him Bhaijan. When she says that, it sounds funny. I always cover my laughter.

The Group is going to fight for Assamese, not for any religion, against immigrants who come without invitation. When I asked Father: why aren't they jailed? Why are they allowed here? When did it start? Why did it start? I was twenty-two years old a decade back. Father was on his deathbed, only capable of drinking water and telling stories. I still remember my talks with him as if it were yesterday that we spoke. I remember his face. The doctor said that he would live for just one more day. But he lived for fifteen more days and talked all day and all night, told me everything that he had kept in his heart all his life. About his wife, my mother; about his work; about his struggle for money; about his love for Assam.

I still remember him telling me about Major Butler saying Assam was a ghost town in the mid-1800s, not even a single bird in sight! Assam was a silent zone.

The British brought Bengalis to look after the administration as they thought Assamese were not the right fit for it.

*They brought people from Orissa and Bihar as labourers in
tea gardens, as they thought Assamese were not hardworking enough. They brought Marwari to encourage trading
in Assam, as they thought the Assamese were not smart
enough. And to commercialize farming, they brought people
from Sylhet, Bangladesh, which was still part of Bharat
then. And they gave the British huge profits. We Assamese
could not. We could not adjust to the changes in society. It
was difficult for us to accept other people bossing on our
land. And these peasants kept coming, forever.*

*Father raised concerns. He asked me to keep my ID ready.
To take care of Mother. To make friends with the police,
politicians, and students. And most importantly, to keep
reading the newspaper. I never read a single word from the
newspaper then. Now I don't spend a single day without
reading the Assam Tribune.*

*I think the fear Father expressed is turning into a reality.
Assam is not at peace these days. There is chaos inside;
there is chaos outside. I do want to sell this small one-room
house and go to rural areas. In Guwahati, there are a lot of
protests going on. I hope that in villages there will be some
peace left. Who would not like to stay in a place surrounded
by green tea gardens? Or in a house amid green plateaus? I
may not have the same surroundings as I imagine, but I can
get a house closer to nature.*

SHABANA

EARLY 1958

'I do not know where we are going, so do not ask me anything about it. And keep your mouth shut all day. If Abbu hears you talking, he is going to leave you behind,' Ammi had warned me several times that week.

The glow on her face had disappeared during those days, knowing that we were leaving the house, which she had set up with a lot of effort and where she had been living since the day she got married to Abbu. She wanted to ask Abbu *why we can't live here, in our own Hakimpur,* but she had no courage. No one had the courage to question Abbu about anything. Ammi's face was pale, and her eyes were puffy and red for almost every day that week. Her voice was thinner than ever. She was going to keep behind all her friends who were unaware of her plan, all her household stuff, her one-room house and her parents. Ammi's parents lived in Golanda, where the Padma and Brahmaputra met. Abbu had a weird fascination with these rivers, and everyone else in the family had somehow adopted the same emotion for these giant water bodies. Abbu would praise them, for they were our food givers.

'Don't be stupid to carry any household stuff. Only clothes, nothing else,' Abbu had urged the three of us. He was not at peace. He would check multiple times whether he had taken all his belongings. Whether Nadim, my elder brother, had checked the bus timetable correctly, whether Ammi had taken only necessary things, and whether I was keeping quiet and not announcing his plan of leaving East Pakistan to anyone. He knew that I knew. His muscles were tense. All morning, he stood with his arms crossed, his brow furrowing and mouth opening halfway with each question about Nadim's travel plans.

The leftover food from the previous night was packed in two big tiffins, which Abbu carried when he would go fishing with Nadim. I never attended school. Nadim, who was four years older than me, taught me the Bengali alphabet and numbers. He taught me full-stop, comma, hyphen and how to use them in a sentence. He wanted to continue his studies, but Abbu asked him to go fishing and sell the fish to earn money. He did what Abbu asked him to do.

Nadim was so bothered that day that he bit his finger-nails, wrung his hands, and looked fixedly at the wall. That morning, Ammi made *chai* for everyone. I would not get *chai* generally, but that day was altogether unique.

I wore my white salwar kameez that Abbu had bought from *Purana Bazaar,* where used clothes were sold. I had two pairs of chappals bought from the same bazaar. One blue, one green. Green was my favourite. I decided to wear green on the day of our journey. Ammi helped me tie my long hair. She held all my hair in a tight grip, pulled it together in a bun, gently placed it on my head and put a rubber band around it. The plastic rubber band, sometimes red, sometimes blue. I did not know where she had kept the packet, but there was always one band on her wrist.

Until last year, nobody asked me to wear *a burqa* that covered the face, but as I turned thirteen, Ammi would never let me go out of the house without wearing it. I wore it that day as well, but not before looking at myself in the mirror. While Ammi was touching the walls of the house and looking at every corner with tears in her eyes, and Abbu and Nadim were busy discussing the travel arrangements, I pulled out a palm-sized mirror from Ammi's purse that was hanging on the wall. The purse was made of jute, square, brown, with a black handle and with the capacity to hold a small mirror, a small tin of talcum powder and something else that was used to colour the lips; it looked weird to me. Ammi never had money in her purse. No one gave her any, neither Abbu nor Nadim. She bought the purse at *Purana Bazaar,* the same place she bought my dresses and *sandal*s.

I looked at myself in that tiny glass and took out a tin of powder from the purse. I was never happy with my complexion. Nadim said that I was fair, but I never agreed with him. I applied powder to my face and looked in the mirror again. *This is okay.* Ammi took the mirror from me after weeping and moved her finger over the curls on her forehead. She had the fair complexion, fairer than the powder. I never understood why she used talcum powder. Ammi took out that weird thing from her purse and applied it to her lips, which started looking different, pink*er.*

'What is that called?' I asked Ammi.

She put it back in her purse.

'You don't have to know everything, Shabana,' she said and covered my face, which was already looking bizarre, with white patches all over it.

'Why do I have to wear this *burqa*?' I changed the topic, but questioning was inevitable. Questions were always on my mind. I felt that someone stored them there, maybe *Allah*. And my job was just to take them out using my smart mouth.

'The *burqa* keeps us safe.'

'From whom?' I said from behind the *burqa*.

She did not answer.

I always asked her about food–aroma, fish–colonies, the Brahmaputra, cats and dogs, but she would not answer. She would talk with Abbu, Nadim, her friends, her parents, sometimes even with herself, but not with me.

That day I was very particular about keeping mum. Nadim, Abbu, and Ammi picked the fishing net – *jal* – and our four bags full of clothes up. I was given no responsibility but to keep quiet. The door was locked. *Chappals* were worn, and four pairs of feet started moving towards the bus–stop. One anxious, one weeping, one worried and one excited. None talking.

Ek, dui, tin, cha, panch, choy, sat, ath, noy, dos–as we passed ten houses and I counted them, we reached a place where the bus was supposed to come. It was still dark. The chirping of birds had just started. There was no light on the road, but I could still tell that we had reached the bus–stop, as there was garbage by the side of that place, and it stank badly. In the daytime, one could also see spit stains on the wall. In front of the bus stop stood a small mosque, though it was still larger than our house. Abbu recited prayers at home. Nadim, too. He used to say, *Allah* is everywhere—why limit us to go to a certain place and pray? You can pray anywhere and everywhere. But I was certain that *Allah* was not there at that smelly bus-stop.

I moved my hands inside my *burqa* and pressed my nose with the index fingers of both hands to avoid the odour going inside my nose.

'Do you know who is talking?' I tried to amuse Nadim with my nasal voice.

Ammi opened my *burqa* and looked at me. I looked at her. In the slight dawn light, I could tell that she was angry at me. I removed my hand from my nose. And kept my index finger on my lips, telling her without speaking that I would not talk further. Nadim smirked, and I pinched him on his forearm. I sat on a bench at the bus-stop. Ammi and Abbu started talking to each other. I used all my powers to infer and interpret their hush-hush, and the only word I could hear was Assam. Nadim was standing by Abbu. He knew all about the discussion.

Assam must be the next stop.

I grabbed a window seat at the rear when the bus arrived. Ammi sat by my side. I opened my *burqa* to witness the half-empty bus and half-asleep Hakimpur. The bus had around twenty seats, and it smelled like rotten vegetables. There were already some people on the bus. Only men, no women apart from me and Ammi.

'The driver has not cleaned the bus; it stinks,' I said. Ammi did not react. She was busy with her thoughts.

The driver shouted at the people to be quick in boarding. Abbu and Nadim sat in the front. They whispered something to each other now and then. Ammi did not open her *burqa*, but I knew she was weeping. Ammi cried almost every other day for one reason or another. Some days she would fight with Abbu, some days she would miss her parents, who were living in the village next to ours. Some days she cried because she had a headache. Abbu said once, 'You get a headache because you cry, not the other way round.' I would always ask her why she cried now and then, but she would not answer me.

'Not in front of Shabana. She has no filter. She will get us all in trouble,' Ammi had once announced while we were having dinner a week before our journey. But I was smarter than they thought. I knew Nadim would go over the fence for me.

'If you promise me to keep this secret, then only I am going to tell you. If Abbu comes to know that I have told you, he will kill me,' Nadim said.

'I promise. I shall tell this to no one.'

'We are going to *Bharat*. We will get more money there for the same work we do here. We can have a bigger house and a farm for ourselves.'

'Why do we need a bigger house? And a farm?' I questioned.

'I will get married soon. With more people, we need more space and more money. Don't you want the green scarf you liked the other day at the market? We can buy it when we have more money,' said Nadim, like a mature man with his chin up.

'I want that scarf. It was made of silk, and it had pearls on the border. Will we come back here to buy it?' I asked.

'No, in Bharat you will get better scarves. We will buy something there.'

Nadim was always brief. Everyone was afraid of my opening mouth and broadcasting Abbu's plan of leaving East Pakistan and moving to Bharat. I had to keep the promise, so I decided to be tight-lipped until we reached Bharat.

I remembered seeing the sunrise from the window and the paddy fields glowing in the morning light. The chirping of the birds became more noticeable when we moved away from the village. The road blew dust that soon filled the bus. We tried to close the glass window, but it was stuck. My *burqa* saved me from the dust; I was slowly understanding its use. The landscape was pleasing, but secretly I was keener to see the other side of the border.

And then there were questions in my head, whether Bharat would be as beautiful as East Pakistan? What did people in Bharat look like? Where would we live once we reach Bharat? Once Abbu said that Brahmaputra was in Bharat as well, was he kidding? Would Ammi allow me to have *chai* every day in the new place? What colour scarf should I buy in Bharat, green or yellow? My inquisitiveness was overwhelming.

What would anybody expect from a thirteen-year-old yet to see the real world?

Ammi was quiet for a long time. Her weeping had stopped. Ammi was thirty-five years old, and Abbu was fifty-two. Ammi was still young and beautiful; Abbu had grey hair. Ammi was fat; Abbu was thin. Ammi was fair and Abbu was dark. To me, they were always the reverse of one another. Abbu would talk all day; Ammi wouldn't talk as much. You could read Abbu's face when he wasn't talking; Ammi's expression was the same in every situation-good or bad. I was like Abbu, loquacious. I loved talking, making inquiries, being curious and being the centre of attention. But Abbu always avoided talking with me. I did not have enough maturity, as Abbu said, but I could understand who liked me and who did not.

'I know I am a girl—that is why they do not like me,' I said to Nadim one day.

'That's not true, Shabana,' he said unconvincingly.

Nadim was in a mood to talk, to share more information, so I continued speaking, but on a different topic.

'Why does she cry so often?'

'She misses her parents,' he continued.

'Is that all? There must be something more to it.'

'You know you are a thirteen-year-old, right? Behave like one.'

These were our usual discussions when Ammi and Abbu would fight and we would be in our small front yard, lying on the ground and looking at the stars.

'Will the sky be the same in Bharat?'

'It is the same everywhere. It is huge, and it covers the whole earth.'

'Do you know how Bharat will be different from our country?'

'Bharat has huge tea plantations. It has many rivers, many jobs, and many people.'

'Will we get to see tea gardens?'

'Yeah, maybe. No more questions about Bharat, Shabana.'

And I shut my mouth. Nadim was good, but he was smart enough to push me away whenever I tried to get more information out of him.

We travelled for around five hours before the bus stopped. East Pakistan was very dusty. The roads were not smooth, and half of the ride was bumpy. Every time the bus bumped, Ammi would look at me. Ammi was wearing her *burqa*, but I knew she was angry as I had chosen a seat at the rear of the bus. On this bumpy ride, we crossed Mapilara, where I had come once with Nadim at a mosque. We crossed a river.

'This is the Teesta River,' Ammi said and murmured something under her breath.

'What did you say?' I prompted.

'Teesta, Padma, Brahmaputra, all *beel*s and ponds are the reason that we could go fishing and earn money. They help us with two times' food. I pray to *Allah* to keep them full of water forever,' Ammi said.

I nodded. The Teesta water was blue, the same as that of the Brahmaputra. But the banks of the Teesta were smaller than those of the Brahmaputra. Brahmaputra was a leader. I wanted to be like Brahmaputra, the leader of everyone around me.

There were some women washing clothes on the bank, and some kids playing around. I looked at Nadim. He was looking out of the window. Maybe he was thinking about his new job in Bharat, maybe he was thinking about where to take me shopping to buy that green scarf, or maybe he was thinking about eating food. And that reminded me of the food that we carried with us.

'Ammi, I am hungry. When are we going to reach?' Ammi looked at me with her big eyes. She was asking me to shut up. The bus came to a halt in a few hours.

'Everyone, get out of the bus now. Keep your bags on the bus, carry your tiffin.' The driver took a sip of water from the water bottle he carried, gargled, and spat the water out of the window. He was wearing a khaki dress, and his mouth was red, the same colour as the spitting stains at the bus stop. He was clean-shaven and looked a little older than Nadim. He was fair, like Ammi. And as rude as Abbu.

Everyone got off the bus. There was no bus-stop, but a poorly built road with *beel*s on both sides. I had the superpower of listening to whispers and murmurs, so I knew we were in Kurigram. The driver parked the bus at the roadside and got out. He joined a group of men. Ammi and I sat on the ground nearby. Everyone was waiting for someone. But no one spoke to each other. What were we hiding, and from whom? Otherwise, chatty Abbu was unusually quiet and seemed tense.

It was always difficult to understand what Ammi thought. Maybe she was still in Hakimpur in her tiny house, or she was here, thinking about the next course of action. No one would know. Nadim came to the place where I and Ammi were sitting. He had carried the tiffin bag with him. Ammi opened the bag, took out the tiffin and gestured at me to eat. I dove into the chicken curry just like the duck dove into the water in the *beel* behind us. The *beel* was small and seemed unused. The water was cleaner than any of the other ponds in Hakimpur. The pond on the other side of the road seemed bigger, and there were tall brown weeds on its border, which partially hid the view. Standing on the edge of the pond, I could see some fish. Blue, orange, grey, black, white, yellow. Tiny, tinier.

'See, kid fishes are near the edge and parent fish are deeper inside the pond. They must be cooking lunch for their kids,' I said to Nadim. He smirked. There was not a single house around. Apart from us, there were no other humans but two street dogs roaming around.

'Are you scared of dogs?' I asked him.

'I am not, but you are, I know,' he said, staring at the water. His eyebrows did not move. He was thinking about something else. The journey.

'When will we reach? It's so boring to travel.'

'Some more time,' he answered confidently.

'How much exactly?' I asked.

'An hour or so.'

'We have already spent two hours here. What are those people talking about?' I pointed to where Abbu was standing and asked Nadim. Nadim did not answer.

'Is it going to rain?' I continued.

'I don't think so,' he answered in the same tone. My brother was the most boring person in Hakimpur. I was certain of that. He took a banana out of his bag and gave it to me. I broke it in two halves and gave one half to Ammi. I started eating my share when I saw a man approaching from a distance on a motorcycle. Nadim went to the place where Abbu and the other men were standing. The new man was tall and had a wide chest. He was wearing a black *pathani,* and he had a long beard. He did not look at Ammi and me and went straight to the group of men. Abbu's eyes lit up when he saw this tall man. He went on talking with every single man in the group, including Abbu. I saw Abbu introducing Nadim to the new man and then pointing his finger at me and Ammi. He must have told the new man that we were his family. Abbu then moved his hand into his right pocket and took out some *taka.* The tall man took the money, looked at me and Ammi, and moved on to speak with the rest of the men in the group and collected money from them.

The bus driver hailed us and asked us to board. The tall man said something to the driver and gave him money.

While we were boarding, I poked Nadim. He knew what I wanted, but instead of talking with me, he hurried to his seat. I followed him and sat beside him. Ammi came to our seat, held me by my arms and took me to my seat at the rear. I sat by the window. She covered my face with the *burqa* and the bus started. We travelled for no more than half an hour and the bus came to a halt.

'Get down fast and take your bags!' the young driver screamed.

My brother quickly picked up our bags, Abbu picked up his *jal,* and we all got off. It was getting dark outside, but anyone could tell that we were in paddy fields. I saw some light in the distance and a thick rope tied at both ends to two poles. I knew that was the border. I had a big smile on my face. We were close. There were some huts where dinner was arranged. One hut was only for women. Ammi held my hand and took me inside with her. It was a small hut. Candles were lit and kept in the middle of the hut. Ammi looked so beautiful in the candlelight. I wanted to be as beautiful as Ammi, but I was not. Almost all the women were in *burqas,* just like us. They were constantly chatting. I and Ammi kept quiet. I could smell the food cooking in the field. On the *chullahs.* Everyone was waiting for his or her turn to leave that country. After some time, two women entered; one carried a large pot of rice; the other, the curry.

'Early dinner?' I asked.

Ammi kept her index finger on her lips and said, 'Not a single word, remember?'

I nodded. I wasn't hungry.

A banana leaf was kept in front of us; Ammi and I were supposed to share the food. A woman served rice and fish curry. I took the first morsel.

'Can I have some salt, please?' I enquired.

Ammi looked at me.

'No thanks, I am okay,' I said and smiled.

'We need nothing, *Didi*. Thank you for the food,' Ammi said to the woman who was serving.

I was waiting for the night to pass and to witness a new day in Bharat. When we were done with the dinner, I and Ammi walked outside. Abbu and Nadim were having dinner in different huts. A man walked from the border and greeted Ammi.

'Are you planning to travel tonight?' he asked.

'Yes,' Ammi answered.

'What time?' He asked again.

'I am not aware of the time. Can I ask my husband?'

'Yes, ask him.'

Ammi rushed towards the hut where Abbu was having dinner. This man was in a green uniform, and he had a thick moustache. He looked at me. I smiled at him. He did not smile back.

'What is your name, uncle?' I asked.

I am called "Sir." What is your name? He responded.

'I am Shabana.'

He bent on his knees and moved his hand over my cheek.

'Where are you from, Shabana?' he asked.

I took a step back and replied, 'Hakimpur.'

'Hakimpur,' he repeated.

Ammi came running, held my hand and pulled me towards the other side.

'I am going to keep you here. You are not coming with us.'

'I am sorry, Ammi. I won't say anything now.'

'I explicitly asked you to avoid questioning others, remember?' Ammi continued scolding me.

'You did, Ammi, I am sorry.'

The man in the green uniform was looking at us and listening to our conversation. I did not like him. He was weird, just like the situation.

Abbu had followed Ammi. He introduced himself to the man in the green uniform.

'Your bus is ready. Keep your bags ready to be checked at the gate,' he told Abbu.

'Thank you, *Saab,*' said Abbu. Meanwhile, one more person in a yellow uniform joined us. Six of us, with these two men, started walking towards the thick rope. Abbu was leading with bags, followed by Nadim, who carried *jal.* Then Ammi. Then me. We walked for nearly twenty minutes to cross the paddy fields. But a man in the green uniform put a hand on my mouth and pulled me into the fields. The man in the yellow uniform followed my family. He kept his index finger on his lips. Then, held my head in both his hands. Came close. Put his lips on my lips and in no time pushed his tongue inside my mouth. It moved like a snake. It was hot. It touched everywhere inside my mouth. It touched all my teeth. He let me go in a minute. Abbu and Nadim were getting the bags checked. Ammi was standing at a distance. When I ran to her, she gave me the other half of the banana.

'Let them go,' the man in the green uniform ordered. I looked at him. He moved his tongue over his lips and winked at me.

'Bharat,' Abbu said, and there was light in his eyes.

Four pairs of feet crossed the East Pakistan border and entered the promised land. One overwhelmed, one hesitant, one excited, one lost.

MAHESH

5 June 1979

I had to get the air filled in the tyres this morning. The bicycle is thirty years old now. It is Father's, and I am still repairing it and using it. His memories are associated with it, and I have no heart to replace it with a new, expensive bicycle. Not that I can afford one.

"Go Away Foreigner"-I read on one wall on my way to the shop. I read many such slogans every day on different walls these days. And like every other person in Assam, I thought about my roots. Had Father been alive today, how would he have reacted to all this?

It has been quiet for the past few years, but this year everything is changing. Both the protests and the sales in my shop have gone up. I saw people engrossed in discussions. About what? Everyone knows.

It took me ten minutes to reach the shop from my house.

Guwahati is a beautiful place. Small houses. Big trees. Long roads. Good people. It has changed significantly,

though, in the last ten years. Guwahati was not this crowd-
ed earlier. Despite population and pollution growth, Guwa-
hati remains stunning and kind. The city still welcomes
and accepts new people.

The sales are going well. Who would spend a day without
chai?!

The shop was crowded today, and the majority of cus-
tomers were talking about student groups and their agen-
das. People are worried about the outcome. No one knows
whether the Centre is going to support it. And if the Centre
does not, then how will the protesters get what they want?
The hot chai and this discussion are now a daily routine. I
am an active participant in these discussions. We discussed
immigrants from Bangladesh and Nepal. The jobs lost to
outsiders, news about local women being raped by outsiders
and outsider women being raped by locals, humans tearing
each other apart for the land. There is news of Hindus
killing Muslims, Muslims killing Hindus, outsiders killing
locals and locals killing outsiders.

Father had said that the major reason is the way the
Redcliffe line was drawn. A messy work, he would call it.
Done by people who knew nothing about Bharat, religion
and ethnicity. They almost separated the northeastern part
of Bharat from Bharat. We are connected to the country just
through a narrow strip of land. Is that fair? Does the Centre
consider us to be part of it? The connectivity to the rest
of the country is extremely poor from here. The Redcliffe
line separated families, and Bharat has constantly suffered
since then.

These discussions about Hindus, Muslims, Insiders, Out-
siders, Assamese, Bengali, the Brahmaputra Valley, and the
Barak Valley are helping me earn more money. I can attract

more customers when I talk and show interest in such topics. I always side with the majority as I don't want any trouble later. No arguments, no fights. But deep down, I fear the unknown even though I am an Assamese. When I confidently discuss these topics, I make sure that Bhaijan is not there. His shop next door is bigger than mine, so there is less chance of him hearing my voice over others'.

The lunch was at the usual place, and I had the usual dish-Khaar and rice. Bhaijan ate duck curry with rice. Good food makes him happy. Good food makes me happy.

The kerosene is about to run out. I need some at home as well as at the shop. I have not cleaned the chai kettle this evening. I must go to the shop early tomorrow to clean.

It sometimes becomes tiring to come home and eat dinner alone. Mother eats before me and sleeps quite early. Bhaijan says to me, 'Mahesh, get married now. It is already too late.' Maybe it is late, maybe it is not. God knows. But I wonder if the comment from someone who did not get married himself should be taken seriously.

SHABANA

EARLY 1958

The wind in the new land was as smooth as the scarf that I wanted to buy-the one with pearls. Even the moon in the sky looked prettier in Bharat. The night was calm and soft. Calmer than that in East Pakistan. Softer than Ammi's silk saree. Softer than wool on a lamb. The lamb that I and Nadeem had seen in Hakimpur and whom I had kissed on the back, whom we had named 'Sona' and whom I had told that I wanted to be free like her-roam in the fields and eat whatever I liked. The smell of Bharat's land offered freshness that I would otherwise only get after having *chai*. That was the magic of Bharat: the land was addictive.

There was a small bus with tinted glass waiting, and everyone was in a rush to board. Men held their wives' hands and pulled them inside the bus to get seats adjacent to each other. Abbu ascended first, and Nadim followed. Nadim held me by my arm and dragged me in with him.

Ammi followed. The crowd was more than the bus could take; some people stood, and some had to stay behind and wait for another bus.

I took a seat next to the window in the second row. But my mind was still absorbing what had happened in the paddy fields. Why did the man put his tongue in my mouth? It did not taste good. It was weird, sickening. I wanted to puke out everything the man in the green uniform had put inside. *No one would notice that I have vomited-the bus is smelling so bad already, just like cow dung,* I thought. But I dropped the plan when Ammi sat by my side. I tried to gulp the bitter taste. It passed through my throat, reached my chest, and then burst up from there to my teeth. The taste of his breath, which was a mixture of the smoke of bidi and *chai*, remained in my mouth, playing, jumping from my palate to my tongue, and vice versa.

'Quick, you fool! I don't have all day,' the driver screamed at an elderly passenger. The driver was fuming and blabbering something under his breath. The old man's relative, who had already taken his seat, went to the bus door and pulled the old man inside.

'This old man cannot go fishing. He cannot sit in the market and sell fish, cannot ride a cycle rickshaw, cannot earn money. He will sit at home and bore his son with tales of his life's hardships,' Ammi whispered in Nadim's ears, looking at the old man. Nadim was sitting next to Abbu in the first row. Abbu had been pinching the bridge of his nose since we entered Bharat. When everyone boarded the bus, the driver asked Abbu to close the door.

'*Ji Saab,*' he said in a thick and unsteady voice.

When the bus started, Abbu's whispers with Nadim resumed, just like Ammi's weeping. The windows were sup-

posed to remain shut as per the driver's order-which explained the foul odour inside. Anybody who disobeyed him
was warned that the person would be thrown off. I waited with my wide-open eyes for the night to pass, replay-
ing the scenes in the fields and holding tightly onto the
jal. Why was his moustache so rough? Were Abbu and
Nadim's beards equally rough? Why are men different
from women? Why don't they wear *burqas*? Why are they
rude, difficult-why? That night I concluded that I did not like
men-except Nadim.

The sudden brakes and the knock on the door pushed me
to stop thinking about men and their rough facial hair. The
driver watched the door with horror, and his eyes widened.
He pushed the hair back from his forehead.

'Unlock it,' the driver said to Abbu in a shaky voice.

The driver was another man whom I did not like. I could
not figure out the need for screaming. Why could not he talk
normally, properly? He was a man—that was an answer
enough for many questions. He could do whatever he wanted. He was free—no *burqa*, no safety needed.

Abbu rushed from his seat and opened the door. Two people in green uniforms entered the bus, and a shiver travelled
down my spine.

'Where is this bus going?' one of them asked.

'Dhubri, *Saab*,' the driver answered.

'And where is this coming from?'

There was silence. The driver felt imprisoned by fear.

'Where is this coming from?'

I imagined his loud voice touching every corner of the bus
but taking too long to reach the driver as he took a long time
to answer back.

'Kurigram, *Saab*.'

One of these men held his hand in front of the driver. The driver struggled at first, but eventually took some cash out of his pocket and placed it in the hand that was put forward. Abbu witnessed this, put his head down, and walked toward his seat.

'You may go now. But no more trips for this week. Tell your man,' one of the men in the green uniform said. The uniform was authoritative; people wearing it could give orders to other people.

'Yes, *Saab. Dhonnobad Saab,*' the driver was pleased.

I liked that someone screamed at the driver. It was proof that there was someone above him, another man. I initially thought that men only screamed at women, but that was not true. They did scream at each other, and the one who could frighten the other was the winner. So, if I could imagine a ladder, women were at the bottom of it. Girls. No. Girls who talk. Then, girls who listen to their parents and keep quiet. Above them, women who talk, one level up, were shy women-women like Ammi. Then, men who are soft-spoken, like Nadim. Above them, men like Abbu who were rude. One step above are the men who screamed and were unkind, like the driver, and at the top-the men in green uniforms who could frighten everyone starting from the bottom of the ladder to the top.

We reached Dhubri when it was almost the middle of the night.

'Get down, everyone. Quick!' came an order from the driver.

All the people grabbed their bags and hurried to the door.

'Here is your address in Guwahati. Get some jobs there. Work wherever you can, earn money.' Abbu took out a piece of paper from his pocket and handed it over to Nadim when we stepped down.

Nadim nodded, unsurprised, as if he already knew we all had to split once we reached Bharat. And he had not told me anything about it when we discussed the journey. I felt like I was giving away my green scarf, even though I didn't own it.

'It has the name of a person whom you must meet. He will give you a place to live for ten days. After that, you must pay rent for it. He may help you get a job. You will have to earn money as soon as possible if you want to continue living here,' Abbu said coldly.

Nadim nodded.

'And learn Assamese.'

Assamese

Assam

We are in Assam.

There was hardly any light on the road where we were standing, but the moon was shining brightly. In that light, I could see tears in Abbu's eyes. His son was going on an adventure. But Bharat was not an enemy; Bharat was a dream, and then it was a dream come true. I was sure Nadim would be all right.

'Shabana,' he called my name, and I looked at him with tearful eyes.

'Take care,' he said and put his heavy hand on my head.

I hugged him. I could not control my tears. I could not speak-my throat was choked.

'Stay as you are. I don't want you to change. I will come back soon,' he said.

'How soon?' I asked, my lips trembling.

'In a blink,' he answered. He knew he was lying, and I knew he was lying.

'Don't forget to bring my green scarf, you promised me,' I said, and Nadim laughed.

Did Abbu know who he was taking away from me? Nadim was the only person I spoke to about stars, planets, rivers, mountains, tea estates, fish, festivals, men, women, girls, boys, *burqas*, beards, almost everything. He was the only one who taught me the *Bangla* alphabet and showed me East Pakistan and Bharat on a map. He told me about the Brahmaputra Valley and the Barak Valley. He told me about tea plantations in Assam. He promised to buy me new dresses every month. Only he took me to *Purana Bazaar* to buy me dresses and shoes. I was upset with him. He did not tell me he would be separated from us. But I was also optimistic that I would get my green scarf sooner than later.

Ammi held my hand and pulled me towards her. Nadim hugged Abbu. Then he sat in a cycle rickshaw and made his way to Guwahati.

Why can't he come with us, Abbu? Abbu, please let him stay with us. Words stuck in my throat. Just like me, they feared Abbu's reaction. Abbu, who would otherwise ignore me, looked at me for a minute. I assumed that he was going to speak to me to answer my plea. But he did not. Ammi held both my hands and looked into my eyes. I wondered what she was searching for. Fear? Pain? Defeat? I looked into her eyes, too. I suspected there was a scolding on my way.

'Behave now! We are yet to reach our destination.'

'I behaved all the way through,' I said.

'Oh, did you?'

I wanted to scream, disappear, ask Nadim to come back
and take me, go back to East Pakistan-all at the same
time. All men-except Nadim-and Ammi were my un-
favourite. Abbu hurried to the cycle rickshaw standing
by our side and said, 'Goalpara, section18'. The cyclist
nodded. We sat on, and he started pedalling. The journey
was not over yet, and I was more than tired already.

'How long will the cyclist pedal? How much money will
he get?' I asked Ammi. But she was asleep as soon as we
sat in the rickshaw.

'Nine hours,' Abbu replied.

'Then why don't we get a bus?'

There was no answer. Abbu had a quota for my questions in a day-zero. That day was unusual in many ways,
so he answered one question. In that old cycle rickshaw,
with a red roof and yellow floor where our tired feet
rested, where there was a sound every time the rider
pedaled the cycle, I slept peacefully.

The sunlight and the landscape of Bharat were more
beautiful than I had imagined. Bharat was cleaner than
East Pakistan. The roads were wider, and there was a lot
of greenery around. I could see mountains in the distance.
It appeared as though someone was asleep under them. A
huge man. And the greenery was nothing but the blanket
he had used to cover himself. There were ponds and *beel*s
now and then, just like in East Pakistan. But still, Bharat
looked different-grander than East Pakistan, more beautiful than East Pakistan, and quieter than East Pakistan.
Just like East Pakistan's big brother. Like me and Nadim.
Nadim was like Bharat, everyone's favourite. I was like
East Pakistan; everyone judged me.

I woke Ammi up to witness the beauty, but she did not seem to appreciate the scene. She was probably expecting to be in Hakimpur. Moving to Bharat was just a nightmare for her.

We reached Goalpara before noon, where Abbu gave the driver some money. It was not *Taka*. Abbu called it *Rupaiya*. I recalled Abbu's words to Nadim – *Come home with a lot of Rupaiya*.

'*Dhonnobad*,' said the cyclist.

'Which direction is Section18?' asked Abbu.

'In the East, it's a ten minutes' walk from here.'

Abbu picked up our bags and led the way to our new house. I, with *jal*, and Ammi, followed him.

Cattle were churning on the roadside farms. The road was muddy. And by the look of it, it resembled many roads in East Pakistan, the ones with a lot of potholes. The *chappal* that Nadim had bought for me before our trip would go deep inside the mud. It gave me a lot of pleasure to remove the *chappal* gently from the dirt and notice the mud sticking to the sole. Some splashes of mud on the strap looked like a mould on leftover curry, specifically leftover for more than a day. The kind of curry Abbu made Ammi eat when she forgot to serve it when it was a day old. I had looked at Ammi when she wept while eating that curry. Nadim looked towards the ground. He was weeping too. Abbu felt nothing. I wept because Ammi and Nadim were weeping. That day, I liked Ammi. Not because she was crying, not because she had to eat curry with fungus. But because she spoke freely with me that day and told me that marriage is not necessary. Women can live without marrying someone. They can earn their own money. They can go to the market and sell fish. They can clean somebody's house and earn

money that comes with their sweat and tears. I had no
thoughts about her speech that day. I was naïve. I only
listened and told Nadim all that she said to me. Nadim
asked me to ignore what Ammi said. She said so because
she was angry at Abbu, he said, and I agreed. I thought
marriage was necessary. Nadim never feared getting
married. Why should I fear it? I would get married. I had
concluded when I was ten years old, three years back.

It was fun to run in the mud. I giggled, and Ammi
turned back to give me a look. I wished I hadn't woken
her up in the rickshaw. She would have gone back to
Kurigram and then to Hakimpur, her favourite place on
earth. Abbu said we were in the Brahmaputra Valley. In
my head, I always referred to the Brahmaputra Valley as
Jannah and the Brahmaputra as Brahma.

'Shabana, this is the Brahmaputra Valley. Do you see
how beautiful it is?'

'Yes, Abbu. It is more beautiful than Hakimpur,' I answered hurriedly. Abbu was in a good mood, and I did not
want to miss the chance to have a conversation with him.
I had a chance to become his favourite when Nadim was
not there.

'Nothing can beat Hakimpur. Never say that again,'
Ammi intervened. She loved Hakimpur more than she
loved Nadim.

'Abbu, the majority of Brahma is in Bharat, right?' I
continued.

'Brahma is one of the Hindu gods. Brahma and
Brahmaputra are different.'

'I don't know the god Brahma; I know only the Brahma
River. My Brahma,' I said.

I had a huge fascination with this massive river. It was around half an hour from our house in Hakimpur to its enchanting banks. She had powers she would use at the right time. And then the world would keep quiet, accept her angst, accept her greatness, accept that she was nature. Our savior, as Ammi would call her.

The valley was greener than the green scarf that I had liked in Hakimpur's *Purana Bazaar.*

In the valley, there was a constant sound of birds. And there was always a mild wind flowing. The hills were taller than the ones I had seen before. There are four words that I could use to describe the Brahmaputra Valley-ponds, trees, mountains and roads. The real sequence from where I was standing was roads, ponds, trees, and mountains. The narrow roads were bordered on both sides by a series of ponds, separated by a thin green line of farms. The ponds were enclosed by tall coconut trees bearing large green coconuts. Wide *Jamun* trees—you had to look closely to see *Jamun* hanging on them—accompanied by coconut trees. The ground below the *Jamun* tree was always messed up with *Jamun*s that fell on the ground with their seeds coming out. I loved *Jamun,* but taking them off the tree had always been a task. There were farms between the ponds and the mountains. The long, wide, green and the yellow mustard farms. You could see scarecrows standing to scare away birds and sometimes animals like foxes. And the beautiful rice crops were arranged symmetrically in rows parallel to each other. They carried dewdrops on their leaves. The drops would move from one place to another with every blow of wind. I stood by the side of the crops and moved with them in whichever direction the wind blew. My *burqa* flowed with me effortlessly. The mud beneath these

crops held these crops tightly. None of the crops were
damaged by the wind. While Ammi and Abbu were
walking ahead, I picked up soil from the ground and put
it inside my mouth. I loved eating soil. I sucked walls
at home when I was alone. There was a different pleasure in doing such things. Different meaning courageous.
Different meaning fulfilling. Being different made me
happy.

The narrow dusty roads in the valley were surrounded
by small plateaus, all covered in green and having cattle grazing on them. I did not see much cattle in East
Pakistan. Abbu had said once that cows in East Pakistan
were imported from Bharat. Why not? I thought. Bharat
had an abundance of everything. Nadim had told me
about tea estates, the long, wide tea plantations which
would cover an area twice the size of Hakimpur. The tall
green mountains would surround the plantation. Nadim
had promised to take me there one day when he earned a
lot of money. With a *jal* in one hand and a *chappal* in the
other, I followed Abbu and Ammi.

'There was heavy rain two nights before, hence the
mud,' said Abbu. 'There is the Brahmaputra at a walking
distance from our house.'

'Will you be going into the Brahmaputra for fishing?' I
asked Ammi.

'Not really. There is a *beel* nearby, Kumri *Beel,* where
many people go fishing. I will go there first. I need to
make some friends first before facing any competition for
fishing in the Brahmaputra.'

'Where have we come? So many changes, so many
risks. Hakimpur was so comfortable,' Ammi replied. 'No
pain, no gain,' Abbu said in a stern voice.

I did not see any risks other than the mud where my feet would get stuck now and then. Bharat was no risk; Bharat was safe. It was big, beautiful, and big-hearted to take us in. Abbu continued, 'You must make some friends, Assamese friends or people from East Pakistan who know Assamese. Learn Assamese and teach Shabana as well.'

Ammi nodded.

Some people were looking at us, staring at our faces. Abbu's walk was faster than usual, and we followed to match his speed. The houses in Assam were strange. They were raised on a platform and supported by stilts. They were not made of mud, like our house in Hakimpur. The houses seemed to be made of wood, and they had stairs to reach the elevated platform. A man, in lungi and *chador* over his shoulder, came down from one while we were waiting. He looked at Abbu from head to toe. '*Salaam*,' he said.

'*Walekum Assalam*, Salim Saab.'

'Welcome to Assam,' he said with a broad smile on his face.

'*Dhonnobad.*'

'I got a message that you would reach here in the morning. You are late,' the man said.

'Yeah, the cycle rickshaw rider was old. He took longer than expected to ride here from Dhubri,' Abbu said apologetically.

'*O kichhu na!* Come with me.' He took us to the house, which was next to his, but separated by a small farm and a small beel.

'This is your house, and this is the key. Get fresh and then let's catch up for some lunch at our place.'

The house stood on just six bamboo supports. There was a wooden ladder that took us to a small veranda in front of the main door. Abbu opened it and then helped Ammi and me. He then picked up our bags and left them outside the entrance. We went inside to find a house almost the same size as the one in Hakimpur. The roof was tin, and there was a stove in the corner. Abbu opened the small window next to the door.

We took a bath, changed into better clothes and went to Salim uncle's house. I was excited to have lunch; I was hungry. Plus, it was the first time that I was trying food in Bharat.

'This is my wife Asma,' Salim uncle introduced his wife to us.

'Welcome,' Asma said. Asma auntie-fat, fair complexion, long hair, thick nose, big eyes that looked at each other. I wanted to laugh, but I looked away. Ammi greeted her. Asma auntie held Ammi's hand and took her inside the kitchen. I followed them. Salim uncle had a two-room house with many cabinets. In their living room were two chairs where Abbu and Salim uncle were sitting. I and Ammi sat on the floor in their small and tidy kitchen.

'I wonder where to get groceries from?' Ammi started the usual questioning. She would scold me if I asked questions, but she herself was no less inquisitive.

'There is a general store where the rickshaw driver dropped you. There is a *bazaar* in Goalpara two days a week, where you can get fresh vegetables.'

'And water?' Ammi did not want to stop.

'Most houses have their own ponds. Brahmaputra is only a five-minute walk, by the way. Did you bring any utensils?'

'My *shauhar* asked me to leave everything behind.' Ammi was about to cry.

I got up and went to the living room. Abbu and Salim uncle were talking about fishing. I went straight to the deck. It was bigger than ours. From there, I saw hills. I saw women carrying water pots, boys playing on the ground, farms, cows, buffalos, sky with clouds. It was overcast, and I could hear the water flowing. Brahmaputra. From the next day onwards, Abbu started going fishing to the nearby *beel* along with Salim uncle. Ammi had gradually bought some utensils for the kitchen. She set her routine very quickly. Every time she would go out with Asma auntie, she would buy something for the house. Either a pan or flour.

Abbu worked almost all the time. He caught many fish every day, and we got enough money by selling them to Salim uncle, who would eventually sell them to a wholesaler in Goalpara. But Ammi said Abbu did not seem happy. Abbu and Ammi would talk every day about Nadim. I missed him. I was keen to know what Guwahati looked like. I imagined him coming home, both of us sitting on our deck and talking about Bharat. I decided I would take Nadim to the Brahmaputra and show him how beautiful that river was when he came to Goalpara.

Some days, I thought that Brahma was like us. Like me. And I was sure that many people hurt her. Maybe someone like the man in a green uniform. She touched so many people's lives. I knew she cried. She was alone. Just like me. But she was fearless; I was not. I wished to learn that from her, but I could not. I went to the bank of the Brahmaputra every day. *Every day.* I liked witnessing the immensity of that river. She was so strong and yet compassionate to feed so many people. People praised her. She had the power to destroy their lives with her floodwater. She had the power to kill them instantly, and no one had the ability to stop her. Brahma's water was different, enchanting, shiny, sparkling. The river knew everything. She knew me, she knew my destiny, and maybe she was not excited about it. Maybe I was not excited about it. The message I received from Brahma was vague.

MAHESH

7 June 1979

*I*t was again a beautiful morning today. I shaved my beard and wore a new kurta that Bhaijan had gifted me. Ever since he told me about the bride he had in mind for me, I have felt love for her. When I heard from Bhaijan about her eyes, I thought of Hema Malini, the Hindi actor-the most beautiful I have ever seen. I have always imagined my bride to be a beautiful lady. And I think I must compliment her in terms of looks. Agha-doesn't the name itself create excitement in your heart? It does. She is younger than I am by fifteen years. Mother said the age gap does not matter. Bhaijan said the same thing. But I am not sure. She would have a different angle from which to look at the world. I have a different angle. How do we match? How do I make her happy? How do I make her feel that she has not married an old, boring man? Even though I am only thirty-two years old, I do feel old. Mother says it is because I spend time with Bhaijan. Bhaijan is old, really old. Not physically, but *mentally. Anyway, Bhaijan said he would soon get Agha's photo for me.*

I again had to fill the air in the tyres.

When I reached the shop, I saw some customers already waiting outside. That's real happiness. People liking the chai you make and coming back again and again. But I know they're really there for the chat, not just the chai. I came to know that tomorrow was a bandh in Assam, a protest against the unhindered migration of outsiders. It affects the state and tribal people of Assam. I must keep the shop closed. I do not want anybody pelting stones and breaking the only source of living I have. Whenever there are protests, rallies, Satyagrahas, or bandhs, I lose money. When I lose money, I can't buy stuff. People who run grocery markets don't earn money. They buy less stuff from farmers. Everyone becomes poor. This is the first statewide bandh against illegal immigration.

The Group has highlighted several issues to the state and the Centre. Last year they had three days of Satyagraha and an all-day Bandh in Guwahati demanding reservation of 80 percent of jobs for people from Assam. They also want refugees who have entered Bharat after the 1971 war to be sent back. And to make Assamese as a medium of instruction for higher education. Will that be acted upon quickly? Or will that be actioned at all? Maybe not. And looking at the pattern of the Centre's treatment of states in the North-East of Bharat, we need to push really hard to get anything from the Centre. We are like stepchildren!

Bhaijan has asked me to lend him some money to pay his electricity bill, pending for four months now, he said. I had kept that money to buy two more benches to keep outside the shop, but I think I will buy benches sometime later. Bhaijan is a good man, and I consider him my elder brother. These days he is bothered too much. I hardly see him smiling. He thinks he may be deported to Bangladesh just like his parents, but I do not think so. He came to Assam when I was ten years old, before 1961. He will be allowed to stay here. I even told him this multiple times. The Group is negotiating to keep people who came until 1961. I do not know why he does not believe me. Bhaijan still refers to Bangladesh as East Pakistan, even though the name change happened more than eight years ago now.

He even seemed upset when I told him about tomorrow's strike. He closed the shop after lunch and went home.

I read the news every day. But the rumors are also spreading rapidly. The one who believes rumours will think that everyone is unsafe in Assam, irrespective of whether they are insiders or outsiders. I believe bad things happen only to those people who have done bad things to others. It is said that all good that happens to you is because of your parents' good deeds, and I am sure that Father has done more than enough good deeds.

Moreover, since I am born and brought up here in Assam, I fear no one.

SHABANA

EARLY 1959

Ten months had passed since we had entered Bharat's territory. Life in Hakimpur and that in Bharat were too different. Abbu would work on a farm and go fishing. Ammi had also started shopping for salwar kameez and makeup for herself. But she did not put any makeup on. Abbu would wear cotton shirts when someone came to our house. The situation was better. Nadim was right; Bharat had money.

'She is no longer a kid. She is a grown-up girl, and it is not good to keep a young girl at home. Do you see any prospects for her here?' Ammi started one morning with a weird question to Abbu.

Why she was after marrying me off, I did not know. I was only fourteen. I barely saw her smile. She was usually disappointed in something or someone. She would stare at the sky. Snap at me for no reason. I saw her taking *rupaiya* from Abbu's pocket when he was asleep, which she later denied taking. She would cry when she was alone. She would curse her parents for marrying her off to Abbu. She would look at Abbu with anger that I had never seen in her eyes before. She was unhappy in her marriage. And she still wanted me to get married.

'I don't know many people here yet to talk about this. This is a sensitive topic,' Abbu said dismissively. He did not seem in a hurry to marry me off.

'Maybe brother Salim would know someone. No harm in asking him,' Ammi insisted.

Abbu and I did not grow closer in Bharat, but his ignoring me never really happened there. One reason could be that I stored all my questions in my head. Hardly anything went out. I had decided to ask them to Nadim and no one else. The other reason could be Nadim's absence. He missed Nadim so much that he forgot that anyone at all was present around him. I never heard him and Ammi having long talks. He would chat less while having meals. He stopped making the noise of food chewing that Nadim never liked. He missed his son, the successor to his throne in the Ali household.

I usually accompanied him to the Brahmaputra after lunch. He would go fishing, and I would sit on the banks admiring the beauty of the river. I would stare at it for hours. Talk with it. In my head, I would go back to Hakimpur. To our small house, to our front yard where Nadim and I would discuss this river. I would go back to the Brahma in Hakimpur. I knew Brahma was the biggest thing in the world, bigger than Hakimpur, bigger than mountains, bigger than Bharat, bigger than everyone and everything else. I wondered whether she was ready. I wondered whether she would accept my plea to hear me out. Or if she would accept my company when we both would not talk. I wondered if that was my love for her. Just like my love for Nadim, unending. Infinite. Massive. Giant. Unconditional.

Why do you struggle to find words? Nadim had asked me one day. I told him, 'I have different thoughts every minute about one thing, one person, one situation. With every passing minute, my love grows, my hatred strengthens, my views get stronger.' And he would say, 'Hate is a big word, Shabana. Do not use it.' And I would ask, 'How big?' And he would say, 'Bigger than your Brahma. She would let you live peacefully. Hate would never let you do that.' I would laugh and disagree. That was Nadim. He would always take the conversation to a different level. I missed him when I was with Brahma. I wondered if I could tell the winds flying over Brahma to carry my message to Nadim. To Guwahati that I missed him. That he had to come back, at least for a day.

In Hakimpur, I had learned how to catch fish with my bare hands. Nadim taught me. We once went to the Dhupa *beel*. Nadim splashed the water in front of him, then dove in. A few seconds later, he came up with a small fish in his hand. My mind refused to believe what my eyes had witnessed! Sure that he had a bag of fish somewhere down there, I demanded that he repeat the feat in another part of the pond, a part of my choosing. Once again, dove under, and this time he came up with two fish, one in each hand! Nadim was out of this world. He asked me to follow his instructions blindly. I splashed the water, dove in and I had a fish in my hand. Nadim laughed. I smiled. My chin was up, thinking that Abbu would be proud of me. But I never told him. Now, in Assam, I had a chance. Instead, I murmured, 'I miss Nadim.' We were having dinner. Abbu looked up and said, 'Write him a letter.' He knew I could read and write. Abbu brought an inland letter in two days, and I began writing to my brother, opening myself up again bit by bit.

Dear Nadim,

How are you? And how is everything in Guwahati? We did not speak after we split at Dhubri. Did you reach Guwahati all right? Do you like the house you live in? Abbu said that he gets your whereabouts now and then from Salim uncle. As Salim uncle goes to Guwahati frequently. But I wanted to talk to you and tell you that Abbu, Ammi and I miss you very much.

I know this is not how I am supposed to start a letter, but I am running out of patience to see you and talk to you. Do you miss us? Do you miss me?

The houses here in Assam are different from how they are in Hakimpur. Did you notice that? When I first saw our house, I wasn't sure if it would stand throughout the night as there was heavy wind outside all the time. The house shakes, though. It has stilts. What if they are weak? What if the wood is chipped?

Salim uncle, who is our neighbour, said that poverty and cultural conflicts are major issues in the Brahmaputra Valley. Abbu kept quiet about that. Salim uncle said, 'You don't have to worry. You can still get some land in the hills, and farming will yield more money than fishing.' Abbu looked upset after the discussion. Does Abbu know farming? Would that be easy for Abbu to give up fishing?

Many questions crossed my mind, and I could not ask them of anyone. You know how Ammi and Abbu are-lost in their own individual worlds. But surprisingly, Abbu speaks with me these days—I mean a sentence per day. I am happy with that. Ammi keeps weeping all the time. Sometimes

she complains about Abbu to our neighbor. Asma aun-
tie. Asma auntie's husband, Salim uncle, helped Abbu
get a spot for fishing in the Brahmaputra. Fishing does
not seem to be as popular here in Bharat as it was in
East Pakistan. Abbu was telling Salim uncle that fish
was smuggled from East Pakistan to Bharat and cattle
smuggled from Bharat to East Pakistan. There is a cow
corridor from where the cattle are pushed across the
border. Isn't it a strange concept, a cow corridor?

I like the vibe here in Bharat. It is so positive, fresh, and
inviting. People here are good, too. Very welcoming. What
do you think? I went to Goalpara Bazaar with Ammi on
Saturday. Ammi said we don't have to buy old clothes
when you start sending us money. Did you get any work
yet?

I still have so many things to tell you, but Abbu asked
me to write only in an inland letter. He said, 'Stamps are
expensive. I miss you; do write back. Write a bigger letter;
I would love to read it.'

Yours,

Shabana

I realised after writing a letter to Nadim that I had
missed mentioning how beautiful the sunset looked from
the veranda of our wooden house.

After a month, Abbu came home with a letter from
Nadim.

Dear Shabana,

So good to see your letter. I am not surprised that Abbu
asked you to write one. See, he knows you can read and
write. And he never stopped you from doing so. He is
encouraging you to write more. He is a good father. Admit
it now!

It took me twenty hours to travel from Dhubri to Guwahati that night. I arrived here in the dark. The houses here are not tall, and they do not have stilts. The purpose of stilts is to protect your house from flood and when the land is unstable because of the mud that you mentioned beneath it. I live in a small room with four other boys. We are all from East Pakistan. I started a small cleaning job as soon as I reached here, where I go to clean the university campus. But that does not pay me well. I get to eat only once a day after paying my rent. The room's owner is demanding daily rent because he fears we'll leave without paying. There is a shop here where they are looking for someone who can help serve chai. I went there this morning. The owner is old and kind. He said he would keep me posted on when to start. I am not optimistic, though, as many other boys visited his shop that day.

Guwahati's aura doesn't bother me. But I liked the Hakimpur better. But we are here for good, so let's keep working hard.

I will write more when I get a good-paying job. Unfortunately, I have only two paise to pay for the stamp. I had to use a smaller postcard than you sent. I know you are waiting for more talk; I will discuss all of your questions as soon as possible. And yes, I miss you, Ammi, and Abbu. I miss you the most.

Kuda Hafiz!

Yours,

Nadim

When I was done reading and re-reading the letter to myself, I told Abbu what the letter said. He seemed content, or he seemed excited. I couldn't tell. But he was not sad. And maybe he was proud of the fact that I could read and write without going to school.

One evening, Asma auntie and Salim uncle came home. She has brought *Maccher Jhol.* My favourite. The fish was fried with mustard paste. My taste buds would jump with joy when the mustard paste touched them. Ammi and Asma auntie sat inside. Abbu and Salim uncle sat on the deck. I was inside, but overheard conversations from both sides.

'My days are longer than they used to be in Hakimpur,' Ammi said to Asma auntie.

'You are getting bored. You can see if you get a job on tea plantations? Do you want me to look for it?' Asma auntie said convincingly.

'No, not tea gardens.' Ammi had a big NO on her face, but her tone was mild.

'Why not? I heard women are welcome to work on tea plantations,' Asma auntie said.

'YOU WILL STAY AT HOME. YOU HAVE CHANGED COUNTRY NOT *SHAUHAR*. I AM STILL ALIVE!' Abbu screamed from outside.

Asma auntie and Ammi stopped chatting. I laughed. I could see wrinkles on Ammi's forehead. She was looking older in just a year. Her hair turned gray quickly. She had stopped using the lip colour. And she had dark circles under her eyes. Asma auntie put a finger on her lips, hinting that I should keep quiet. Everyone did it when Abbu got angry.

'Aren't you here to earn more money, have a better life and land for yourself? This is your only chance. Things are going to get complicated from now on.' Salim uncle whispered to Abbu. 'With paddy fields, you will get a portion of paddy for you. You won't need that much; you can sell some of it. That should be enough for three of you for a year,' he continued. I had heard this conversation in the past.

'Fishing is in my blood, Salim,' Abbu said.

'Farming will give you more money. You must work in the fields first. Work long hours. They are not as hardworking as we are. Take good care of their farm. And then you ask them if they want to sell their land,' Salim uncle said. He had a plan.

'And?' Abbu was curious to know more.

'And they will say *yes*,' Salim uncle said and smirked.

'Why would they say yes?' Abbu's eyebrows twisted and his eyes narrowed.

'They don't like outsiders. They don't like lights around their houses. They don't enjoy having people around them. So, they will sell their land and move further into the hills. They would sell it cheap,' Salim uncle said. He knew everything.

'Wise people won't sell land for cheap,' Abbu said.

'There are very few wise people here-hence we can grow here, right?' Salim uncle winked at Abbu.

'Why are we here when they don't like us? Is this manipulation, Abbu? Nadim said this word in the past,' I interfered confidently.

Abbu gave me a sharp look. He told Salim uncle to stop talking through his eyes and neck movement. He did not want to discuss in our house, where three more pairs of ears were witnessing the plan. But I knew he had decided. He was going to get land. Someone's land. Assam's land.

MAHESH

10 July 1979

*W*hen Bhaijan came home, Mother started complaining about the noise from the neighbour's house, that she had to be alone at home every day and that I was not getting married. She even started complaining about the influx from Bangladesh. That the immigrants snatched land, jobs, earned more money than us and created imbalance in society. Bhaijan had a glass of water and left.

There was an agreement to detect and deport Bangladeshis from the voters list in a meeting hosted by the Group-the decision was supported by youngsters, teachers, councils and different groups, sub-groups and tribes. The overall support may mean that next year's elections will be boycotted.

Isn't the world created through migration? But there must be a boundary, a limit, a stop, and, at times, strict laws. We common people can do nothing. Shouldn't the Lady at the Centre act? At least listen to the Group and propose *logical next steps. Dismissing things will only complicate the situation. No one can manage this situation peacefully. People involved are stubborn. I miss Father a lot. I witnessed the accident when he was killed by a truck. I remember people gathering around him, some people coming forward and taking him to the hospital. Had he been alive today, the situation would have been different. Mother was never this torturous. Surely Father's death has taken a toll on her mind. Father would have supported me to complete my education. He may have helped me get admission to the same university where these students gather. I would have been one of the students in their union, which Father may or may not have liked. I am not sure.*

Bhaijan has repaid me the money that he borrowed some time back. I wasn't very sure whether to take it or not, but he forced me to. He has helped me immensely in all aspects of my life since I have known him.

The protests are still going on in some way or another. The slogan 'arm yourself' is even painted at the back of my shop. I can do nothing. Bhaijan said that I am lucky to have been born and brought up in Assam. Who would tell him that I was not? Who made Assam what it is now? Every tribe wants its separate land. Some of them even have their own languages. They do not accept Assamese as their language. There are people from Bangladesh, Nepal, or even people from other states, snatching the jobs and lands. Our identity is not secure in our own land. We are threatened by the Bengalis. We are threatened by the Bangladeshis. We are Otithi in our own land. Protests, satyagraha, and marches are happening in Assam. Then there is police firing. There are deaths. Sometimes outsiders do something violent in reaction to these rallies. Then there are more deaths. Then there is this Lady at the Centre, not paying attention to the Group. Who suffers? We. The poor people. Those who have families to feed. Those who are born in Assam are still under the radar of speculation-because of their language, their religion, and sometimes their attitude. Father loved Assam very much. He suspected chaos would be created. He suspected that people would kill each other. But did he suspect that almost everyone would suffer for different reasons? Tribes, land, language, money, jobs, religion, insider, outsider. Sometimes it is too much to ponder, too much to accept, and too much to let go. It feels like a bad dream. A nightmare. Can I wake up tomorrow morning and find a peaceful Assam? Can I? Can I request all the deities to nullify these pressures and let people live peacefully?

SHABANA

EARLY 1960

Another thing that changed after we moved to Bharat was my making *chai*. I would also get a cup of *chai* everyday morning and evening. But it wasn't a cup of *chai*. It was an emotion.

After keeping the pan on the stove and pouring two-and-a-half cups of water into it, a broad grin would appear on my face. Two spoonfuls of sugar and a spoonful of *chai* powder would lighten my eyes. The boiling sugar water with traces of *chai* powder in it would smell out of this world. The smell would enter my nose and travel straight to my head, energizing my eyes, ears, nose, lips, and everything. Sometimes I would dance to the mild sound of boiling *chai*. With my hands parallel to the ground, my palms directed upwards, my legs folded beneath my thighs, my teeth biting my lips, and my eyes closed. On every boil, I would move my shoulders up and down and move my head sideways. Every subsequent boil would give me more fra-

grance and more energy. After enjoying the magical smell,
then came time to put milk into the boiling brown water. In the way white milk mixed with the brown *chai*,
I thought of us Pakistanis mixing with people in Bharat.
Muslims mixing with Hindus. Outsiders mixing with insiders. Bengalis mixing with Assamese. And then you pour
the *chai* into a glass, a steel glass. Then you hold the glass
in your hand, smell this drink that only *Allah* could have
invented, and take the first sip. It goes through your lips,
to your tongue-touches all the taste buds-and then you feel
the warmth of this *chai* in your throat. It does not go to
your stomach. It is not to fill your tummy. It is to fulfill
your soul, where the heart is, on the left side of your body.
It goes to your heart. Gives it more energy to pump the
blood. When your heart pumps more blood to your body,
your eyes widen further, your brain becomes sharper, and
then you see Ammi is suffering and Abbu is as careless as
a stranger.

One afternoon, while I was just waking from my nap, I
heard Ammi speaking to Abbu. 'I am not at peace! This is
not our land. These are not our people. We are outsiders. We
have come here without any invitation and are using things
that belong to the people here. It is their land. It is their
country. The fish here belong to them. The jobs here belong
to them. Their way of living is different. Ours is different.
Eating beef is a sin in this land. But we cherish beef, right?
This is just one difference. There are many such. Tell me,
aren't we in somebody else's territory?'

'SHUT UP!' Abbu screamed.

But Ammi continued. 'Don't you miss Hakimpur? Our
small house. Our small front yard. I miss it. Even the
sky here looks different. Evenings are darker here, and the

nights are lonely. The days are empty. I miss my mother. She always said I lacked the courage to manage my marriage. She was right. I am a failure.'

I heard a bang on the door. Abbu had left. That was the moment I decided to write a letter to Nadim, to talk to someone sane. Abbu had brought some more inland letters. I picked up one.

Dear Nadim,

Hope you are well. Haven't received your letter in a long time, so writing this to know your well-being. Are you eating well?

There are so many things that I want to tell you, and I am not sure where to start. Let me start with Abbu. Abbu has started working on the farm, day and night. He gives no money to Ammi, but she thinks he is earning more than double the money he was earning in Hakimpur. Tribal people here do not like living amongst outsiders, so they sell their lands cheap to new people and move further inside the forest. Ammi suspects that Abbu has bought such land. It is a good thing, right? But Ammi says that the locals will realize one day that it is their land, and we are capturing it-buying in less money and making more money than they ever made on this land. I think Ammi complicates things. What do you think? Is it our fault that the people here are lazy?

I do not like that Abbu sometimes talks rudely to Ammi. Ammi still wants to go back to Hakimpur. I heard her telling Abbu that people are getting killed for entering Bharat's space. Is that true? Do you know what a Muslim is? The one who wears a burqa, or the one with a long beard? Oh wait, you don't have a long beard-but you are still a Muslim. How come? And what is a Hindu? Those

who do not eat beef. Aren't our faces similar to Hindus?
And our hair is black, just like theirs. What do you think
differentiates us from them or them from us?

I don't think I ever mentioned this about Salim uncle to
you. Salim uncle eats food cooked for three people in one
go. He ate all the machher jhol that Ammi had prepared.
Ammi and I did not get any. He has a big tummy, which
sometimes comes out of his shirt. His lungi slips from his
tummy, so he ties his lungi low. His eyebrows are thick.
We have this space between the two eyebrows, right? He
does not have that. He has one long, thick eyebrow that runs
from one end of his forehead to the other. When he smiles
and when his eyebrows twist and turn, they look like an
earthworm. I have never seen an earthworm as long and as
thick as his eyebrows, though. You also have joint eyebrows,
haven't you? I am laughing now. Salim uncle also talks a
lot, more than Abbu used to. More than I used to.

I am learning to cook these days. I can cook aloo bhaja,
machher jhol, and murgir mangsho. I wanted to cook beef,
but Ammi said I should not expect to get beef here. Ammi
is how she was when we left Hakimpur-wet eyes, frowned
forehead, round lip line. I asked her why she was upset. She
said she had no idea where she should start. She did not
scold me. She said that I have grown up—is that possible in
two years?

I want to say one final thing before I conclude this letter.
I have this fear. Yes, don't say I am fearless. I have this
fear that the real Bharat may not be like our dream Bharat.
Is that a baseless fear? Do you have such fears? How has
Bharat treated you so far? Do you know the real Bharat yet?

I shall wait for your response. Take care; we miss you!

Your-not at all changed-sister;

Shabana

I handed over the letter to Abbu the next day. He seemed pleased to see that I had used the whole paper to write, not a single paisa wasted.

'I shall post it tomorrow,' he said and kept the letter in his shirt pocket.

I showed my teeth. My chin went up. Abbu looked healthier than before. He had started wearing better dresses-the ones coloured black and blue as opposed to his previous pink and red shirts. He would eat at least three rotis. He looked cheerful some days, and on some days extremely gloomy. My evening walks to the Brahmaputra continued. On one such evening, when I was appreciating the beauty of this massive river, I noticed a boy sitting a few steps away from me and staring at me. He smiled at me. I smiled back. His name was Amir, and he was holding the *Kopou Phool* in his hand.

MAHESH

27 August 1979

*C*ustomers discuss every piece of news in the Assam
*Tribune at the shop. I am planning to keep some news-
papers for sale as I am sure I will sell all the newspapers in
no time. Everyone wants to know what's happening. People
are curious.*

*Last month and this month have been busy. I have ex-
tended the working hours by at least three hours. There
are many crowds at the university these days, and people
keep coming and going inside till late. I bought more nimki
and bidi yesterday, just in case. I bought two more types of
biscuits. The shop looks better now, with more material to
sell. The best-selling items are bidi and chai. Currently, the
meetings between the Center and the Group are the main
topic of discussion. About some students flying to Delhi.
And about some big people coming to Guwahati. I have
already told Bhaijan that he had not taken someone's land.
And the shop that he had established some ten–twelve years*

ago is something he had earned. He did not have to bother much about these things. God will help him.

My journey home was on foot, with my bicycle. Silent Guwahati is a gem. I sometimes feel short of words. Such a warm wind and houses with closed doors, no noise, no slogans, no queues, no rallies. Everyone is quiet. Peace.

I am of two minds. One which supports the Group, one which does not. I wonder why we can't seal the border and keep all the people who are already inside. I can't say this aloud; I may upset people. I would be called insensitive. But sometimes very few people think about both sides. Some people want a solution; some want justice; some want ex-citement. Sometimes I think everyone involved in the dis-cussion wants different things, and it may lead to no reso-lution at all.

I also think that I should not bother about these things. I am an Assamese, and as long as I am not touched; I am fine. But I am also concerned about the land that we are losing to outsiders. Why would they snatch land from poor tribal people? Or pay a cheap price? Are they smarter than we are? Do they think that what we have is enough? Do they think that people here are not struggling and that taking a little land from them won't bother them? Some people are also concerned about losing the culture. Assam has a rich culture. Rich language. Our festivals, food, attire, songs, and celebrations are so precious. They say outsiders multiply fast. Why not take the Centre into confidence and close the border? This has become so much more political than anyone else would have ever thought.

Father had told me that when Assamese was declared the official language of the state after independence, the Bengalis fought. The tribes fought. Satyagrahas were held.

People were killed in police shootings. It was unfair to impose Assamese as an official language on the hill people. They asked for separate states. Assam was further divided into different states based on the hill tribes. Some tribes that stayed in Assam have not yet accepted Assamese as their official language. But the core of Assam has remained the same. Assamese is the official language, and there is enough support from the Assamese people to give it priority.

SHABANA

LATE 1960

'I may be a stranger today, but tomorrow I will be someone you know very well,' he said when I had denied
sharing my name with him. We were on the bank, sitting
beside each other, just a foot away. He came there every
evening. I went there every evening. His bicycle was parked
beside him. The bicycle looked old. Very old. He must have
borrowed it from someone or bought it cheap, I thought.
Abbu had given away his bicycle in Hakimpur.

'And how is that possible?' I continued the discussion. I
felt the sand beneath me moving when he shifted towards
me.

I had never seen anyone as beautiful as he was. His face
was as white as wheat flour and as smooth as the glass
mirror that was in Ammi's purse. His nose was straight
like a stick, and his beautifully carved eyes reminded me
of those of a deer. He was indeed a deer, shy and beautiful.
Afraid? No, he didn't seem afraid of anyone.

'I will let you know tomorrow,' he said in my ear. His voice was warm, like *chai*. He smelled of something familiar, *bidi*.

I moved away. 'What do you do for a living?' I asked.

'I work,' he said.

'Where?'

'On farms.' His hands did look like the hands of someone who would work on farms. But they were nowhere near Abbu's.

'Whose farm?' I wondered if he worked at Abbu's farm.

'Not on your Abbu's farm,' he winked at me.

How did he know? *It means he might know my name already. And where I live,* I thought to myself.

'It is late. I must go home now,' I said.

'Tomorrow at the same time?' He asked.

'Yes, same time,' I answered.

It rained for the next two months. So, I did not go to Brahmaputra. But I remembered every word he said. His deep dimple on his right cheek and his uniform teeth. My eyes stared at his lips, and his stared at mine. His thick black hairdo made me think of Dilip Kumar, an actor in Bharat, whose picture Asma auntie carried in her purse without Salim uncle's knowledge. He had long hands. I wonder if they wanted to touch mine. I thought of his lips, his talk, his smile. I craved meeting him. I sat on our veranda and prayed for Brahma to stop the rain almost every day. I noticed Ammi's eyes on me sometimes, but I knew she knew nothing. She was never interested in my life. She was still in Hakimpur.

I went to the Brahmaputra a month after it stopped raining. There was mud all over Goalpara. But I wanted to go, to see Amir. When I tried to step down from our house, my leg went in the mud up to my knee. I had to wait until the sun soaked the water and the soil became hard.

Amir was late for our first meeting after a break of three months.

'I went to fix the puncture, hence the delay,' he explained.

I wanted to hug him tight. Just stare at him. But I did not. 'That's all right. I wasn't expecting you.' I immediately thought that he would know that I was lying.

'But I wanted to see you. How have your days been since we last met?' he asked.

'Nothing different. Same. How about you?'

'I could not sleep. I was thinking about you all the time,' he said, looking directly into my eyes.

Me too. I wanted to say it, but I did not. 'And why so?' I knew the answer. He liked me. But I wanted to hear that from him.

'Because I like talking to you,' he said.

'Why?' I asked and looked at the ground.

'Because you seem innocent.'

'Am I?' I blushed.

'Yes,' he held my chin in his hand and looked into my eyes.

'Is that a good thing, though?' I asked. I wanted him to say yes. I wanted to hear him praise me. I moved a little away. He took his hand off my chin.

'Yes, why not?'

'My brother, Nadim, says I am too innocent for this world.'

'That is so not true. If you meet the right people, you are good for this world. Do not listen to Nadim,' he winked at me.

'You know, I like to colour my lips and face. And wear new dresses every day.' I had changed the topic. I was excited to talk to him.

'Are these your hobbies?' he asked.

'These are my future hobbies. I have never done any of these before.'

He laughed until there were tears in his eyes. 'That is called makeup, you fool,' he said.

I never liked Abbu calling me a fool, but when Amir said that, it sounded cool. Like a compliment. If I could make him laugh, I was good.

'Do you like Hakimpur or Bharat?' he asked.

'Hakimpur.'

There were frowns on his forehead. His eyes were wide open. He wanted me to justify. I rushed through my explanation. 'Because I know Hakimpur very well, I do not know Bharat. This is a land unknown to me. And while we are welcome here, we might have also hurt some sentiments. How long is this river?'

'I don't care about sentiments,' he murmured. 'This river, however, is unimaginably long. We will take a boat someday and go to the other side.'

I ignored the first sentence. 'How beautiful it would be to cross this river!'

'Yes,' he said. He then took my palm and kissed it. *Electricity,* Nadim always spoke about it. I had just felt it. My cheeks were heavy, and I was smiling. I looked at my hand. It had started glowing. Maybe that was love. People glow. Smile. Laugh. Talk. A wave of emotions passed through me. I couldn't name it. It was happiness, but the best happiness in the world. To be in love. We both were sitting on the bank of the Brahmaputra. She was witnessing our conversation. She was noticing me and Amir. And I got a message that she approved of this chat. She didn't mind me talking to a stranger, a man. It could be taboo in the society for a girl to talk to a stranger in a secluded place. But it was not tabooed as per Brahma. So, I feared no one. I was right to talk to Amir, to meet him, to fall in love with him. I sat there and chatted with him until sunset.

I told him about our house in Hakimpur, Sona, my conversations with Nadim in our front yard, and our journey to Goalpara. He listened intently. No complaints. Though he did not ask any questions, it seemed that he was attentive. For a few minutes during our conversation, he would look at Brahma and then back at me. He was thinking of something in parallel.

'What are you thinking?' I asked.

'No, nothing. I am simply listening to you.'

'No, you are not.'

'I was thinking about your lips. Are they naturally pink? Or you apply something to them?' I didn't answer. I bit my lip and looked away. He looked away, too. I was shy; he was shy.

'Who's in your family?' I asked him.

'It is you,' he answered.

'Me?'

'You will become one day, won't you?' He asked and held my hand.

'What do I have to do to become your family?' I asked. His hands were very soft. I tightened my grip on it.

'Talk with me every day; just the way you are doing now. I cannot chat as much as you do. You just have so much energy. And you have so many stories. You can talk for hours about people you love. But I can hear. Yes, I am all ears-you can share everything with me.' I moved close to him. With our hands entangled in each other's, we witnessed the sunset together.

'Is it okay if I leave now?' I said as the darkness was descending on us.

'Yes sure. You are obedient.'

'Aren't I? Ammi will never understand,' I said and left barefoot with my *chappal*s in my hand. I noticed my footprints on the sand. They went deep inside the land on the riverbank. *If we dig here, would we find Brahma running from beneath the land?* I had a thought that I decided to ask Nadim. My footprints reminded me of Ammi's feet. She would create them on the cow dung that covered the floor of our one-room house in Hakimpur.

I did not look back, but I knew Amir was looking at me. He was thinking of me. His eyes were on my back. He was noticing my walk, my *burqa*. I reached home. Helped Ammi in cooking that night and slept. I could not stop thinking about Amir. He was so handsome. He came into my dream that night, and we spoke for a long time. I told him everything about Hakimpur again. He listened to everything again, and he also told me about his life. That he was from *East Pakistan* itself, from Sylhet. His parents lived in Sylhet, and he had one younger sister and four younger brothers. There was a huge responsibility on his shoulders as the eldest son. He didn't follow any. He wanted a life of his own. He ran away from his house to live his dream life. Where he earned money and spent all that money on himself. I opened my eyes midway through that dream. I wasn't in a bad mood. I knew Amir was nothing like my dream. I could hear birds chirping and see a ray of light coming from behind the hills through the window.

MAHESH

8 October 1979

*B*haijan showed me the picture of Agha and her sister Rani. Both are beautiful. But Agha is more beautiful than any other woman I have ever seen, be it in real life or on television. In fact, she is more beautiful than Hema Malini. I am going to show this picture to Mother tonight. Bhaijan thinks she would be a great match for me. Yes, she definitely is. He planned to speak with Mother soon. Best if he talks with her now.

Mother openly sides with the Assamese, especially tribal people. She says they are innocent, naive. They could not understand the world. They could not understand the hunger for money, the hunger for land the rest of the world has. And that they could not identify opportunities. But also, that they have been punished enough. Now the Lady must help. She must help us.

SHABANA

EARLY 1961

'Less milk, we pay for it here,' Ammi said when I was making *chai*. I liked more milk in my *chai*.

'It's not much, Ammi.'

'For two cups of *chai*, we use half a cup of milk, and the rest is water,' Ammi said to me. Her nose was red, and her eyes were big.

'Why are you angry?' I asked.

'That's because I have to tell you one thing multiple times,' Ammi continued. 'You have no brain.'

I got up from there and went onto the veranda. I cried. And I missed Amir. I wanted to go to him and hug him tight. I didn't even know where he lived. *Why do we live with our parents? Why can't I live on my own-or with Amir? With someone who understands me.* Ammi came to the deck and sat in a chair beside mine. I looked the other way. At the sun.

'You know, Shabana, I had four babies after Nadim and before you,' Ammi said.

'FOUR!' I was surprised. That was a new piece of information.

'And where are they now?' I continued out of curiosity.

'They are with *Allah!* She looked at the sky.

'Why? What happened?'

'I do not know. I could never solve that mystery. All of them died when they turned one, strangely. One of them had a fever, and he died. Another one had a cough, and he died. The twins had heart problems. All boys. After your delivery, the doctor begged me and Abbu not to have any more kids. Your Abbu wanted sons, more sons, to earn more money so he could relax when he is old, and they would take care of him.' Ammi wiped her tears and continued, 'But I was exhausted, lonely, and felt inadequate.'

'Is that why you are always upset?' Ammi looked at me in anger. I had asked the right question. Her anger towards me was constant. 'And is that why you do not like me?' I continued. I was angry too. *Was I the punching bag to take blows from everyone?*

Ammi left saying nothing.

But I knew that when she left Hakimpur, she felt that the only thing that belonged to her had gone. Abbu had taken that from her after he took himself and Nadim away. Nadim was raised by Abbu, not Ammi. Abbu would spend all the time with Nadim as Ammi's punishment for not giving him any more sons. Nadim grew closer to Abbu. That was Abbu-rude, cruel. But Abbu did not stop Nadim from getting close to me; we were the best brother and sister. Ammi was left aside-that was Abbu-inconsiderate. Ammi was curious about Bharat until we moved to Bharat.

She wanted to know how the tea plantations in Bharat look like? If the Brahmaputra in East–Pakistan and the Brahmaputra in Bharat are different? Can we eat beef in Bharat? If Bharat has any fish? She thought East Pakistan is the only place on the globe to have fish. When she ate fish in Bharat, she declared that the fish in East Pakistan is the best. But Ammi was also losing her mind, not ready to overcome the loss of leaving Hakimpur. She told me once that she saw Abbu talking to Salim uncle on the farm. In reality, Salim uncle and Asma auntie had gone to Sylhet that week to see their relatives. She would see animals flying in the sky, fish on the ground and birds swimming in beels. She would cook *aloo* and say that was chicken; she would make three rotis and say she had made six. And many such things.

I did not tell Ammi about Amir. She never had freedom. I wasn't sure about her reaction to my freedom-freedom to love a man. A beautiful man. He did not think that boys are better than girls. He was not money–minded. He did not scold me or get angry with me. I was enjoying the freedom to walk to Brahma every evening; I would not risk that. I continued meeting Amir that year. He would stare at me for a long time, sometimes even without dropping his eyelids. He would keep his hand on my hand. Our hands would rest on the sand. He would move his fingers on my fingers. Each hair on my finger, however small, could feel his touch and his love for me. He would then move his hand on my forearms, and a shiver would run through my body. But then he stopped at my elbow. He did not move his hand anywhere else.

Some days, he would touch my feet and fingers. Then move his hand up from there-inside my salwar. That would give me goosebumps. He would touch my foreleg. He would stop at the big mole near my knee. The hair on my legs would entangle with each other after he moved his hand away. When I looked into his eyes, he would avoid my gaze. Sometimes his hands seem tough, and sometimes delicate. Both. My hands were in a rush to touch him. To touch his cheek, his forehead, his lips. But I would try not to dwell on that thought. After touching my hands and my legs, he would stare at the river and say nothing. And I was still comfortable. He would move his hand from his hair and look at Brahma. He was a thinker, a deep thinker. He would stare at my lips and say that he loved my lips the most – pink, delicate lips, with a mole on the right side of the upper lip—he would describe them. I would look at his eyes, narrow—I could not look through them some days, and some days they were full of love. Love for me. Love for my hair. Love for my lips. Love for my hands. Love for my feet. I would go home before sunset. Some days, he would hold my hand and ask me to stay back longer. I would do so. But he would remain silent. Abbu hardly spoke to me; Ammi scolded me. I was not comfortable around them. But Amir was different. I wanted to get closer to him. Whether he talked to me or not.

'Where do you live, Amir? Is this to the north of the Brahmaputra or south?' I asked about the one thing that had been bothering me for days. I did not know him well enough.

'Does that matter?' he asked.

'Yes, it does. I have told you everything about me. When will I know everything about you?'

'Don't get upset, Shabana. That is not you. You are patient. You trust me. You know I would keep nothing from you,' he said and kept his hand on my shoulder. *Then tell me, where do you live?* Words remain inside my mouth. His touch made me lose myself. I instead moved forward and hugged him. He was taken aback.

'You are quick,' he smirked.

'How do you mean?' I was offended.

'I mean, you don't have to attack me. Be patient.'

My heart started racing. I felt as if I had been stabbed in my stomach. *Why would he say that? He does everything that he wants to-why am I under restrictions?*

I got up from there, put on my *chappal*s and started walking towards my home.

'Shabana, Shabana, wait!' he came after me.

'I have work at home; I have to go,' I was quick to answer.

'I was kidding.'

'No, you were not. You are rude,' I stated a fact.

'I am not. Here..,' he said and pulled me close to him. Close to his chest. I could see his chest hair from the top buttons of his shirt. I could smell him. My face was close to his neck. His body was warm, and he was bigger than I had thought. I wanted to close my eyes and just feel the heaven I was in. And I also wanted to keep my eyes open and see every bit of his neck, his chest, his chin. I felt his love at that moment. I felt his care. I felt his craving for me. I loved him. He loved me. He was Amir. My Amir. He put his lips on mine. I felt the heat inside my mouth. I felt the softness of his lips. He retracted. I had just closed my eyes. I had just started feeling his love for me. He took a few steps back.

'You better go, Shabana, it's late,' he said.

I instead moved ahead to kiss him. He moved farther away.

'Next time,' he said. That was Amir, unpredictable. I walked back home. I did not turn back to see him. I did not feel his eyes on me. That was Amir. At moments, he was my world, and, at moments, I did not know him at all.

MAHESH

20 October 1979

*B*haijan, who was otherwise not interested in any of
the Group's meetings or discussions, went to attend
the gathering at Judge's Field last week. Newspaper articles
indicate that voter turnout in many parts of Assam has
more than doubled. Possibly, the voter list would be revised.
Outsiders would be identified and deported. But the meeting
that Bhaijan attended directed people's focus onto something else.

He did not tell me what the meeting was about, but some
customers were discussing it at the shop. The Group will
use the word "foreigner" instead of "outsider" for their
movement from now on. The protests and rallies and
marches will be against foreigners now and not outsiders.
This is to clarify that the movement is not against any
religion or language. It is against anyone who has crossed
the border and come to Bharat illegally. That is not a relief
to Bhaijan.

After that meeting, I saw the marches increased. People would march from Guwahati University, shouting slogans and carrying placards in their hands. "Boycott Foreigners!", "We want sovereignty!" written on their placards. Some rallies were held a few kilometers away from the university, where people carried fire torches in their hands. I saw many women taking part. I would wonder whether Agha would ever take part in these rallies, or if she would be scared like her maternal uncle, Bhaijan. Sometimes the marches went on and on throughout the day. Sometimes I had to close the shop as there was not enough space on the road for these people to walk, and the door of my tiny shop, which opens on the road, was a kind of roadblock. No one ever asked me to close the shop, because some people stopped at the shop for some chai and bidi, but I wanted no risk. The back door worked fine. I served chai from there.

It is not possible for an Assamese to spend a day without at least two cups of chai, so rallies or no rallies, I am earning enough money these days.

SHABANA

LATE 1962

That evening, I saw him clean-shaven. He let me kiss him on his cheek. He kissed me on my lips. We did not speak much; we only kissed. I liked his soft lips, the smell of his breath, his clean cheeks, and his bony chest. He pulled me closer to himself. Moved his hands up my legs and between my thighs. He slowly raised his hand upward while looking directly into my eyes. I pushed his hand away. He repeated his act. I again pushed his hand away. Rage flowed through him like lava. The veins in his neck were bulging. His nose became red. The winds were stronger than on any other day, but I still witnessed myself perspiring. *What should I do?* I thought to myself. I kissed him; he pushed me away. I moved further closer to him and hugged him; he pushed me away. He got up and started walking away.

I panicked. 'Amir, wait!'

'WHAT FOR?' he screamed.

'Please sit, please. I beg you.' I was on my knees, holding his hand.

He did not respond, did not move. I stood still, staring at Brahma.

I held his hand and kept it on my chest. He moved his hand onto my chest, still did not look at me.

'Please come to me,' I said, pulling his hand close to me.

He sat down. Gave me a kiss and moved his hand inside my kurta and all over my chest. I liked it, and I did not like it. Both. He gently put his hand again between my thighs.

'Amir,' I said gently. He did not like strong voices, I had realised.

'Yes.' His eyes were closed, and his voice was soft. His hand was still roaming between my thighs.

'I cannot do this with anyone other than my *shauhar.*'

'Are you asking me for marriage?'

Well, I had not asked him to marry me. That was a blunt question. But I also thought that he was only spending time with me and would not marry me. 'Why not? Don't you like me?' I said.

'Well, I do. I do love you, Shabana. Let's get married,' he said. But I sensed doubt in his voice. I did not go to Brahma for a few days after that. There was no reason to be surprised at my proposal. Was he thinking that I would do whatever he asked me to without getting married?

I felt as if good times were just around the corner, and then they disappeared. I felt so happy and lucky with Amir. He listened to me talking all the time. Unlike Ammi and Abbu. I cursed myself for not going to Brahma to see him.

'Ammi, what is the meaning of marriage?' I asked Ammi one evening when we were having *chai.* Abbu was at work.

'Marriage is when a man and a woman live together.'

'From what age?'

Ammi glanced at me. The *kajal* in her eyes was thicker than on any other day; she had not cried that day.

'Why do you ask?'

'I want to get married.'

'*Ya Allah!* You are a woman. You should never show a desire to get married. People will judge you.'

'How would they judge me?'

'They would think that you are a bad woman,' Ammi said.

'What is a bad woman?' I asked.

'A woman who falls in love with a man. Lets him touch her before *Nikah*. Asks a man to marry her without waiting for a man to propose to her. One who is keen on getting married. Likes another man after marriage. Talks too much. Talks aloud. Does not cook food for her family. Wakes up late. Argues with her *shauhar*. World does not like such a woman,' she answered. I sensed there was an unending list.

'And why are men allowed to say such things? Or show desperation? Or behave the way they want?' I asked.

'Because this is a man's world. Men make decisions. We follow. Men order. We follow. Men tell us what to do and how to do it. We follow,' Ammi said.

'That is not true, Ammi. Some men listen to women,' I said confidently.

'And where do these men live? Are they on some other planet?' Ammi mocked me.

'Well, do you think Nadim would ever treat his wife like that?'

'You never know!'

'You raised him, you would.'

Ammi interrupted, 'I did not. Your Abbu raised him. I was responsible only for feeding him. He spent hardly any time with me.'

'But I know Nadim. He would never expect a woman to follow his orders blindly.'

'We shall see!' Ammi laughed.

I kept quiet. Had I made a mistake by asking Amir to get married to me? I might not. Everyone's experiences are different, as Nadim told me once.

When I went to the river, after almost fifteen days, I saw Amir. Staring at the water and intermittently throwing stones into it. I sat next to him.

'Let's get married,' he said.

'I have not yet talked about you to Ammi and Abbu,' I answered plainly.

'Will they approve of our marriage?' he asked.

'I am not sure,' I answered.

'They do not care for you, do they?' He looked into my eyes. I looked at him. I thought about what he had said. He was right. I had given him that information.

'But no girl has chosen her *shauhar* ever in Hakimpur. Ammi and Abbu would not like it. Won't I be remembered for eloping and getting married without my parents' consent?'

'It's different. Yes. But not bad,' Amir said, not convincingly.

It was different, yes. I loved different. Different made me happy.

'What about Nadim?' I blurted.

'Let's get married first. You can always notify Nadim by letter. He can come see us when he can.' He pulled me close to him and kissed me.

'I love you more than anything else in this world, Sha-bana,' he said. Those words sounded magical. His madness for me mesmerized me completely at that moment. I agreed. I agreed to be different. To be courageous. To elope and get married. At that moment. Instead of going home, we went to a mosque.

MAHESH

1 November 1979

I did not take part in any discussions at the shop today or for the past few days. I have realised that I do not have a concrete opinion about this issue related to outsiders. I get stuck between two minds. Some days I support the Group, some days I just want peace. Some subgroups in the past have accused the Group of filing false complaints against them that they are not insiders. I have no opinion about that. There is no compulsion to have an opinion. I find that safe. Not hurting anyone's sentiments.

But deep down, I want everyone to be safe. Be it insiders or outsiders.

SHABANA

LATE 1962

The bus stopped in the dark. I got down first, then Amir. I carried my luggage. Amir carried his small bag. I couldn't see the road in the dark. But I could hear the river water flowing. We walked for a while before entering a village. I couldn't see the room we entered properly. There was no light. 'I will fix the light tomorrow,' Amir said. I nodded.

We kept the bags in the corner. I was hungry, but Amir had no intention of letting me cook. He locked the door, dragged me close to him and kissed me on the lips. His cold lips made me shiver a little, but I got used to them the next moment. Then I felt his teeth on my neck, his hands on my waist, his hair on my cheek. My hands were on his back. I unbuttoned his shirt. He unbuttoned my blouse. We were on the floor, kissing each other. I loved him. And I knew he loved me. He moved his hands onto my thighs and kissed me on my chest. He was sweating but also laughing. He slept quickly. I stayed awake, looking at the ceiling. I wished for many more such nights. I had no regrets about leaving Ammi and Abbu's house and marrying Amir.

***

The next morning, when I woke up, Amir was not in the room. The door was closed but not locked. I opened the door and looked outside. It was a narrow lane with small rooms on both sides. I could see straight inside those rooms where other people were living. Everyone was awake, and almost all the houses had their doors open. I closed the door. There was a cup of *chai* covered with a saucer. There was a small earthen pot with water. Clearly, there was no bathroom inside the room. In our Hakimpur house, the bathroom was inside the house, and there was a public toilet outside that we used. Here, the situation was rather worse. I went outside to hunt for a bathroom. On the right side, there was a never-ending series of one-room houses. I walked towards the left. There was a narrow road going behind these houses, which I followed. Farther left, there were two doors, half-broken. I opened one of them, a bathroom, and it was bigger than Amir's one- room house, and there was no bucket. No mug. There was a tap. The water was cold. I washed my mouth, face, feet, and hands. The bathroom was made of asbestos sheets, and it surprisingly, it had no roof. It had no lock inside as well. I had not brought a towel, but there was someone outside the bathroom holding a small towel for me.

'I am Dimi. I am your neighbor. Amir did not tell us about his *Nikah*,' she said. She had to bend to enter through the door. Her hair, neck, and hands were longer than those of an average woman's, and her dusky skin tone was shinier than the silver earrings that Asma aunty used to wear.' He comes home once a month and doesn't talk much to anyone. What's your name?' she continued.

'Shabana.'

'Congratulations, Shabana.' Her lips parted in a smile, showing her uniform teeth.

'Take this towel. And here is some ash for cleaning your teeth,' she offered her help.

'Thank you.'

'I will see you after some time?' She asked.

I nodded.

Usually people are good, I remember Nadim telling me. *Very few people are evil-minded and want to hurt others.* Leaving Ammi and Abbu did not make me cry, but the memory of each word that Nadim had told me that was stored in the cabinet in my heart, in my soul, did. There was a difference between wiping your face with a towel and wiping away your tears-the latter can never conceal your red eyes.

I walked to my house. I wasn't sure where Dimi lived. I carried the remaining ash and the towel with me. I lit the stove to warm my *chai*. I put the chai in the pan, smelled it and saw the steam rising up and going all around the room. Using the half-broken filter, I filtered my tea back into the cup. The colour of the walls was light yellow, and it seemed that the room hadn't been coloured for years. I wasn't sure since when Amir had been living there.

I opened my bag, folded all the salwar kameez, Ammi's two sarees that I had put in the bag without her noticing, a *burqa* and kept them on the shelf in the corner. I opened

Amir's bag, took out three pairs of pants and a shirt, and hung them with nails on the wall. His bag was empty except for a pink handkerchief at the bottom of it. It wasn't mine.

'Where did Amir go?' Dimi was at the door again.

'He must have gone to find some work. We are going to settle here,' I said.

'Sure, I live there.' She pointed at a house. The big house. There was a small playground between her house and the colony where I had lived for a night. A small boy came running toward her. 'And this is my boy, Chandan,' she said, smiling.

'Do you want to come in?' I asked her.

'You seem to be in the middle of something,' she said, looking at the open bags. 'You can continue your work, we will talk later,' and she started leaving the room.

'Dimi, do you know where the grocery store is?'

'Yes, just outside the colony. What do you need? Do you want company?' She offered her company this time.

'How about in an hour's time? I will clean the room until then,' I smiled.

'Good, just shout my name from the door. I will be here,' she said and left.

There was a small window on the same wall as the door. Through the door and the window, I could clearly see Dimi's house. I wasn't sure why Amir had gone out without waking me up. I went to the bathroom to take a bath. Dimi came as soon as she saw me walking towards the bathroom.

'Shabana, it is better to take a bath early in the morning when no one is awake. It does not have a lock. And it is shared, right? There is always someone using it,' she offered her advice at that time.

'Oh, will you wait at the door? I will be quick,' I asked.

She nodded. With that awkward experience, our friendship started.

In the afternoon, I made some rice. There were limited
groceries for making curry. I had a few rupees-picked up
from Ammi's purse while packing my stuff- that I used
to buy potatoes-my favourite-and a few spices. I thought
Amir would come home for lunch, but he did not. There
was no way for me to find where he was. He came home in
the evening. He seemed tired. I made some *chai* for us and
handed the cup over to him. He made no eye contact.

'How was your day?'

He kept quiet.

'You will get the job, Amir'. I put my hand on his hand.
He had a frown on his forehead. I wasn't sure whether to
continue the conversation or not. I was afraid of him, but I
also wanted to speak out. I spoke.

'There is nothing here, no food. No blanket. No water,' I
continued. He kept quiet.

'I can buy some stuff if you give me some money,' I said.

'I don't have any money, Shabana.'

'What happened to the money you earned in Goalpara?
Did you spend all?' I asked him. In my view, the questions
were asked in a gentle tone. But he did not like them. He
looked at me with anger.

'That is none of your business,' he said in a stern voice.

'It was not my business-but now it is. How do you expect
me to stay here with you? We need some basic things...,' he
did not let me finish my speech. He threw the cup against
the wall. His eyes were red, and he was fuming.

'Do not ask me about MY MONEY. I decide what to do
with it. ALWAYS,' the usual Amir has spoken. I realised
that I had made a mistake by asking him about money. He

was already stressed, and I had made his situation worse. Tears began to well up in my eyes. He stormed out of his tiny house. Everything was calmer in a moment, except my soul. It was disturbed, badly disturbed. I blamed Abbu-he had asked us to leave Goalpara to save his reputation. Because of him, Amir was jobless. Because of him, we were fighting. And because of him, we did not have a proper place to sleep. Poor Amir. He suffered because of me.

I got up, cooked dinner and waited for him to come home. When he came home drunk, we ate, we made love and slept. He did not look at me when he kissed me, nor did he say anything. I loved Amir's touch. I put my hands through his hair. He was calm. I knew it was my love that brought him back home. I had decided not to ask him anything about the job or the money. I had to stand by him in his tough time. Unlike Ammi, who constantly tortured Abbu with talk of Hakimpur.

MAHESH

20 November 1979

*O*nly so that Mother could feel better, I decided yesterday to gift her a statue of her favourite deity. Maa Durga. Mother's eyes softened when she saw her gift, and she had a wide smile on her face. Mother is a big supporter of women-especially women who change the world-those who dare to go against the tide-dare to fight and win-just like the Lady at the Centre.

Mother is Hindu; Father was Muslim. Mother is Assamese; Father was Bengali. Both were born in Assam. They eloped from their respective houses and married, but their families accepted them in no time. Mother married Father on two conditions-one, that she would not have many kids; in fact, she would have just one—and the other that her kid would carry her surname, not Father's. People called her insane. But Father agreed. Mother raised me as a Hindu; Father did not object. Mother taught me Assamese; Father never taught me Bengali.

Father was living with his family, surrounded by tea gardens, before eloping with Mother. His father, my grandfather, was a tea labourer. He had migrated from Bengal in the early 1900s. He started working as a labourer and soon became an administrator. Father followed my grandfather's footsteps and became a labourer and then an administrator. His mother was an Assamese. When Father met Mother, he decided he had to do something for Assam, for Bharat. She intensified his patriotic feelings. They eloped, and he became a land administrator in Guwahati. He said the job was difficult, as sometimes he would become emotional and give people the benefit of the doubt. Some people made use of his nature and approached him frequently to resolve disputes related to land. He had realised soon that Assam was in danger. That the Assamese had to pull up their socks, take control of their jobs, and land. But he also predicted that this problem should be resolved sooner and peacefully. Violence would not help. When people expected him to bend his morals, he decided it wasn't the right job for him. He quit. He bought a shop for cash near the university.

Father was focused on good, inclusive thinking. He said all gods are the same, be it Shiva, Krishna, Allah or Jesus. Only the names are different. No one promotes violence. They promote only love and acceptance. He said that before independence from the British, Bharat and Bangladesh were one. We were all from the same country. Then there was the problem of interprovincial migration. Now, it has become a problem of illegal immigration. To me, this seems more serious, though.

SHABANA

EARLY 1963

Amir started working on a farm. He went to work every day. *No holidays,* he said. But when he came home, he was never tired. Never lacking energy. Or that was my love for him. I liked him no matter how he looked. Good, bad, tired, active. He would make *chai* most mornings while I would take a bath.

One day when I saw he was in a good mood, I asked him, 'May I go out with Dimi to the *Bazaar*? She said scarves and *chappals* are sold for a cheap rate there.'

'Stay away from Dimi,' he said.

'Why?' I asked. 'She has been very helpful since we came here. She even helps with food and groceries sometimes,' I murmured.

'Why do you take food and groceries from her? Were you raised in a royal family where you had a kitchen stuffed with food? I bet your parents had not have much food at home, nor did they ever buy good clothes for you. You were poor. What's the problem if I am poor?' he said.

'That is not true. I never had to ask anyone to lend me anything.' I murmured.

'If you are ashamed of me, you may leave. I can get any Assamese girl,' he said.

I apologized to him. But I had so many questions in my head. *Why is he talking about my leaving him? Where do I go if I leave him? Abbu and Ammi would never take me back. And why does he want an Assamese girl?* I did not know who Amir was and what he thought. However, I had decided never to stay away from Dimi. I did not go to the *bazaar* with her, but I would take her for walks without Amir's knowledge. I would not wear a *burqa* when I was out with her. Amir, however, had gotten two *saree*s for me-they looked old. He did not like my wearing anything but a saree. So, I would wear a *saree*. I gave Dimi some of the *salwar kameez* from my bag. Not sure what she did with them, she gave me a few *saree*s in return, though. I tore the remaining *salwar kameez* and used them to clean the floor, window, door. Sometimes wipe my sweat, tears.

My question and his answer never changed. What changed was the way he responded. Sometimes he would answer patiently. Sometimes he wouldn't. Sometimes he would make love without being drunk. He would stare at my lips but would not praise my beauty as he used to. I convinced myself it was because of my old *saree*s and oily hair. I would talk then. I would tell him how much I love him and how much I miss Nadim. How much I liked Bharat and how much I miss Hakimpur. I told him about missing Brahma and our pending boat ride to the other end of Brahma. He would never respond. I did not know whether he would listen to me or ignore me.

Months passed by—I set up my routine. I would wake up early every day, have a bath, cook food for Amir to carry in his tiffin, talk with Dimi, take a nap in the afternoon, make *chai* in the evening, cook dinner, wait for Amir to come home, eat and sleep. Some days, he would bring groceries and vegetables on his way home from the farm. Sometimes I would borrow sugar or salt or oil from Dimi. He would not know. He would give me two rupees sometimes. Sometimes, he would not give a single *paisa* to me. I would rely on Dimi on such occasions. In the afternoon, sometimes I would write letters to Nadim and then tear them up. He had not tried to contact me even once, and I would not contact him either.

Dimi became my best friend. We both talked every day after Amir went to the farm. Discuss every other household in the colony. Discuss her husband, Viju, and my husband. She would tell me about Bharat, and I would tell her about East Pakistan. She would tell me about people from East Pakistan entering Bharat and snatching land. She would tell me about people in Bharat not liking outsiders coming in. I would tell her that people outside Bharat thought Bharat had a lot of resources. She would say yes, but Bharat also has many people. Bharat's resources are for Bharat's people. I would say, but outsiders respect and love Bharat. She would say yes, but there is a process, a way to enter. Why do they sneak in? I would not answer. I had sneaked in.

I, however, did not know where Amir was from.

One evening, when he came home, ate, and slept, I checked his pockets. There were ten rupees in his pocket. I took out three rupees to buy the groceries the next day. I also found a pair of earrings. I smiled to myself. That was my Amir. He was still thinking about me—my likes, my dislikes. I kept the earrings back in his pocket. I also kept back the three rupees—I would ask him for money when he would gift me the earrings in the morning, I thought. My Amir. My love. I lay down beside him. I did not care that I was living in a small house with less food—poverty does not hurt when you are surrounded by people you love. I remembered Nadim telling me this—I had a man who loved me and cared for me. In my view, I was a fortunate woman. I was so fortunate, though, that I never got those earrings, and I also missed the opportunity to steal the three rupees.

MAHESH

01 December 1979

*Y*esterday, a girl came to Bhaijan's shop and stared at me for quite a while. She was beautiful. Bhaijan told me I was staring at her. I don't take him seriously sometimes.

Few students flew to Delhi last month to see the President. They have asked him to postpone the upcoming elections in Assam. No conclusion. That's Assam's destiny. Action from the State, no reaction from the Centre.

Bhaijan and I had a fantastic dinner outside this week. When I tried the alcohol for the first time, it tasted terrible. I did not want anymore but Bhaijan pushed me to have one more glass. That night, I stayed with Bhaijan because I could not ride my bike home, and he worried about Mother's reaction, affecting our future alcohol plans. He says that I am still a kid to her. When Bhaijan was drunk, he started telling me about the day when he and his family travelled to Bharat. He told me how excited everyone was. He told *me about his younger sister, Shabana, and how much he loves her. He told me how his parents were deported to Bangladesh the year Shabana got married. And that his mother was killed in the stampede in the deportation camp. She never reached back to her homeland. He cried hard. He misses his mother. He misses his father. He said their decision to come to Assam had broken their family. He said he did not share the news of their mother's death with his sister. He did not know how she would manage the pain.*

SHABANA

MID 1963

That morning when I woke up, I felt dizzy. I slept all day long, did not give tiffin to Amir, nor did I cook for myself. Dimi came knocking at the door in the late afternoon. When she found me still lying on the floor, she gave me some warm water. An elderly woman, who also lived in my village, performed some checks on my wrist. Dimi went out with the lady and got medicine for me, along with some rice and fish curry. I had food and took the medicine. I slept again. I woke up in the evening. Dimi was sitting on her veranda. She rushed to me when she saw me at the door.

'You are pregnant,' she said and put a piece of jaggery in my mouth. I smiled, but I was not sure how Amir would react. I touched my tummy, but I did not feel any change in my body. It was indeed good news. Ammi had said once that children bring stability. I hoped the sign of our love would lessen Amir's anger and bring peace to our life. I made *kheer*. Ammi had made it when Nadim started helping

Abbu fishing, assuming that there would be more money coming home. She had made it whenever she wanted to tell Abbu something when she was happy. When Amir came home tired, I offered him *kheer* instead of *chai*.

'What's this for?' he asked.

'I have good news, Amir.' I said. He nodded, but did not look up.

'I am pregnant,' I said, smiled and looked at the ground.

'I have no money for *our* food, so where do you expect me to get money to take care of a baby? And are you sure it's my baby?' He asked. He did not flinch. Even though the weather was very hot that day, I was frozen by Amir's words. My stomach twisted. I ignored his questions to continue the conversation.

'Do you think I should work? I can work, Amir. I see some ladies working on the farms,' I asked.

'Do you want to tell the world how incapable your *shauhar* is? Is that your intention? Or your lover is working on the farm, and you want to join him,' he continued his aggression.

'No, Amir, I am thinking of making our life better-'

'By working outside, Shabana?'

'Yes, because women work.'

His palm hit me hard on my cheek. I controlled my tears. I put on my *chappals* and left the house without a *burqa*. I knew it would anger him further that I went out without a *burqa*, but I did not care that day. The narrow lane felt longer than usual that day, and when it ended, I walked for some more time to reach a river, the Kopili. Dimi and I had come here many times. I sat there alone. Looking at the slow-moving water. Looking at the *naukas* docked on the bank of the river and noticing the *Kopou Phool* swinging with the wind. I looked around, and when I saw no one, I let my tears flow freely and let my cry come out. Not my vision, but life had blurred in front of me. I thought of Amir, who had asked me about my dreams. Dreaming was far–fetched for me; I was desperate to live a normal life. A life that Amir had promised me. I wanted to speak with *Allah*, and I knew no other way to see him and talk with him apart from dying. What Dimi said about Amir seemed correct that day. Amir wanted a good life, but without any responsibility. He wanted to have a house, a lot of money-but only for himself. He wasn't built to think about others, or even his own wife, for that matter. He was a liar. I wasn't sure if he had ever loved me. I thought about the pink handkerchief found in his bag, which was not mine. I thought about the studs, which were never given to me, and disappeared from his pocket the next day. The smell of the talcum powder from his neck-when we did not have any talcum powder at home.

My visits to Kopili stopped when I was in my ninth month of pregnancy. Kopili reminded me of the Brahmaputra. But the Brahmaputra was like East Pakistan, known to me since my birth, and Kopili was like Bharat: I did not know what it held for me. There was something more. Something more that I was looking forward to, something more that would bring me closer to something else. I could never grow closer to Kopili. Maybe because it was born in Bharat, and it died in the same land. It had no connection with East Pakistan and, hence, with me. It was different.

I was bad at making new relationships, or maybe I had become bad. Or I had developed a mentality to keep myself safe. I did not know. But I had started liking silence, being quiet, being invisible. That helped. Dimi said that there was chaos in my head. That I was a mess. But how would she

know the unannounced pain of leaving your parents, of assuming that they never loved you and of trusting a stranger
only to see that your life has turned upside down? I missed
Nadim. My only constant. Everything since the night we arrived in Bharat seemed complicated to comprehend. There
was no clarity, only confusion and only questions.

Time changed more quickly than I could ever have imagined.

MAHESH

15 December 1979

I sometimes wonder if we are too gentle with the Centre and too harsh with certain subgroups. I am not really sure, but some people were saying such things the other day at the shop. I also heard that some people are forced to go back to West Bengal as the violence is increasing day by day. Their state government has set up a few camps for them. They are mostly farmers and fishermen. Some Nepalese farmers have also been deported. Bhaijan heard this conversation too. When the discussion was over, he took out his handkerchief and started wiping the sweat from his brow.

SHABANA

LATE 1967

When Ammi had seen me with Amir, she did not believe her eyes. Abbu was sitting on the veranda, smoking a *bidi*. He stared hard at me.

'Is this why you went to the Brahmaputra every evening?' he asked. Either he wasn't surprised to see me and Amir, or he hid it well. I kept mum. Ammi started crying.

'What have you done, Shabana? This is not a good sign. You should not have done this,' she let out a loud cry after saying this. Her eyes were red in no time. Amir kept nudging me at the elbow, asking me to leave.

'Abbu, I love Amir. I did not know any other way to do this,' I confessed to Abbu. I wanted to impress Abbu by being honest, even when I had done the worst thing possible for a girl of my age.

'Does he love you, Shabana?' Abbu asked.

'Yes, yes. He does, Abbu. Amir, tell them,' I asked Amir to take part in the conversation.

'Let's go. It's late,' Amir replied. Just a few hours back, he had confessed his love to me; now, in front of Ammi and Abbu, he was not saying it aloud.

'Where do you live, Amir?' Abbu asked him.

'I have a tin shed on a farm, close to the Brahmaputra.'

'Okay, listen, both of you,' Abbu continued. His tone did not change. His face did not flinch. 'Leave Goalpara, right now. I do not want you to stay here in the same village and torment my reputation any further. And Shabana,' Abbu continued. I had a smile on my face when he said my name. He was going to say something to me.

'Yes, Abbu.'

'Do not come here again. You are dead to us. I was right about you since your birth. You brought only misery to this household. Now go and never show your face again.' Abbu said. But his breath was rapid, and his eyes were half closed. He was going to faint. My eyes widened, and I gritted my teeth. I was breathing rapidly. But I started crying. I could never impress Abbu, and I would not get any more chances to do so. I went inside. I packed my clothes, an extra pair of *chappals*, and a few rupees from Ammi's purse. I looked at Ammi. She was facing the wall and crying, screaming. I had never seen or heard her crying so hard-even when she had left Hakimpur against her will. I wanted to touch Ammi's shaking shoulder, but I did not. I should have.

Five years had passed since this event, but Ammi and Abbu still slipped into my dreams. *Life is not what you think it is*-Ammi's words were chiming in my ears. I haven't received a single letter from Nadim. I wasn't sure if I was ashamed of admitting my mistake to my parents or if my ego was too big to talk to them. In any case, I had admitted that marrying Amir was a mistake.

When I was on my delivery bed for the first time, I felt just an inch away from my death. I had sweated all day. I had cramps coming from my lower back, travelling to my neck. Then they would travel back to my thighs. My back hurt with every cramp. I felt the tension in my cheeks. I wondered *why people have babies. Most importantly, why did they get married? Or why they fall in love.* I could not sleep even for a minute. After battling the physical and mental pain, I delivered my first set of babies. Amir had not gone to the farm that day.

'I am waiting for my prince to arrive,' he had said to everyone in the neighbourhood. People nodded. Smiled at him.

To Amir's disappointment, I delivered two girls in the late 1963-both beautiful, with brown curls and deep dimples-Agha and Rani. They looked very much like Amir. Everyone in the neighbourhood came to see them, their beauty. One was loud. The other one was quiet. I witnessed Amir leaving the room without even looking at them.

They are not mine, he murmured, even in his sleep. He had a frown on his face. He did not eat at home for a month after that. Dimi helped me with food for a month and taught me how to breastfeed. Amir, even though he was upset, made *chai* everyday morning. Agha was easy. Rani was the easiest. When she was six months old, Amir lifted Rani in his arms for the first time. Rani shrieked.

'This cannot be my baby. Who did you sleep with? You *harami!*' Amir blurted and handed over Rani to me.

'Do you want to know?' I spoke.

He kicked me in my stomach. 'This is so that you don't give birth to such creatures next time.'

'There is no next time.' I was adamant when I said that. It was hard taking care of two babies without much help and with no money.

His hand hit my cheek hard. 'There is always next time until you give me a boy.'

His love for his unborn and non-existent son was too much for him to love his actual daughters. I loved my girls more than anything else in the world. Their first smiles, first words, when they started walking, when they started crawling-everything was carved in my brain never to be forgotten. Both my daughters looked gorgeous, like the women who came on TV. They had soft voices. I could hear them all day. Unless they would cry. When they cried, I cried. And then Dimi had to manage the three of us.

Life got busy. The money that Amir gave me was not enough to take care of two daughters. When they were two years old, I gave birth to twin sons-Rashid and Sajid. Amir took them on his shoulders and ran through the neighbourhood. He accepted he had become a father. Father of two boys. His princes had arrived.

'They are my boys,' he repeated after having sons.

'Yes, they are your boys,' I would answer.

'And these-these are not my girls. Liabilities,' he would continue.

'These are your girls,' I murmured.

'What did you say?' I asked. It was actually a warning never to say such a thing.

'Nothing, nothing. Yes, they are liabilities,' I said. The blow from the last beating was still hurting in my stomach. Dimi attempted both deliveries. In three years, I was blessed with four kids. If I had to admit it, I would say life before having kids was better. As only I used to suffer. I had developed coping mechanisms to live with Amir, his anger, his moods, his mysteries. But I was unsure of how my kids would cope. Especially my daughters. They grew faster than boys. Dimi had suggested the name Rani, and Rani grew closer to Dimi. Agha spent time alone since her childhood. I knew she spoke more to herself than to anybody else. Rani would ask everyone to talk twice, the second time in a louder voice. I had asked her not to talk with and in front of Amir, as he would get irritated. All my kids were close to my heart. But I had a special affection towards Rani, the kindest of all, who was too naïve to accept that the world was not fair.

Dimi introduced me to some people, for whom I started doing the cleaning chores. I would get two rupees to clean the big house. Once a week. But they would not summon me every week. So, I was still running tight on money. They had everything. Big house. Good furniture. A lot of food. Good clothes. Books.

***

Back in Hakimpur, Nadim and I had spoken about envy one day. Ammi and Abbu were fighting, so he and I stayed in our front yard. Looking at nowhere and thinking did not know what. He said, 'Do you know what envy is?'

'It sounds like someone's name, right?' I said.

'No. It is wanting that somebody else has. You feel the lack of it only after seeing other people having it.'

I had a frown on my forehead.

'I think Abbu is envious. Because people in the village went to Bharat. Bought a big house. An enormous piece of land. Became rich. Abbu never wanted to leave Hakimpur. He loves the peace we have here. He never spoke about earning a lot of money until recently. And that urge has become very intense in a brief time. Now he wants to do the same thing that these people have done.'

'Why is that a bad thing, though?' I asked.

'Look at these five fingers,' he showed me his palm. I widened my eyes and looked at his fingers. 'What am I looking at exactly?' I spoke.

'Are these fingers the same?' He replied.

'No, why would they be?' I replied.

'We all are like these fingers. Different from each other. We are not all meant for the same thing. Especially when we don't opt for the right ways.'

'Why don't you tell Abbu to stay here in Hakimpur?' I asked.

Nadim took a pause, looked at me and said, 'I am an obedient son, Shabana. Unlike you. Listen to Ammi and Abbu always. Do you understand me?' he had changed the topic and was scolding me.

I wondered if I was envious of those people who had big houses and a lot of food where I was doing the cleaning jobs. Maybe I was not. But there was someone whom I knew I was certainly envious of.

Amir did not change after having kids, except in two respects. He stopped making love to me, and he grew wary of the tension in the society. He ordered our kids to call me Ma instead of Ammi and call him Baba instead of Abbu. Dimi told me Amir introduced himself as Himanta to the people outside. He got some documents with him one day and asked me to keep them safe.

'They are proof I am from Bharat,' he said. 'Don't lose them.'

'But I am not from Bharat,' I argued.

'That is your problem, Shabana. You might have to leave Bharat soon,' he said. Coldly.

'What happens to my kids?'

'They were born here. They can stay here. Take your daughters with you, though.' He was his usual self. I never knew where Amir was from. In reality, I did not know who he was. No family. No friends. He never told me. But he would sweat thinking about the protests happening in Assam against outsiders.

AGHA

We have our exams next week. I don't want to study; I don't want to attend the exams. But Ma won't let that happen. She will start her lecture about borrowing money from people to buy us notebooks and pens. I have been hearing the same irritating lecture for years now. I am going to take the day-off today. And this is my last year of school. I am not going to study in the tenth standard.

'Ma, I have a headache. I don't think I can walk that long to school,' I say. She believes me. I barely recall her questioning anyone at home, including me.

Baba has gone to the fields, and Rashid and Sajid have already left for school. Rashid is very adamant, like Baba-he will not eat food if it is cold. When he does that, I am the happiest person in the room, as I get more food. Ma does not convince him to eat; Baba does. But he does not listen to Baba. He also gets angry quickly, like Baba. And he rushes out of the house. Baba, or Sajid, or Rani has to go out to convince him and bring him home. I do not go. Ma does not go. Ma does not like his behaviour, but she is never vocal about it. Baba never scolds him. In fact, he secretly encourages Rashid. Sajid is a gem, Ma says.

They are twins; Rashid appeared six minutes before Sajid. When he came out, Baba was so excited to see him that he did not want to wait until he was wrapped in a piece of cloth. He lifted him up, put him on his head, and started dancing. He did not care that the baby was crying. When Sajid came out, Baba ran into the chawl like a crazy man, chanting, "*I got boys, I got boys.*" He changed from that day. He walked with his chin up. He walked with his shoulders tight. He walked with his chest broadened. Ma has told met this. I asked Ma how he felt when I was born? She said that he was happy. But I knew she was lying. She knew I knew. Neither of us continued the conversation. Naturally, he had never liked Rani since her birth. The boys are handsome. Ma says they look just like her. Baba says they look just like him. I think they look more like Ma. Ma is beautiful. Baba is not as much. In terms of nature, Sajid is more like Ma, the good one. Rashid is more like Baba, the bad one.

Rani is getting ready to go to school. Why she always has to be so disciplined, I shall never know. She never bunks school, even gets good marks. Better than mine. She is kind. But she lost all that because of her hearing issue. No one likes her. She is not carrying tiffin to the school. She can stay for seven hours without eating, but that's difficult for me. Sometimes we come home from school for lunch. Ma tells us what days to come home and what days to skip. Everything depends on whether we have enough rice and curry at home for lunch. Or if Ma has been successful in getting food from Dimi auntie. Or if Ma has gotten any cleaning job and the payment for it the same day. Or if Baba had no breakfast in the morning, we came home and ate the food he had not eaten. In the harsh sun of the afternoon, we run from school and stop only when we reach our home. The road is hotter than the pan that Baba had thrown at Ma that bruised her cheek. Ma had fainted. Baba, instead of getting a doctor, stormed out of the house. Rashid kept looking at Ma. Rani started crying and kissing Ma on her cheek. Sajid ran to Dimi auntie. She came with cold water and straps to cover Ma's injury. I don't remember what I did. I was probably finishing my *chai*.

Ma does not eat breakfast, not sure if she eats lunch. She eats dinner. She is thinner than I and Rani. Our breakfast is *chai* and roti in the morning. Today there was no milk in the *chai*, so I did not have it. Baba did not have it either. He threw it into the gutter outside the house. Looked at Ma in anger and left home. I could not tell how Ma felt about it. I could not read her face. She is usually expressionless. With those dark circles around her eyes and messed up hair, I always see her as someone who is deep in thought-but I cannot name those thoughts. I cannot name the emotions she goes through. I cannot name the emotions that I go through. I think I understand hunger, sleep, my admiration for Masha's life and something else when Chandan gives me an envelope. I had secretly liked that.

Ma drank *chai* after Baba was gone. Rani ate roti with *chai*. Whenever Baba gets angry at Ma, Rani holds Ma's hand. Ma calls her a kind soul. But why a kind soul would not get good treatment from the rest of the world is some-thing I always wonder. That was an indication enough for me never to be kind to the world. Rani got ready for school. Her school uniform has a tear near the knee. She doesn't mind wearing it. She closes the door to wear her school uniform, she brushes her hair and ties it in a ponytail. Who ties such long hair in a ponytail? I tie my hair in a braid. She applies powder to her face. She gives me a smile every time she notices that I am looking at her. I do not smile back. She picks up her school bag and leaves. I walk to the door and look at her silhouette from there. I wonder what makes her so calm, happy, patient and 'kind' as Ma says. I have no idea what Ma says about me. Maybe rude, selfish, someone who keeps everything to herself-what's the word-private. But Ma is a private person too. She does not tell anything to anyone-she might be talking about her emotions to Dimi auntie though. Ma talks to Dimi auntie everyday afternoon after and before lunch. She sometimes has her afternoon *chai* at Dimi auntie's place. Dimi auntie is exceptionally beautiful, more beautiful than Ma. I wonder how Chandan is that ugly. He looks like his father. His father is not handsome. Dimi auntie does not talk with Baba. I have heard her calling him *Chhapri*. I should get angry, but I don't. I wonder why that is so? I don't feel part of this house. Or even a part of this family. I wouldn't mind if I got a new Ma and Baba tomorrow, with no sister or brother, for that matter. This house has such a sad environment. Even if I want to smile, I can't. Something inside me tells me, not now. Probably Ma's always expressionless face makes me think that way. Or Baba's frequent anger. Or Rani's frequent smiles and unnecessary love for me. Rashid's carelessness. Sajid's inconsiderate attitude towards me. Everything good and everything bad in this house makes me sad.

Ma has done washing clothes and dishes. I am sitting in a corner of the house, holding my head. Even though it does not hurt, I have to act. It is easy to fool Ma. Baba does not care, and Rani would give me water to drink and massage my head without me asking her to do so. While I am sitting here with my legs close to my chest and both my hands on my temple, I notice Ma walking to the door, washing dishes. Drying clothes. Her feet are thin and decorative. You can draw them and look at them for hours. Her fingers are thin. They are delicate, and I think they can go deep in the sand, like sand on the bank of Kopili. I look at my feet. They are broad. They are like Baba's feet. Ma says I look like Baba. That I am Baba's carbon copy. My feet are not delicate. Ma's hands are delicate too. And she has a mole in the middle of her palm. I heard Dimi auntie telling her that having a mole in the middle of the palm means having a lot of money. Ma laughed. I wanted to laugh, too. I think money runs away from Ma. She does not ask Baba for money. She takes some out of his pocket instead. And she cannot do that skillfully. Once Baba got up in the morning, he saw he had less money in the pocket than he expected. He shouted at everyone and asked where his money was. I knew Ma had taken it. I simply looked at her. I did not know Baba was looking at me. Baba slapped Ma hard, pulled her hair and pushed her out of the house. He asked Ma if she needed the money to give to her lover. He called her *randi.* I do not know what that means, but I knew that was bad. Ma calmly came inside, wiped her tears, and started cleaning the floor that Baba had made dirty after throwing *chai* and leftover curry. I looked at Ma. She looked so calm even after such a massive humiliation, but she had cried almost every day after that day. That day I had cried too, even though for a few seconds. But I do not know why. I do not ask myself such questions. I think knowing the details is a waste of time.

Ma says that Baba likes me a little because I am his first child. Two minutes older than Rani. So, he does not beat me. He does not beat Sajid and Rashid. He beats Ma and Rani. The bruises on Ma's cheek and Rani's hand do not look good. I used to feel special, but now I don't as Masha asks me about Rani's bruises, and I do not know what to say.

Masha has a happy family. Her Ma is fearless. Her Baba does not beat anyone at home. And most importantly, they have a lot of food at home. Once she bought puri for her tiffin. Ma has asked us not to peep into other people's tiffins. But the smell of Puri was so fresh and enchanting, it took me to a different world. A world where my tummy is full. I could not control my hunger, my greed and I told Masha that Rani wanted to eat a Puri from her tiffin. Masha offered her one. I tore that in half, handed the first half to Rani, and took the rest for myself. Masha was done with her lunch before us. She went to wash her hands. I took half of what was left on Rani's plate. She smiled at me and said nothing. That day again, I decided never to be like Rani. People will eat your food from your plate without your permission, and you just smile.

My headache is over as Ma has gone to Dimi auntie. I decided to take a nap. Make the best use of my time. I closed the door. Close the window curtain. The room is now dark. I like that. I take my usual place by the side of the wall, place a sheet on the floor, and take one blanket from the shelf. The one complete blanket is for myself-I am content! Whole house for me, the whole blanket for me-today, indeed, is a special day! I close my eyes, and then there is a dream. I see two people on the farm — a man and a girl almost my age. The man is standing behind the tree, and the girl is standing by his side. They are holding hands and cuddling. I open my eyes. It is not a dream; I had seen these visuals in real life many times when I was coming back from school from a different route. The man was always the same, but the girls were different. I close my eyes again after I brush off all my thoughts about them, and I go into a deep sleep.

Ma comes home in the late afternoon. Her eyes are swollen. Not sure what she spoke about with Dimi auntie for such a long time. A part of me wants to ask her how she feels when Baba beats her. A bigger part of me tells me not to get involved. To think only of myself. Everyone has come to earth with an agenda. Ma's agenda must be to get beatings, to satisfy Baba's ego. They are not my words. I heard Dimi auntie scolding Ma one day, as Ma never answers Baba back to not to hurt his ego. Mine must be to think of food. Rani's must be good to everyone. Baba's must be to hurt people. Rashid's to become like Baba. Sajid's to take care of Ma and Rani. And Chandan's to follow me everywhere I go.

Ma does not eat anything. I am hungry, and there is my share of roti that was made in the morning. I have it with some oil and salt. Ma uses my sheet and blanket. She is going to take a nap.

'Ma, I am going to Kopili. Shall be back in an hour,' I announced my plan.

'Don't be late, Agha. You know that your Baba doesn't like you and Rani going out of the house unless you are going to the school.'

'I will be back before Rani comes home, Ma,' I said.

Ma looks at me. She knows I am lying. She knows that I skipped school because I said I had a headache, but now I am going to walk for more than half an hour to reach Kopili. But she also knows my love for Kopili. My Kopili.

Sometimes, Ma also likes to go to Kopili. Ma likes the sand on the bank. She removes her chappals while walking on the bank. She closes her eyes and welcomes the breeze on her face and in her hair. Every time she does this, I realise that Ma is beautiful: beneath her dark circles, her newly appearing wrinkles and her gloomy eyes, there is beauty, there is shine, there is truth. Her eyes are sharp, her skin is delicate, her brown hair is smooth, and her straight nose and the mole on the right side above her lip are evidence that *Allah* might have taken a long time to create her.

I wear Rani's dress. I like to use her dresses so that my dresses remain good. I wear my *burqa* over it and step out. Some days I feel that Kopili calls me. She wants to see me. She has a message for me — a vague message. Nature must know what's going to happen to us, to me. She will know whether I can do that makeup course. She will know whether I can ever have a kitchen full of food. Whether I will earn money and buy good dresses just like Masha. Whether I will ever be happy.

The weather is cold, but still warmer than yesterday. I walk looking inside other houses. Almost all the doors are open. Somewhere, a child is crying, people are chatting, and some are cooking lunch. Not everyone is poor like us. People have enough food at home. I wonder what I can trade for food. I am okay with getting a beating from Baba if I get three times the food. I am okay with getting bruises every day if I get good food three times like *puri,* or butter or *aloo bhaja* with a lot of *sorshe.* I wonder what else I can trade for good food. My thoughts are interrupted when I hear the bicycle bell. I move to the side, but the cycle does not go ahead. I look back-it is Chandan. I start walking without looking back any further. Chandan must have had his lunch, I thought. I am sure he never has to think about food. His Ma must be cooking delicious food before he gets hungry. I walk along the sides of paddy fields, tall trees with leaves fallen around them. I like dry leaves. I pick one up and keep walking. I do not hear the cycle ring anymore. The road to Kopili is not smooth. None of the roads in Matiparbat are. Masha says the roads in Guwahati are better. She has been to Guwahati many times. Her mamu lives there. Even my Mamu lives there, but he never invites us there. He looks at us as if we are the cause of Ma's suffering. Sufferings-what are they? Suffering is the same as being beaten-someone spitting on your face-someone holding your wrist so tight that you get bruises around your wrist-cursed words hurled at you. Ma and Rani suffer. But not getting enough food should also be suffering. So, I suffer too. Rani suffers more than I do-she does not get food. She gets beaten, and Baba shouts at her often. Ma suffers more than Rani-she does not get food, gets beaten almost every day, and Baba shouts at her at least twice every day. People in the colony sympathise with her. Only Baba does not suffer. He makes everyone else suffer.

I stop when I reach the riverbank. I see some *Naukas docked at the bank.* My heart is pounding, as I am not certain whether Chandan followed me or not. I look back, and I see no one. There is relief. I sit on the big rocks, looking at the slowly moving water. My *burqa* is moving with the wind. I open the face cover. I see this water clearly now. Sometimes there are *nauka*s docked on the bank of this river. I wonder if my grandfather used this kind of *nauka*. Ma tells us sometimes that he was a fisherman in Bangladesh. Ma still calls it East-Pakistan. She says she does not like the new name. It is specific to the Bengali people. The Pakistan she knew was open to different languages. Open to different religions. Open to different people. *Why did they still come here?* She does not answer this. She thinks that the decision wasn't under her control. I do not doubt that. She does not exercise any control even now. I sometimes think that she can beat Baba back. Or shout at him. Or spit in his face. Push him out of the house. At least one of these. She can show her anger in some way. But for this, she has to get angry. I am not sure if she gets angry at all. I think she gets sad.

I see a fish, a small fish swimming close to the bank. I think of *Machher jhol*. I haven't had it for quite some time now. Ma cooks it better than Dimi auntie. But we hardly buy any fish. Dimi auntie makes *Machher jhol* frequently.

'Agha.' I hear my name.

I look back; Chandan is there. I say nothing. He hasn't gone to college. He skips college more than I skip school.

'This is for you,' he says and hands over the blue envelope again.

This time I ask him, 'Why do you give me these envelopes?'

He answers, 'I am going to write you letters. You store the letters in these envelopes.'

I ask, 'Why will you write me letters?'

He answers, 'Because I have many things to tell you, and I don't see you often. Even if I see you, you are reluctant to talk to me.'

I look down. I open the envelope. It is big and empty. I ask, 'What are you going to write in those letters?'

He answers, 'My thoughts about you, and about everything else and everyone else around me.'

I ask, 'Why do you want to tell me about everything and everyone else around you?'

'Because I want you to become my best friend. Will you be?'

'I don't think so.' I hand the envelope back to him. He does not take it.

'I will send letters through Rani. I have told her. She is going to accept it on your behalf.'

I look at him. His big nose is where I look at first. The pimples look bigger than the other day. His complexion is black, charcoal black, and his oily hair is combed backwards. I like his shirt though — light yellow — and it has brown buttons. He is wearing khaki shorts. He is looking into my eyes. I do not know what he was looking for. I looked into his eyes, too. They are big in the middle but become narrow immediately and end quickly. They are like a pebble. A round pebble. The whites of his eyeballs look yellowish today. He smiles at me, showing his long teeth and a big gap in the front teeth. He pedals back.

'Tata,' he says.

I look away to Kopili. I am not sure why he is after me. But secretly I like the attention that I am getting, even though he is the ugliest person I have ever seen, even though I know I am not going to read any of his letters. I am thinking about the smell of puri that Masha had brought in her tiffin. And the texture of that puri. So soft, so crispy. I hear a bicycle ring again.

'Agha.' Chandan is back. He is panting. 'I missed telling you one more thing.'

'What?' I am annoyed now.

'The other envelope that I have given you is for the money.'

'Money? I do not have any money.' I am startled. *Where do I get the money? And why does he need money from me?* I wonder.

'No, I will give you the money when we get married. You can use the envelope to keep the money.'

'Okay, first, I am not marrying you. I am not marrying anyone. I am going to do the makeup course in Guwahati. I am going to earn my own money,' I said confidently.

'I am okay with that. I will give you money for your make-up course.'

'I did not ask for your money or your permission,' I hit back at him.

'But you will need money, right? Your Baba does not have money.'

I do not like what he says. I do not like the fact that our poverty is known in the world. I do not like that he thinks that I am weak.

'LEAVE right now!' I scream. I do not know why. I do not know how. I start crying loudly. I howl. My hunger and my poverty are in front of the whole world. My anger with Ma and Baba is at the peak. My dislike for Rani, Sajid, and Rashid is stronger than ever. Why do we need so many people at home? None of them is good. None of them is worth my time, my sharing my problems with them. I am done keeping everything to myself. I am done. I wipe my tears and walk to the Kopili. I take a step forward, straight into the river. My legs are deep in the water up to my knees. My *burqa* is wet. The water is splashing all over my body. The mud on the riverbed is coming up. The color of the water is changing. My feet are deep in the riverbed. I feel small and big pebbles in the mud. Some are hurting me. Some are escaping from beneath my feet when I move my feet forward. The water is cold. I close my eyes and keep walking. I hear Chandan taking my name. I pay no heed. The water is up to my chest now. A fish has entered my *burqa,* and I feel the tickling on my stomach. I want to laugh, but I know if I do so, the water will enter my mouth, and it will be easier for Kopili to take me in.

I decide to ask Baba for money for my makeup course. I decide to first talk with Ma. I decide to ask Mamu, who has helped with school fees. Maybe he is able to give some money for my course, as well. I decide that I will repay their money. I decide to give it a try before trying to die. I feel the Kopili water at my chin and then I take a step back. I return to the land, to this mysterious riverbank, which sometimes asks me to follow my heart and sometimes to give up.

MAHESH

30 December 1979

*I*f I could speak with God, I would ask him when all this would stop. Bhaijan says that this has just started, and I have to believe him. The new year is just a day away, but Assam's situation is genuinely worrying. To cancel the elections, the Group tried many ways, including kidnapping the election supporters. One of the Group supporters was killed. When the body of the supporter was taken to the hospital, there were again clashes, and a doctor was killed. Then there was a curfew. I closed the shop that day and almost ran to my house. Bhaijan asked me to be at his place until the situation stabilized, but Mother was alone at home, so I came back home.

My initial fear of violence is coming true. There was a lathi-charge this month and some police firing as well. I now regret having a shop so close to the university. Had it been somewhere else, I would have at least kept it open. I *judge the situation every day and open the shop only when it is safe.*

From the small window of our one-room house, I have seen protestors pelting stones at the shops, beating up the shopkeepers and setting fire to the places open during the curfew. I have seen police hitting protesters with batons and running after them until they couldn't get hold of these disruptors. The roads in Guwahati, which always have so many people walking over them, were clear for many days, and there was a pin-drop silence even during the daytime. Mother is scared to go out even to buy vegetables. She was at home almost all month. Only when the emergency was declared was she a little calm, but she still thinks that curfews are going to come back. She says there is going to be fire everywhere, that we are all going to die. I am sure most of the people in Assam who have seen curfew are thinking like her now. This month, numerous people took an oath to continue the fight until all foreigners are kicked out. The state has declared the closure of schools and colleges until mid-January. The President's rule is imposed in Assam now. As there was a probability of violence, the railway service was cancelled three days in a row.

We open the shop, but we do not know how long we can do business on a particular day. I have not spent much time with Bhaijan recently due to the chaos. I wanted to know more things about Agha from him, like her likes and dislikes, her favourite food, her favourite colour, her favourite dress. Mother liked Agha's picture when I showed it to her last month. Mother wants me to get married as soon as possible, but something is stopping me.

The oil blockade started by the Group a few days back is continuing. Thousands of people have participated in the *protest. A statewide week of noncooperation is currently underway. Overall, the year is ending on an incredibly sad note. I am not getting married, and the chaos is not stopping.*

AGHA

LATE 1979

I wait on the riverbank to dry myself. The envelope is lying beside the rock. Chandan has parked his cycle and is sitting on the rock. His mouth is half open. He is trying to figure out what just happened. I stand next to the rock, allowing the wind to wash over me. He does not talk. I do not talk. We spent the time quietly until sunset. As soon as I feel dry, I start walking towards the house. Chandan follows at a distance. I am carrying the envelope with me.

When I reached the house, I hid the envelope in my school-bag and changed my dress.

Ma is awake. The sheet and the blanket are folded and kept on the upper shelf. The *chai* is boiling, and the smell of it makes me feel that life is not that bad. I have a weird fascination with *chai*. I like the smell, especially when it is boiling. I like to filter it through a steel cup. And then look at it. I don't like to drink it, but I like the fact that I *have* a cup of *chai*.

I help Ma cook. The dinner is *aloo bhaja* and roti. Rani comes back from school with a wide smile on her face. I empty the flour tin onto a plate and start kneading the flour. Ma is observing me. She must be thinking whether my headache is over or not.

'I don't have a headache anymore,' I react as soon as I doubt she would ask me something. Even though she usually does not.

'I did not ask you,' Ma answered while cutting the aloo. She does not look up.

'Ma.'

'Yes, Agha,' now she looks up.

'I do not want to go to school.' She looks into my eyes. She says nothing. She keeps staring at me. I stare at her. Deep inside, I think she was a different woman earlier. Her dark circles never suit her. They did not belong there. Her hair is embarrassed by its grey shade. And proof enough that she has become old at a young age. I hear her saying, *your Baba did not want you to go to school. I have taken a lot of beatings to send you to school. Have borrowed money from Dimi, Nadim Bhai. I work in other people's houses to buy notebooks and pens for you. Why do you say that?*—but her lips do not move. She is quiet.

'I want to do the makeup course. Masha said they teach to do makeup in Guwahati. I want to learn it.' I noticed Ma's eyes lighting up. But the light immediately went out.

'Baba won't allow that, Agha. It is not for people like us.'

'Who is it for, then? For rich people? Everything here is for rich people. And why aren't we rich? Why do we struggle for two times meals?'

'Agha, things are not easy.'

I put the dough back on the plate and stormed out of the house. Just like Baba does. Keeping quiet increases my anger. But I do not know whom to talk to. Ma has no control over what happens at home. Her submissiveness frustrates me but also makes me realise she must be in pain. Even when I do not speak with her, I feel that understanding her is just one step away from me. But I am afraid to take that step, as I know that her pain is deep, and I may not be able to handle that.

I go outside to the playground. Rani follows me. She sits by my side. She looks at me and gives me a smile. I do not smile back. The playground is between our house and Chandan's lavish house. I look at his house. The door is open. I do not see Dimi auntie. She must be cooking. Chandan's cycle is parked outside. I do not see him either. I sit on the playground, facing our tiny household. *Ma must have felt bad, so I should be considerate towards her. No one talks with her properly.* I go home in a few minutes and sit, touching my back to the patched wall. I notice Ma. She is cooking dinner. She looks at me as I walk in. She has pity in her eyes for me, or is that sympathy or care or love? It is love. She loves me. I close my eyes to revisit what happened at the riverbank. Rani comes home and sits by my side. When I see her, she shows me a broken plastic glass that she has found on the playground. I do not understand what is special about it, nor does she. She is happy that she has found something-anything. Her brown eyes are brightened up. I do not participate in her happiness until she gives that glass to me. It is pink. I have never seen a colored plastic glass.

'What do I do with this, Rani?'

She cannot hear what I say.

'What are you saying?' she says with patience and with that effortless smile.

'WHAT DO I DO WITH THIS?' I scream.

She smiles, giggles, and says, 'It is a gift for you-my dear elder sister.' Her voice is sweet, and her teeth are all uniform. She is the most beautiful girl in the family. I think she does not understand that I do not like her. She is always good to me. In fact, she loves me. Sometimes I think it is her sweet nature and the goodness of her heart that makes people take her for granted. But again, that is not my problem.

I keep the plastic glass on my right side. She still has an innocent smile on her face. I close my eyes again to avoid her. But she keeps sitting by my side. When I look at her again, she is digging her nails into the ground. Her expression has changed. She is upset.

'What happened?' I asked her.

She cannot hear me, and I am not patient enough to ask her again. Rani leaves after some time. I do not speak with Rashid and Sajid much unless I need some help from them in household work like getting water from a *beel* for cleaning plates. Or sometimes when Baba has some paisa, he asks me to buy *Nimki,* and then I delegate that work to Rashid or Sajid. They never say no. They like going out. They feel trapped in this small room, just like me. Sometimes you struggle for fresh air, so many people, so little space. I move on to dreaming about becoming a makeup artist.

In the night, Baba brings a dress for me—of course, a used one. It is a *salwar kameez,* a blue gown, and a pink pyjama with a pink dupatta. I do not understand where he gets that from. Ma says nothing. Rani is happiest to see that I have got a gift from Baba even though she does not get any. Rashid does not react. Sajid leaves the house. He wants to keep everything to himself, but he cannot. His face says what he won't. He is not happy about the gift.

After we finish our dinner, I go to the bathroom to try on the new dress. It fits me well, and I think it looks good on me. I think of the person who wore it before me. Could that be a rich girl? Can her luck pass on to me after I wear her dress? I wonder if that is possible. If yes, I would never wear Ma's saree or Rani's dress.

While I am thinking this, Rani looks at me and gestures that I am looking like a princess. She has a wide smile on her face and her hands on her head like a crown. I change into my old dress, fold the dress Baba brought me, and keep it well, along with my school uniform. Baba seems in a good mood today, so I decide I am going to ask him about my makeup course the very next morning.

Ma cries when everyone is asleep. I hear it and still pretend I have not and start licking the wall to taste that delicious mud. Everyone knows Ma is not happy, and nobody cares except Rani. Probably she does not know. She sleeps as soon as her head touches the pillow. Every night, I wonder what Ma thinks about. Is it about Baba? That he is not well behaved. Or does she miss mamu? Or does she miss her parents? Ma tells me she saw her parents last when she left their house to marry Baba. I want to ask her if she misses them now, but I stop myself. I do not want to unwrap her past or her problems. I have enough of my own.

I think about Chandan. I think he is a kind soul. He makes me feel special. No one has made me feel like that until now. I think of his house-at least three times bigger than ours. I think of his kitchen-full of food. He even has a bicycle. Everyone in the chawl says that he has money. And he is after me. He wants to marry me. I think that if I can unsee his nose and the pimples over it and his big teeth and the gaps between them and his broad lips and his coal-like complexion, then I can marry him. But I am not sure how to unsee what is visible. I think of his cycle bell; I like that too. I like Dimi auntie. She is Ma's best friend. But I will not get married until I ask Baba about my makeup course. I may even get some help from Mamu. I will not give up so soon.

MAHESH

15 January 1980

*M*other's crankiness has reduced a bit, but that is because I am here to help with every small thing.
Sometimes I wonder where she gets all that frustration.
There was no electricity, some issue with the wiring. I have
fixed the problem to the best of my capabilities.

Mother wants me to get married soon. She said that she
wants to see the face of her grandson and then she can die
peacefully. But what if I have a daughter and not a son? How
will she react?

The new year started with the 58-hour Assam bandh.
Bengalis were attacked in Assamese-dominated districts,
and Assamese attacked in Bengali-dominated districts.
The governor had to call the army three times this month.
The situation in Guwahati is worsening, and the Army
was here last week. Only the army can control protesters.
I haven't been to the shop since the emergency. Somehow, it
doesn't feel safe. I, however, went to the shop last week late at

night to check if everything was alright. I am an Assamese, and I still fear. What must the foreigners be thinking? I am sure they are packing bags ready to leave. Mother says that not everyone is as panicky as I am. Foreigners are determined to settle here, and that angers the protestors.

SHABANA

MID 1970

My children would play together on the playground that was between my tiny house and Dimi's grand house. Chandan would also play with them. He was fond of Agha, but Agha never liked playing with him.

I heard a noise from the ground one day, when I was dreaming of eating fish. Fish would bring back memories of Hakimpur and of Goalpara. There were ample fish in my house. In Amir's house, if I ever cooked fish, I had to justify where the money had come from. Every time, I would say that Dimi offered fish in return for the Aloo curry that I offered her. My children loved fish. I had no idea when I would be able to cook fish next. I rushed to the ground and saw Rashid screaming at the other children. Rashid was arrogant. He would beat other children from the neighbourhood and sometimes his own siblings, too. I went close to him and held his hand. He dismissed me and looked at me in anger. He looked like Amir for a moment. The same anger. The same attitude. Agha, Rani, and Sajid hid behind me. Rashid's nose became red, and he murmured something.

'What did you say?' I asked him.

'Well done, my boy!' Amir shouted from the door.

He had come home early that day. Rashid was just five years old, but I could already see him following Amir's footprints. He rushed to his father and gave him a high-five. Amir looked at me—I saw pride in his eyes and a sense of having won something. I looked at the ground. Sajid, Agha, and Rani stayed outside. I walked home. I cleaned the stove. I put the cooker on the stove. I put the washed *rice* and *daal* in the cooker. I put turmeric and salt in it. I closed the lid.

'Make *aloo bhaja, Harami!*' Amir shouted at me. He was sitting in the corner of the room. He opened the bottle of *hathbhatti*. He asked Rashid to get a glass of water. He added the liquor and took a sip. It was going to be a long evening.

***

I wasn't sure what Ammi and Abbu did after I left them. Or when they notified Nadim about me and Amir. I wasn't sure how Nadim reacted. I wasn't sure why they never contacted me. And I wasn't sure how I had survived this marriage with Amir. I would sometimes open the box, having all my memories of Ammi, Abbu, and Nadim, our Hakimpur house, Sona and Brahma. But these memories were accompanied by tears. And they would hurt more than the blows and the punches Amir gave me. I would then imagine closing this box, tightening the lid and then throwing it far into the Brahma. I would see it floating on the water and travelling away from me and disappearing. But then I would feel the pain in my heart, in my soul, on the left side of my chest where the heart is. And that pain would never go away. Even after crying hard, talking to Dimi, or seeing my children happy. It was there to stay forever. So, I decided to write to Nadim. To gain support. Mental support. Financial support. And to show Amir that I had someone strong to rely on. I did not need him. My brother would take care of me. But I was not sure what to write. I was not sure how to admit my mistake. I gathered courage one day. I had his address, but I wasn't certain if it was still current after so much time.

My dear brother,

How are you? I have been thinking about writing to you every day. But life would get in the way. I see you are busy too. I am doing perfectly fine. I thought you would like to know that you are now a Mamu! Mamu to Rani, Agha, Sajid and Rashid. Four sounds too many, right? I had them in two goes.

Take care of yourself, brother. Hope, Ammi and Abbu are fine? Please pass on my love ~~and apologies~~ *to them.*

Your sister,

Shabana

'I will ask Viju to post it. Don't worry, Nadim will get it,' Dimi said, when I sought her help to post it. She never said no to anything. I wondered what good I had done to have found her.

'Why are you so good to me?' I asked her.

'Because you are good to me,' she said.

'But I do nothing for you,' I continued.

'You do. You kill my time,' she said, and we both laughed.

After a month's time, a gentleman came to the door - well dressed. I was cooking in my half-torn saree. He pushed the door open, stood at the door, kept his hand on the left side of his chest, on his soul, and started crying aloud. My Nadim, my brother, had come.

SHABANA

MID 1970

Nadim hugged me and cried longer and harder than I did. He moved his hand on my face over and over again. He kissed my forehead. In no time, his eyes were red and swollen. I cried too, but I would wipe off my tears quickly. They kept coming as long as Nadim was crying. I struggled to get a clear view of my brother, my Nadim. When we were done with our drama, as Nadim called it later, I made a cup of *chai* for him.

'Where are my nieces and nephews?'

'The boys are with Amir on the farm. You will see them in the evening. The girls are outside on the playground. Let me get them home,' I said. I went outside. But instead of going to where the girls were playing, I first went to Dimi's.

'I need a bowl of flour and a few *baigans*.' I blurted my demands to her. She was sitting in her big chair. 'Is that your brother?'

I smiled and quickly added, 'Yes, yes—plus a bit of sugar.'

'You look exactly like him without your bruises,' she said. Dimi had never cared about the situation. She would taunt and mock me as and when she desired. I took the bowl full of flour, four *baingan* and a cup of sugar from her. Agha and Rani accompanied me. His eyes lit up when he saw them both.

'This is your mamu,' I said and nodded at Agha and Rani so that they would repeat after me. Only Rani repeated — MAMU — in her loud, inconsistent voice. Agha stared at him. He picked up Agha and kissed her on her cheek. He then took Rani close to him and cried again. That was my brother, a crybaby. He gave them both chocolate. Agha thought that no one was watching her and took half of Rani's chocolates. Rani did not react. She was happy with what she had left. Agha was happy that she had more than Rani. I did not scold Agha.

'Now, go play outside,' Nadim said, while staring at their dirty clothes. He then stared hard at the stuff that I carried with me. He stared at my torn saree.

'They play on the ground all day. I will change their clothes,' I said.

He nodded.

I did not change their clothes. That was the best that they had. He looked all around my modest house. He said nothing. I said nothing.

'I am not staying for dinner. I will, however, stay until Amir comes home,' he said.

'Do you still believe that I can't cook? I cook the best food. Ask my kids.'

'I am sure, Shabana,' he smiled. My brother smiled, showing me those uniform teeth. His forehead shone. We spoke about Hakimpur. We spoke about Sona. He told me about

his house in Guwahati. His shop. That the owner of the
shop where he worked sold the shop to Nadim in return for
two year's earnings. Nadim agreed and became the proud
owner. We spoke about his fears. He told me about the
protests and the chaos all around. But for me, chaos in my
head, chaos in my life, was more than enough to grab my
attention. We spoke about Ammi and Abbu.

'If they forgave me, then why didn't they write to me? Or
come to see me at least once? Do they know that I now have
kids — four of them? That I cook food, good food. That I
wear a saree on my own. I fill water buckets from the public
tap and carry them home, one in each hand, without spilling
the water?'

'Do they know how to read or write, Shabana?' Nadim
asked. I shook my head. 'And Abbu has moved to Hakimpur,' he continued.

'What? When did that happen?' My voice was unsteady.

'The year you got married. Shabana, they were...'

'And you are telling me this now,' I interrupted Nadim. My
heart had skipped a bit. Abbu, after struggling so much to
settle in a new land, moved back to Hakimpur. I could not
believe it.

'Why would Abbu go back? He had so painstakingly built
his life here. Why would he?' I asked him or I asked myself.
I did not know.

'That is what I was telling you. You don't let me...'

'You know what? They must be ashamed of my actions.
That I eloped and got married. I was sure they would not
approve of my decision. It wasn't about Amir; it was about
me. I was never given freedom, and I wanted to snatch it,
experience it. I wanted to feel grown-up. I wanted to be in
control. In control of my own life.'

'I know. Shabana, the night they left –'

'But I am happy that Ammi is back in her home where she belonged,' I said.

Nadim looked into my eyes. I was crying. I was missing them, so he pulled me close to him.

'You can write to me; I will convey your regards to Abbu. And his to you.'

'Why only Abbu? Is Ammi still upset with my behavior? I am not sure when I will be able to travel to Hakimpur. Can you tell them that I now have kids? And that they want to see their Nana-Nani.'

Nadim nodded. I continued, 'I don't think they will travel back here now. Did I make a mistake, brother?' He did not answer.

He rolled his finger on my knee in circles like he used to do when we were kids, when I was still his little sister.

'You are still my little sister!' he said.

I smiled.

Nadim kissed me on my forehead. I was wondering how to store these moments. In a treasure box.

'Now, is this your lover?' Amir said. He was standing at the door and smirking at me and Nadim.

'Amir,' I said and moved away from Nadim.

'No, say no word. I thought you were smart enough never to get caught, but you are not. Sajid, Rashid, this is your Ma's lover. Say hello to him,' Amir laughed. Nadim kept staring at Amir, not uttering a word.

'No, Amir, this is my brother. Nadim. He has come from Guwahati to see us. To see kids.'

'Oh, did you tell him that the girls are not mine? Tell him,' Amir said. He sat in the corner of the room and kept the bottle of *hathbhatti* on the floor. Nadim was still quiet.

'Sajid, Rashid, go play outside,' I said. I did not want the boys to witness that conversation.

'I am leaving, sister,' Nadim blurted.

'No, no. You must eat dinner. You have come here for the first time,' I said and held his hand. Nadim still went outside and wore his shoes. I begged Amir to stop Nadim. 'Please ask him to stop, have dinner and then go,' I said.

'Why would I? We will save one man's food,' Amir responded. There was so much pride on his face. That he had insulted my brother. That he had insulted me in front of my brother. I rushed to the door. Nadim held my head, kissed my forehead, and bid me goodbye. 'Take care of yourself,' he said. I nodded. He went to the playground, kissed all my kids, and left. With tears in my eyes, I couldn't get a clear view of his silhouette escaping the narrow lane.

MAHESH

30 January 1980

*T*he Group has received an invitation to meet and discuss the matter of foreigners with the Lady at the Centre. I hope they have a conclusive discussion, but the chances seem poor. I always think that newspapers should write about the real problems Assamese people have with foreigners. People may forget the real problem over time and grow only vengeful. I think if the intensity of the problem is restated each time, locals can manage the situation peacefully.

This morning, I took a bath, wore a blue kurta and dhoti and went to open the shop. It is after more than a month that I am walking on these streets again. The day started with washing every single cup again. I bought a new tin of biscuits yesterday. The regular customers were there. I somehow did not like the chai that I made. When I told this to Mother, she said that to make a good chai, you must notice how sugar melts in the milk, how chai powder mixes with *sweetened milk changing its colour from white to brown, how grated ginger spreads throughout this brown fluid enriching the taste and how the cardamom sits at the edge of the kettle and still flavours the tea as much as ginger does. When she talks about chai, her eyes brighten. Isn't that the case with every Assamese? I think it is.*

SHABANA

LATE 1971

'And who would pay for their school uniforms, books, paper, pencils? Your Abbu?' he screamed.

A long blade came out of his mouth the moment he parted his lips. The blade had serrated edges. It extended until it reached my neck. It cut me. I started bleeding. Pink-colored blood. I thought of the *Kopou Phool* around Kopili. And those near the border. And those behind my house in Goalpara. They were different, but not bad. This blood would not be bad as well. I touched it. It felt like the green scarf that I had asked Nadim to give me. It disappeared as soon as I touched it. I never told Dimi about this blade. I knew she would think I was absurd. When did that blade grow there? I wondered. Was it there when we walked along the banks of the Brahmaputra? Was it there when he kissed me? Was it there when he asked me to get married to him?

'I have never heard or seen of girls going to the school. They will not go to school. Sajid and Rashid will attend

the school only until they know how to write and read Assamese. Then they will join me on the farm. Six mouths
to feed with only one person earning the money. Why don't
you die out of shame before putting your husband through
such a shame?' That time, I saw snakes coming out of his
mouth. Sliding all over my face and cheek and chin and
neck. I saw his eyes narrow. I saw him smirking. His nose
was bleeding. I stepped back.

Abbu never beat me the way Amir beat me and my daughters.

'I have never gone to visit him since marrying you. I can't
go back to him now when I need help and he has already
moved to Hakimpur. Moreover, where would poor Abbu get
this much money? Nadim has promised to pay for their
school,' I heard myself saying in an unsteady voice. I lied,
but I knew I would be able to convince Nadim to help me. If
not, I would earn my own money. But I was determined to
send them to the school.

'Moved to Hakimpur? He asked me to move away from
Goalpara, and they moved out of this country. This is what
you get when you do bad things to other people,' he said. His
chin was up.

'Ask Nadim to give money to me. I will keep that for the
girls' marriages,' he continued.

I could see no snakes, no blades-I gathered courage
to speak. 'We should be paying for their marriage, not
Nadim.'

'Let me see those horns on your head. Have they grown
so much that YOU TELL ME who should be paying for
what?' Amir said this and held my braid in his hand tightly.
Sajid and Rashid ran outside as soon as they saw Amir
misbehaving.

'Please let me go, please!' I begged. But secretly, I preferred the physical pain to his harsh words. I preferred the bruises on my face and body to the deep scars on my heart.

'Write a letter to Nadim and ask for two hundred rupees. I am short of money. You want to feed your kids, don't you?' he said, hissing at me and tightening the grip on my braid.

I felt the snakes around my neck. I pinched myself, but the snakes did not go away. I shivered. My daughters were shivering too. Their eyes were wide. Their mouths tight shut. Their hands clasped. Their legs close to their chests. My daughters. The future wives of two men, who might be like Amir. I couldn't let the snakes kill me. I had to live for my kids, my daughters. They suffered when I was alive. I wondered what would happen to them after my death. They should be gone out of this house before the snakes kill me, or the blades hit me hard. Should they? What if they fall in love? With someone like him. There were people out there just like him, waiting for girls to get trapped. 'Yes, I will write, I will write.' He loosened his grip. I felt relieved, but I was sure that I was going crazy. It was recently that I would think of Amir's tongue as a snake or a blade. I knew he was bad, but I also knew that I was overthinking and giving him too much control over my life. Those were Dimi's words, and maybe I was agreeing with her that day.

Amir came home late that night and for many consecutive nights after that. I wondered what he must be doing on the farm when there was no daylight. Does he go somewhere else? Who were his friends? What does he eat in the evening? I asked him nothing. He told me nothing. But I found Student Union pamphlets in his pocket. They were old, printed at least a year back. There were words written on them - *Foreigner Go Back!*

I wondered whether he wanted us to go out. *US*-me, Nadim. And all such people like us who travelled to Dhubri from Kurigram on that bus with tinted glass. And I had no idea why he would think like that. When I found those pamphlets in Amir's pocket, the first thing I did was to show them to Dimi. She was not surprised.

'Why are *you* surprised?' she asked me.

'What do you mean?'

'Why are you surprised? Why do you think he should not go to those rallies?'

'He learnt Assamese just a few months back. He is not an Assamese.'

'Then where is he from?' She asked.

'I do not know,' I smirked.

She laughed. 'You married a guy without asking where he is from?'

'I am stupid. I do not understand people.'

'You surely don't.'

I had seen Amir and Dimi exchanging awkward glances.

'Why don't you like him? I don't think he likes you either.'

'I think he is a liar,' Dimi murmured.

'Yes, he is unpredictable. He might tell me tomorrow that he is not going to work anymore. He will tell me that he has no money when he has but will use that money for a bottle of *hathbhatti* or a packet of *bidi*.'

She looked at the pamphlet in her hand. I snatched it gently.

'I have to put this back in his pocket.'

She nodded.

'What is happening with the war?' I asked.

'More people are coming in,' she replied.

I nodded. People like me. People are coming from East Pakistan to Bharat. 'And is East Pakistan intact? I worry about my parents.'

'Your parents are far away from the border. Don't worry. But the war is not beneficial to anyone, you know. The viol ence..,' she said and looked at the ground.

I nodded. It was a war between East Pakistan and West Pakistan. Bharat got involved when West Pakistan attacked Bharat's army. Bharat was helping East Pakistan become a new independent country. Bharat was in the truest sense the elder brother of East Pakistan, as Nadim had said once.

That afternoon, I wrote a letter to Nadim to understand what's happening between West Pakistan and Bharat and how East Pakistan is coping after being at war for eight months with West Pakistan.

Dear Nadim,

Salam!

How are you?

I hope everything is all right with you! I hope you are making enough money at your shop. And I hope your health is good.

I have a new cleaning job just around the corner. Dimi helped me get it. The people there are good. Sahib some-times gives me more money and says that I do more work than I am expected to do. I like the days when my work is appreciated. I go to work when Amir is in the field. I pray to Allah that Amir remains blind to my visits to that place. I wish I could continue the work forever and earn money to feed my kids.

Dimi tells me about the ongoing war. When is it going to be over? Are Ammi and Abbu alright? Is our house in

Hakimpur intact? I worry about our little house; it holds all our memories. I think about it almost every day, do you?

Dimi tells me that there are many refugees coming across the border, especially from our country. Does that mean there are fewer people in our country now? Will that make our return to Hakimpur easy? Do you want to go back? I sometimes want to. There was peace in Hakimpur. I don't find that peace in Bharat. Is it because we were not supposed to come here the way we came? Why do some people ask if we are from across the border? They asked me once when I was walking to the Kopili with Dimi. Amir has asked me to deny it. Say that you are Assamese and that you have evidence for the same, even though you don't. So, I denied. They looked at me from head to toe and asked me in Assamese. I answered in Assamese and left. That is the situation. Do you like that we hide our identity for a few rupaiya? And a job? And a piece of land? I never wanted rupaiya, or a job, or land. You wanted it. Abbu wanted. Do you think it was unfair for I and Ammi to accompany you both here? If I had married someone in Hakimpur, I would have liked that more. In an unknown land with an unknown man, I feel threatened. I say unknown man because Amir is no longer the person I loved. I loved a boy who loved the Brahmaputra and the walks on the banks. The boy who said that he would respect Abbu and Ammi. A boy who said that he would take me to Hakimpur one day. Can people change, Nadim? Do you think it is easy to hide your real self for two straight years? I can't do that even for one minute.

How are Ammi and Abbu? I do not have the guts to tell Amir to shut up. Ammi never had the guts to shut Abbu up. I learned that from her. Abbu was better than Amir, though; I don't remember his beating Ammi. Amir loves *showing how powerful he is, not to other men but to women, especially to his wife and daughters. Anyway, I did not write to tell you about my life. It is not as sad as I may write about in my letters to you. Amir is a good father. He does not beat my daughter every day. He usually spends time outside the house. His drinking has reduced to a certain extent. So, not that bad. Do not worry about me. I am content!*

I want you to keep me posted about the war. Most importantly, about your well-being. You are important to me. I miss our talk. Things have changed so much. Bharat changed everything. Why did we come to Bharat? I know I am repeating the question, and I know the answer. But I ask myself this question every day when I see Amir. When I hear about the war. When I hear about East Pakistanis snatching land and jobs. Why did we create insecurity in people here? We were happy in Hakimpur. I now know that Ammi never disliked Bharat, but she loved Hakimpur. And Hakimpur was everything to her. I wish I could go back to Hakimpur just to see our small house, once.

Write to me!

Your sister,

Shabana

I was a special person when I wrote to Nadim. I was his smart, intelligent, curious sister. But when I was surrounded by Amir, my brain would surrender. I would not think. I would do as I am told. I was a slave. His slave. But I was happy that my kids would go to school. I decided to put all of them to the same standard. They were late for school. First standard when they were almost nine years old. But I was okay. The schoolteacher did not object either. I was happy that they got an opportunity to read and write. I did not have it. I had not completely failed as a mother, after all.

I handed over my letter to Dimi and asked her to post it for me. That woman, Dimi, was my only happiness other than my kids. She had been there through thick and thin. And she never asked for anything in return. Never. But I had to give her something. If not now, then later when I would be capable of doing so. Dimi. My saviour.

MAHESH

10 February 1980

*T*he Group's discussion with the Lady at the Centre
wasn't fruitful, though. The Group wants 1951 to be
the cut-off year, while the lady says she has to take into
account other agreements done around 1971. She also mentioned that people living in Assam for a long time are almost like citizens and can't be called foreigners. But she has
promised that the issues will be looked at with a sense of
urgency. I have even seen some ministers, of course, from
a distance when they came to meet the Group a few days
back. I like students' power. The discussions have started
with the Lady at the Centre; the ministers are coming to
meet the Group. The Group has truly shown its potential to
the people in power. But these big people need oil refineries
to continue working, and when the Group stopped these
refineries, the Centre was losing a lot of money. Bhaijan
says that, in Delhi, a press statement is issued saying that
the country is going to face an oil crisis. If Assam is so im-

*portant to them, why can't the decisions be quick, I wonder.
A common man is suffering because of their inaction.*

*There are constant rumours floating about locals' deaths,
but nothing came in the Assam Tribune. I tell Mother to
believe in content that she reads in the newspaper, not
things heard from neighbours. It takes no time for rumors
to spread, while the facts remain hidden.*

SHABANA

MID 1975

I sat in the doorway of our house one evening with my cup of *chai*. A small gutter ran from the front of the door. Some days it stank; some days it did not. That day, it did not.

Viju had come early; Dimi was with him. The door was closed, but I could see from the window that she had brought some *chai* and something on a plate for him. They sat together on their *charpayi* that they had kept in the living room. He kissed her on the cheek, and she kissed him back. She put her head on his shoulder, and they both kept chatting and laughing.

Viju had never said no to Dimi for anything, Dimi had told me. Dimi wasn't restricted from going anywhere alone. She had no restrictions on wearing just a saree and *chador*-she could also wear a gown. She was allowed to wear whatever makeup she wanted. She was older than I was and still looked way younger than I was. I wanted to be like her. I wanted what she had. I closed my eyes and imagined myself in that big house. Imagined myself being respected. Imagined me bringing *chai* to Viju and imagined him kissing me on my cheek, my lips. He moved his hands on my back, my waist.. No. I opened my eyes. A girl can't show desperation to get married, and a married woman can't think of being with another man-Ammi had said. I had not listened to her once. I am not going to make the same mistake again.

Viju wasn't a good-looking man—short, curly hair, dark, big nose. Amir was a good-looking man—tall, carved lips, fair skin tone, sharp nose. I wondered how an appearance had misled me or was that was destiny. Only *Allah* could tell.

MAHESH

27 February 1980

When there are riots, rallies and marches, when people have to close their shops, a common man loses his daily wage. Some people eat dinner only when they work hard all day, and I am sure many people have spent days without eating anything when these protests or bandhs have happened. I sometimes think that the common man is the lowest priority for rulers, even though the common man, I mean literally, runs the country.

I like when Mother talks about this topic. She has clear thoughts in her head. I have seen the Lady at the Centre giving speeches, of course, on television. Mother talks exactly like her. Chin up, no hesitation in her voice, clear mind, structured thoughts, except that Mother provides reasonable solutions, the Lady does not. And Mother tucks in her philosophy and complaining in between–the Lady does not. When Mother does that, I lose interest in her speech.

SHABANA

EARLY 1980

Eight years had passed since the war. East Pakistan was named Bangladesh as it was dominated by the Bengali people. Assam, even though, belonged to Assamese people, was made of – Assamese, Bengalis, Bangladeshis, Marwaris, Nepalis, Biharis. I wondered how big the heart of Assam was. And how generous Bharat's land was to outsiders.

One day Amir told me he loved the *chai* that I had made. The day before, he had told me he loved the *aloo bhaja* that I had made. He was in a good mood. He was gentle with Agha and, surprisingly, with Rani, too. He even enquired about Rani's studies. She was the only one who was interested in studies. Agha was more interested in learning about make-up. While I remained silent, I approved of her choice. My boys never studied; I did not know how they cleared any of their exams. Agha's hopes that her father would pay for her make-up course strengthened that day. Rani was like me, would crave her father's attention, and she got the attention that day. Beyond her expectations. She was on cloud nine. Amir raised my hopes of having a normal life. I enjoyed living a life knowing that the future was better. Happier. When I gave Amir his tiffin, I looked into his eyes. They had not changed. Those brown pupils and long eyelashes were still capable of capturing all my attention. He looked into my eyes, took tiffin from my hand.

'*Khuda Hafiz,*' he said.

I knew he was shy. He probably wanted a moment just with me to confess his love. Maybe he still loved me. Our visits to the banks of the Brahmaputra flashed through my mind. For the first time, I wanted my kids to leave the house, and to go anywhere — to the playground, to their friends, to Kopili. Just go. Give me one moment with my love. It had been years since we had last made love to each other. I needed him to look at me once more. At my grey hair. At my torn saree. At my untimely wrinkled hands. I wanted him to tell me that I still looked beautiful. And then we could go to Kopili to walk on the banks. We could sit in one of the *naukas* and explore the river. We always spoke about exploring Brahma, but we never did.

Amir left without saying anything. Sajid and Rashid followed. I went to Dimi when Agha and Rani went to school. It was a tough job to send Agha to school. She always had an excuse. That day, she did not have any. Sajid and Rashid would skip school. I had asked Amir to scold them, but he never did. They would not go to school; in fact, they would help Amir on the farm.

'You have pampered them way too much,' Dimi would say.

'Not me, their father,' I would answer.

And she would give me a hard glance. 'When will you be strong, Shabana? When? Do you use your brain ever?'

She was right. I was just passing the days. But that day was still special. That day gave me hope. Amir was on my mind all day. I spoke about him to Dimi. Dimi ignored most of my talk and nodded unconvincingly for the rest of the time. She never liked Amir. But she would always listen to me without interrupting. I told her about my walks on the banks of the Brahmaputra.

'Does your Amir give money at home?' Dimi asked.

'No.'

'It means he does not care, doesn't it?'

'HE DOES.'

'AND HOW? I have never seen a woman as stupid as you.'

I did not know what to say. I instead treated Dimi with *chai*. Sometimes, it was better to avoid the topic than to continue. Especially with Dimi, she had a very sharp tongue and the freedom to take decisions. I wondered if Nadim had been married to someone like Dimi. She talked a lot, managed things on her own, in-fact supported her *shauhar* in everything that he did. Not an overhead, like me.

I had a cleaning job that day. After Agha and Rani were back from the school, I asked Agha to come with me. Cleaning an empty house. The owner mentioned he would send my payment through Viju. I did not mind. Agha got ready in no time, but I knew she never liked this kind of work. She was ashamed. Of me. Of herself. Of our house. But what could I do? I saw a light in her eyes when she would speak about her friend Masha. I had no power to give her a life that Masha had. I always wished that she accepted reality.

Though I liked the fact that she wanted a better life. With more food. More money. Fewer people.

It was four in the afternoon. I wanted to finish the work and be home before six. I had asked Rani to take care of the house until I was back. We left our lane and started walking on the road beside the row of coconut trees. Amir's farm was close by. I made sure that I walked fast so that he would not see me. If he did, he would ask me questions. He would ask me to go back home. He would come home in the evening and beat me and Agha. I wanted to avoid all the drama. What I did not know was that Amir, too, wanted to hide from me. Behind the mango tree, I saw him. There was *Kopou Phool* on the branch, the *Kopou Phool* as beautiful as my Agha. He was with another woman. A girl. She did not look older than Agha. Or did she? He was kissing her. He looked so young with her that I wanted to hide my grey hair. I kept walking, stopping only when I had reached the empty house. I wasn't sure if Agha had seen them or not, but she was her usual self. Stuffing her mouth with food from their kitchen when I was not looking. I completed my work in two hours. I dared not look in the field on my way back. Why would I do things that will later cause me pain? Instead of going home, I took Agha to Kopili. The wind soothed my face. We sat on the bank. I imagined my heart resting in my palms. And then being broken into pieces. I tried to put the pieces together. But they kept on falling. Sometimes away from me. I started collecting them from the sand. They were all over the place. Some of them even scattered close to the Kopili. I had to get them back before they found an embrace in Kopili. I ran after them. But they had gone. Long gone. I shrieked. I missed Ammi. I missed Abbu. I missed Nadim. My people. My only people.

***

When Amir came home that day, he handed me a letter. A letter from Nadim, which he had written to Amir. I was surprised, but not as surprised as I was in the afternoon. I kept the letter aside. Amir looked young. Maybe he had always looked young, and it was me who could not see it. I wasn't sure whether I should ask him about the girl. I did not.

I lay down on the floor and revisited what I had seen on the farm that day. Nadim would say, be careful. But he never mentioned being careful of what or careful of whom. I blame him for my misfortune. He could have, but he did not tell me anything about people like Amir. *You trust people too much,* he would say. But he never explained exactly what that meant. I liked to believe that Amir was not completely unhappy with me as I gave him sons. Two sons. One of them was exactly like him. Beautiful, tall, thin, stubborn, arrogant, careless – Rashid. Rashid would talk like Amir. Walk like Amir. He knew everyone feared Amir. He would take advantage of the situation. In Amir's presence, he would feel the most confident. 'Do not go to Kopili, Ammi. Your legs will hurt.' What he meant was that women were supposed to be at home, only at home. Amir would look at me for my reaction. I would nod.

'Agha, Rani, if you go out other than to school, I will break your leg,' Rashid would say and laugh. Amir would laugh, too. My daughters were older than he was. But they uttered no word against this ragging. It was my duty to shut him up, but I did not. I was afraid. Unsure whether I was afraid of Rashid or of Amir.

Like Abbu, Amir raised his sons. Like Ammi, I was help-less. But Sajid would talk to me. He would bring me flowers, sweets, and fruit. He would say, 'Ammi, make *aloo bhaja*. You make it the best.' I would buy potatoes and make *aloo bhaja*. He would eat it heartily. Sajid would make *chai* for me and say, 'Ammi, I will dry clothes. You sit. Have this *chai*. I have put ginger in it.' I would follow. I saw Nadim in Sajid. He would care for Rani. But he wasn't well connected to Agha. My Agha, my first-born. She did not know that she loved us. She did not know that she cared for us. But I knew she would realize it one day. Rani loved people uncondition-ally and had trust in them. That was dangerous, hurtful. I knew she, too, would realize it one day. I thought I should be grateful to have such kids, to have Dimi in my life. And that Nadim still loved me as much as he loved me when we were in Hakimpur. My life was not bad!

AGHA

EARLY 1980

I made chai for Baba that morning. I hand him a cup. He does not look up. Ma is taking a bath. This is a good time to have a chat with him.

'Baba, I want to do the makeup course,' I blurt.

'What is that?' he still does not look up.

'They teach you how to do the makeup of brides and other women.'

'It is not your fault, Agha. It is your mother's. I had told her not to send you to the school. The people there have messed up your head. Your job is to cook, clean and make babies. I am going to find a *shauhar* for you. Enough of this stupidity.' He now looks up in the eye.

'No, Baba, no. I do not want to get married.'

'I did not ask you.' His nose is red and eyes are big.

I am sweating.

Rani is awake. He looks at her.

'This *harami* will be with us all her life. No one will marry her. LIABILITY!' he screamed at Rani and threw his cup at her.

Ma is at the door. She rushes to Rani. Her head is bleeding. Baba leaves. Rani looks at me and smiles. Ma cries. My cheeks are wet.

***

Baba was in a bad mood for a few days after that. He asked neither Rani about her injury, which he was responsible for, nor did he speak with Ma. In my mind, I had ranked our positions in Baba's life. The first position was for his boys, Sajid and Rashid. The same day he hit Rani with a cup, I saw him chatting and smiling with the boys. Baba knew that they never studied in fact, they failed one class for two consecutive years. But that was never a concern for anyone. They were boys, assets! He particularly liked Rashid. He had never called me his liability, but he also did not speak much with me. Maybe I am a liability to him, too. I guess I am his third favourite, as he had not screamed at me or hit me like Rani. And in the last spot are Ma and Rani together. Baba did not like any of them.

Sajid is like someone who does not share his opinions. He is a quiet one. He looks at me and says nothing. He looks at Ma and says nothing. But he secretly cares for us. He brought bananas to Ma one day when there was no food. And he only offered them to Ma. He insisted she eat both of them in front of him. Ma did. He loves Ma, but never consoles her when she is crying. I think he does not like Baba, but Baba likes him. He is a son. Rashid likes Baba.

He is closest to Baba out of all of us. Baba never cared about our school, our studies, our results. He himself never liked going to school.

Summer was too rough that year. Baba had a lot of work on the farm. He would go early before we even woke up and come home late after our dinner. Baba had asked his farm owner to let Rashid and Sajid work with him, and I understood that they both earned some money, too.

One night in the summer, Baba again brought a *salwar kameez* with him. There was a red gown, red pyjamas, and a yellow dupatta. The dress stank of sweat, as if it hadn't been washed in months. I did not like it, but I did not show it on my face. Without trying it, I folded it back and kept it on the shelf. The look in Ma's eyes was strange; she did not seem happy with these gifts. After our dinner, Baba went out with the boys for a walk. I don't like to, but I took the plates outside to clean them, and then I saw Chandan. Sitting in the chair, he stared at me.

There are no lights on the playground. But the moonlight is intense enough. He does not look as ugly as I thought initially. I had not seen him since our meeting last week at the riverbank when he handed over a blue envelope to me. He must be busy at his college, I think. He is constantly looking at me. I look at him occasionally; our eyes meet, and then I lower my gaze. I have a tickling sensation in my cheeks. I want to smile, but I don't. I look at him again. He moves his hand through his hair and winks at me. I smile. I show my teeth. I like that. And I convey that to him. I want to continue cleaning the utensils, but I have already cleaned the dirty ones. I decide to clean utensils every day. It is not that bad. I pick up the pile of cleaned dishes and go inside.

Ma closes the door. We put the sheets on the floor and lie down.

'Ma, where does Baba get these dresses from?'

'You have to ask him,' she answers in a cold voice.

I look at Ma. She is looking at the ceiling. She knows something. I know something. But none of us speaks. Rani was quiet. I was sure she was listening to us. She picks up both her legs at a right angle and keeps them in that position for some time. Ma pushes them to the floor; she lifts them again. Ma smiles and calls her joker. I smile. She smiles. I turn to the other side and think about Chandan. I think about Dimi auntie, and I think about Viju uncle. I wonder why Dimi auntie is so loud. Her voice manages to reach our small room, crossing the ground. When she sometimes scolds Viju uncle and we hear her, Ma laughs. Dimi auntie also fights with all the neighbours. She does not have to. But she fights with them if someone puts garbage on the ground. Or if someone does not close the tap in the bathroom. Or if the water in the gutter overflows onto the ground. Or if clothes drying on the string outside flow with the air and land on her veranda. She fights almost every day. Either with Viju uncle or with some neighbour. But she is particularly good with Ma. They are best friends. Ma tells her everything, and Dimi auntie tells Ma everything. She tells Ma that Viju uncle is rude to her sometimes and that Chandan does not eat food if he does not like it. I heard it when I was sitting on the ground on a lazy afternoon. But I ignore such information immediately. I do not need to know.

Viju uncle seems simple. The complete opposite of Baba. Calm and quiet. I always see sympathy for Ma in his eyes. People in the Matiparbat like him. They call him Dada. As

Viju uncle helps people. They take their problems to him. They discuss the situation in Assam. They all sit on the ground. Viju uncle sits on his veranda. They ask what is happening. Viju uncle says everything will be alright soon. They ask, why people are abducting women and raping them. Viju uncle says, don't believe the rumours. They ask, why do police shoot so often? Viju uncle says that someone has to maintain the control. They ask, why isn't the Centre helping? Viju uncle says, they are not agreeing on many things with the Group. I do not know what is happening in Assam, and I do not want to know. Does anyone bother about what's happening in my life? Whether I am getting enough food or not? No one does. That's my formula. Think of no one but yourself. Your hunger.

I sleep. I see a dream where a man and a girl of almost my age are kissing. I open my eyes. I hear Ma crying. Baba, Sajid and Rashid were back a long time ago.

***

Today is Sunday. We have no school. Baba sometimes does not go to work on Sundays. He is gone today, early morning. Rashid is with him. Sajid is at home.

In the afternoon when Ma is at Dimi auntie's, Rani is outside on the playground, reading through the book that Dimi auntie has given her. Sajid and Rashid are not outside. I do not know where they have gone. I hear a knock at the door. I get up and I open the door. It is Chandan. He immediately slips in.

'What do you want? Why are you inside?' I ask him with irritation in my voice.

'Here,' he hands me a yellow envelope.

I look at him with my face full of questions.

'Just hold this. We will speak later.' He says and leaves. I look outside to see if anyone has seen him there, but it is a quiet afternoon.

I close the door and look at the envelope in my hand. It is not blue. I keep it in the school bag. After some time, Ma comes home with red and swollen eyes.

'Ma, why do you cry every afternoon and every night?' I am not sure if I am concerned about my mother, or if, deep down, I already know why she's upset.

Ma looks at me. Her gaze is full of despair. 'You need not know the reason, Agha.'

I do not like her response. There is no one at home who is concerned about her, and she does not pay any heed to the one who cares for her-even though it is just one time. I do think, however, that she would have told what we saw on the farm to Dimi auntie. After some time while Ma is taking a nap, Rani comes in and sits by my side. When I look at her, she hands me a chit. I have all the questions in my head, but before I ask her anything, she rushes outside again. I open it:

Agha

Thank you for accepting my gift today. I know you were scared when I came in without an invitation, but don't worry, I was careful. Can we meet at Kopili today at three-thirty in the afternoon?

Chandan

I close the chit and keep it in my bag. I look at the small clock with cracked glass hanging on the wall beside the window. It is three. I do not like Chandan, but I want to go to meet him, maybe to hear what he has to say. I wear the red salwar kameez Baba had brought for me, the one with the yellow dupatta. I had not liked it, as it smelled of sweat.

It still does. But I want to wear it because the colour of the envelope matches the colour of this dupatta. I am going to carry an envelope with me. I need to know what it is for.

I do not see Chandan at his house. His bicycle is not parked outside. I walk straight to the riverbank and sit there. It is warm outside; I open the *burqa* and feel the wind on my face. I hear the cycle ring.

'How are you, Agha?' he asks.

I do not look back, nor do I answer him. I keep the yellow envelope beside me on a rock. I hear him leaning his bicycle against this giant mango tree.

He comes forward and sits by my side, keeping a good distance.

'What did you eat for lunch?'

I did not answer.

'Here, take this.'

He hands over a roti and *sabji* wrapped in a newspaper. I remember Ma telling us to deny politely if someone offers us food. But I am hungry. I cannot say no. I almost snatch it from his hand and start eating. He stares at me. I can sense that, but the food tastes so good that I do not want to let go of any moment to look at it and eat it. I am going to eat first, finish it and then talk back to him.

When I am done eating, I throw the paper in the bushes and go to Kopili and wash my hands and mouth. I wonder whether he brought the food because he didn't like it and didn't want to waste it, or if he truly cares about me. I turn to go back and see Chandan looking at me. At my dupatta. He must have liked it. It matches the color of the envelope. But he does not say anything about it, and as soon as he catches my gaze, he looks away. I take my seat on the rock beside him but keeping my distance.

'Here,' he hands me a two rupees note.

'Where did you get this from?' I ask with surprise.

'I have earned this.'

'How?'

'I am working at a petrol pump. Baba helped me get a job there. This is what I got after working for seven days.'

'I can't take it, Chandan.'

'Why not? Once I earn enough money, I shall ask your Baba for your hand. Just give me a few more months.'

The memory of our past discussions flashed before my eyes. I felt humiliated that day. But today, I am okay to continue the discussion. I am okay with knowing that the world knows about my hunger, my poverty, my weaknesses.

'I don't want to get married to you,' I found my tone milder than ever. I deny him my time. My life. I should have been louder, stronger.

'Take this money and keep it in the envelope I gave you. Use the blue envelope for storing my letters and the yellow one for saving money,' he said.

'What is the other blue one for?' I got carried away in the conversation.

'For this –,' he says and hands me over a pair of earrings. I look at them. They are exactly like Masha has. I want to accept them, and I do the same. I clasped them in my palms.

'My Baba and Ma do this. They have envelopes for keeping money safe, for small jewellery, for important papers,' he continued.

'Shouldn't we keep jewellery in a jewellery box?' I speak from my discussions with Masha. She had told me that rich women keep their jewellery in a box, however small that might be.

'I will get you a jewellery box one day,' he said.

I look at him. I wonder where he gets his confidence from. He looks ugly. But he still dreams of having me. I am so beautiful. I should dream big as well. I should dream of having my beauty parlour one day.

'I saw what happened that day. I saw you standing in the doorway, shivering. I feel bad when I see you like that. I told you your baba has no money to spare on you.'

I look at Kopili. I feel a lump in my throat. But I do not cry.

My likeness shoots up for Chandan considerably. I wonder why I am so clueless about others' struggles. I have no intention of knowing about others, actually. When you have so much on your plate, you struggle to manage your life. No energy to attempt to understand other people. It is difficult. Chandan still has a better life than mine.

'Let's get married soon. We will shift to Guwahati,' Chandan ensured me. I hold the two rupees note, the earrings tight in my hand. We both look at the calm water and feel the wind on our faces. I wonder whether Chandan is telling the truth. I wonder whether he really would pay for my makeup course. I wonder whether he will change his plans after marriage. I wonder whether Dimi auntie will approve of our marriage. She is not like Ma, quiet. She is like Baba, loud and dominating. I wonder if Chandan would provide me three times meals and milk *chai* with ginger. I wonder whether marrying him is the right thing to do. I look at the two rupees note. *Kopou Phool* falls into my lap. I keep the flower, the earring, and the note in the yellow envelope.

We sit in peace, neither talking. But we listen to each other's thoughts. He wants me to look at him, I know. And I deliberately look away. I know I would blush if I looked at him. I know I would smile and give away my desire to be with him. To be with him. I want to be with him. I like the fact that he likes me. I like the attention I am getting. I like his eyes on me. I secretly look at his fingers. They are long and thick. He has a strong palm. He wears a ring on his right index finger.

He leaves after some time without saying anything. I follow him. But he pedals his cycle fast and disappears with the turning road. I walk this road from Kopili to my house alone. Thinking about the envelope and the two rupees note inside it. My heart is heavy with something good. I think of Masha. How beautiful her life is! I think of Chandan. He has a beautiful life too! But I am not sure if I can ever ignore his nose. I have no real issues with his teeth, though. And there are people with dark complexions. He is not the only one. It is not good, but definitely not bad.

MAHESH

11 April 1980

The Lady at the Centre has come to our Guwahati, and though from a distance, I see her. Such a powerful walk. Impressive. And that haircut! I can never say this thing to anyone, but yes, I like her haircut. It's way too modern or courageous, if I may say. I wonder why women in Guwahati are not as modern as the Lady at the Centre. And not only for her haircut but even for her courage, and talk, and achievements. I don't think a man can have a walk that is powerful and modest at the same time. Only women seem to have that special ability.

But the meeting was not fruitful, just like all the previous meetings. Centre and the Group are still not agreeing on the cut-off year.

I like how the Assam Tribune attracts readers with optimistic headlines about these meetings. And at the end of an article, puts a line that the talks failed. They have the technique to create gripping articles.

At the shop, customers talked about who was right, the Centre or the Group. Centre established 1971 as the cut-off year, and the Group wanted it to be 1951. This has been going on for a while now, and my brain stops working when I come across these kinds of talks; we waste only our time. The Group will find it difficult to persuade the all-powerful Centre.

I have even stopped talking about it with Mother these days. The situation outside has calmed since the talks between the Centre and the Group started. But Mother reads my expressions and starts her philosophy that if I continue to be afraid, I will attract problems. Instead, I should be calm and proud as I am an Assamese. I don't always worry about myself; most of my worries are about other people. Especially people like Bhaijan, who are stressed by this movement.

Bihu is here. Mother bought some Kopou Phool to put in her hair. Mother used to dance at the Bihu and cook delicious Til Pitha and Coconut Laddoos. She has not done that since Father passed away.

AGHA

MID 1980

J ust like Sajid and Rashid, I have stopped going to school as well. Ma does not push me to go. She did say that I should complete the tenth standard, but I am not going to. I do not like books; I like combs, powder, lip colour, kajal and mirrors. As we have more money coming home, we get *chai* with milk these days. And I do not see Ma going to Dimi auntie to ask for food. Rashid does not, but Sajid gives some money to Ma. Sajid also bought a saree for Ma one day. I saw tears in her eyes. One day, he bought a dress for Rani. Rani was happy, smiling. She hugged Sajid. I smiled, looking at both. I felt the same emotion that I had felt after seeing Rani cry the other day. Rani never hugs me. Sajid buys nothing for me. I am happy that I am getting enough rice for dinner. Sajid and Rashid come home tired. Baba is not as tired as they are. Sajid once told Ma that Baba disappears in the afternoon and comes back in the evening. Ma said he must be going to look for new work. As the boys are now settling in the paddy fields, he can move on from there and get some easy work for himself. Sajid was not convinced of Ma's answer. I don't think Ma herself was either. I hear Ma telling Dimi auntie that Sajid and Rashid have decided to focus on earning money. Ma was happy when she said that. I am assured that there won't be much food shortage at home going forward.

I am not going to accept what Baba has said to me about getting married. I am going to ask mamu once if he can pay for my makeup course. If he agrees, I will not get married to anyone. I will go to Guwahati. Stay there. Do my course. Have a job. Earn money. And then marry a rich man. Yes, I have a concrete plan in place.

Today after the morning *chai*, I asked Ma for mamu's address, which she gave me reluctantly. I am going to write a letter to mamu this evening, and I shall ask someone to post it. I do not know who. I have never posted a letter myself. Ma writes letters to Mamu sometimes. But she tries to hide it from us when she writes. I have never really spoken with him properly. How will I ask him for help?

***

I sit close to the door; Chandan is at home. His bicycle is parked outside. I wonder what he must be doing. Chatting with his father. Eating breakfast. I wonder what Dimi auntie cooked for breakfast. There is a meeting happening on the ground. Viju uncle usually gives judgments if there are conflicts, fights. Do we need to know both sides to make a judgment? Can we be biased and ignore the other side? Is that at all accepted by the world? But is the world fair?

When I hear Viju uncle talking, I think that the world is not fair. I think hunger is the biggest problem. But, as per Viju uncle, the Centre and the Group not discussing the issue in detail is the biggest problem. I do not know what the Centre is, and I do not know what the Group is. And I don't care what's happening between them. I think only that they should resolve their problems quickly so that these meetings on the ground will stop. They are irritating, and they block my view of Chandan's house. I am sure Chandan finds them irritating, too.

I see Rani on the ground. She is looking at the tree beside Chandan's house. Listening to the grave discussion between Viju uncle and the mob. Not sure how much she can hear, though. I see Chandan walking to Rani, sitting beside her, and handing her something. They both give each other a high five, and then Rani walks home. I wonder why she is comfortable with everyone around her. How is she so forgiving? How is she so calm and patient? Why doesn't she get angry? She has a right to get angry, as very few people treat her well. I wonder from whom she learned this-forgiveness. She has a clean heart, a calm mind. I wonder if I can ever learn something from her. But do I want to? No, I am happy the way I am. Kind people suffer the most-Ma and Rani are examples of it. I should learn from them not to be like them.

Rani comes in and hands me a chit. I do not know whether Ma has seen this or not. Ma is cutting beans. Not looking up. I clasp the chit in my hand and walk to the other corner of the room. Sitting with my back to the wall, my legs folded up to my chest. I opened the chit in a way Ma cannot see it.

Dear Agha

I miss you so much after our last meeting. Did you miss me? Did you try the earrings that I gave you? Please try them. I dreamt of you and the Kopou Phool. In my dream, you were in a pink saree, and you had Kopou Phool in your hair. And you know, the colour of the flower was not pink but blue, so it matched the colour of your eyes. You will look so beautiful in a saree. Have you ever tried a saree? I think you should. Also, I want to touch your curly hair once. I moved my hand through it in my dream. It felt like silk-soft. I want to do that in real life. Will you let me do that someday? Also, yellow suits you better than any other colour. You should wear that color often.

I saw a fight happening just beside the petrol pump yesterday; there was also a shooting. Not sure if anyone was killed. But afraid for my life, I ran back home. Baba is going to find another job for me in a better location. But until he finds another job, I am going to continue working there. We need money, right? To settle down.

I woke up early today. Some people were going to come to see Baba. He has to resolve issues people have with each other. People who have come from the other side of the border are creating noise– Baba says. Ma interrupted him, saying that the people on this side of the border are creating noise. You know how Ma is! She won't agree with anyone easily. Anyway, my morning went by listening to their chatter. The new mob has now come to Baba with new complaints.

And what do you like to eat?

Only yours,

Chandan

I smile.

'Why are you blushing? What's in your hand?' Ma asks me.

I must know my surroundings. My cheeks go red when I think of Chandan, when he winks at me, when he looks at me, when he writes to me. I am startled. I never thought Ma would pay attention to what I was doing.

'Nothing Ma. Just thought of writing something.' I take out my bag, take out a book from it and slip the chit inside it. Ma looks away. I write my response on the chit.

~~Dear Chandan~~

Chandan

When I came home that day, I kept the envelopes in my bag. I shall wear the earrings soon. I will have to tell Ma that Masha has gifted her. For that, I have to go meet her. She will ask me to come to school. I do not want to. I love Kopou Phool too. Aren't they pretty? You know what their specialty is? They bloom only once a year. We wait for them to appear. They make us happy on their arrival and sad on their departure. In stark contrast with those across the border.

I only want these issues to be resolved. Ma worries for mamu as he is in Guwahati, where major protests and marches are happening. What if something happens to him? Ma is not in touch with her parents either; I think. I do not know. I wonder sometimes how you feel when you know you cannot see someone ever again? Is that hurtful? Or you move on with your life? What happens? I do not like to cry. I do not like getting upset. I sometimes think I want to know everything that is happening around me. I want to care, love. I even want to know what these walls think about me. Or even the patch on the wall that I have created by sucking the mud over it. I want to know how they see me. How do they feel about me? How do they like me? And then I think I do not want to know. I do not have the capacity to feel this. To feel emotions. I fear I would become like Ma someday, crying all day. Following all of Baba's orders. I fear!

I think your decision to continue working at the petrol pump is correct. We need money to move to Guwahati.

Regarding my hair, I don't think I will like you putting your hands through it. ~~I am happy as long as I get some food.~~ In terms of food, I like anything, really anything.

Agha

I fold the chit and think if I have written anything that I should not have. And if I am opening myself too much to him. But I ignore that thought. I hand over the chit to Rani, who is staring at me and smiling whenever our eyes meet. She leaves the house. I wonder if she knows what's happening. Ma is noticing everything. I believe she's aware of Chandan's feelings for me. And I think she supports us. I bit my lip to hide my happiness. The dream of Guwahati clouds my mind. I put the bedsheet on the floor and take a blanket. The room does not need to be dark for me to sleep. I don't have a problem in that I am not alone at home. I want to lie down quickly and plan my Guwahati stay in my head. I am going to ask Chandan to get a room close to the parlor. So that I spend less time walking and more time learning. But his work should be closer to the house as well. Anyway, he will cycle so he can manage even if his work is not close to our house. I close my eyes, and I see *Kopou Phool*, the wildflower.

Rani handed me a chit when I woke up from my nap.

Dear Agha

I am so pleased to read what you have written. You want to know what walls think about you? They like you. They

like your being around them. Just like I do. Everyone, every-
thing around you, likes you. I think you can always love and
care for people. That is the only thing that makes us human,
right? I love with a full heart. I care with a full heart. And
I want to tell you that I love you. I love you more than I love
my bicycle. I can do anything for you.

If you do not know whether your mother is in touch with
her parents, you should ask her. I am sure she wants to talk
about it. I like Shabana auntie. She is so calm, so patient. I
don't think she raises her voice to anyone, does she?

Don't you think people on the other side of the border are
human, too? Baba says I am not old enough to put forward
my opinion on these issues. But I have sympathy for people
who suffer. And here, everyone is suffering. I cannot take
sides. I agree with Ma and agree with Baba. People on both
sides are creating issues. They are just like us, after all.
What do you think?

I will keep moving my hand through your hair in my
dreams. Until one day I will win you over. I love you.

  Yours only,

  Chandan

I think about it. I ponder his assertion that they are human. I have a hard time thinking that other people are just
like us, like me. In my world, it is only me. I am not sure who
to let in and who to kick out. But I have started thinking
that I can include Ma in my world. I can let her in, maybe.
Maybe not. I am not sure yet. I look at Ma; she is stitching
Rani's torn salwar. I see my salwar lying on the floor-she
has already stitched my dress. She wipes sweat on her head
with her saree drape. I wonder what goes on inside her head
that is covered by those curly hair and, most times, by her
saree drape. I write my response.

Chandan,

I shall ask Ma about her parents one day. I am just not sure when.

I have mostly seen one side suffering and the other side dominating. There are people with whom you can talk who give you hope that everything will be alright one day. But that does not really happen. The situation does not change. I also think people who suffer should take control and resolve their problems on their own. Beat the opposition up, treat them the way you are treated, and pull their hair. Disrespect them. I have learnt that we should take control into our hands. Enough of humiliation.

Having said that, I don't really care as long as I get three times' meal.

And yes, you can touch my hair in your dream. I won't mind.

Agha

I hand it over to Rani; I received his response in no time.

Dear Agha

I am a little scared after reading your response. You are not talking about people from the other side of the border, right? You are probably talking about your situation. Is that correct?

I don't think we should really care. I don't care what's happening outside as long as I get married to you.

Only yours,

Chandan

I do not answer back. Yes, I am talking about my own situation, and it is also applicable to all other situations where we are mistreated. But I will let him interpret it the way he wants. Ma is at Dimi auntie's all afternoon. Rani is at home, sitting at our open door, but constantly looking at Chandan's house. She looks worried.

'WHAT IS GOING ON?' I ask Rani.

'Nothing, Ma does not seem well,' she answers. She is as upset as if something big has happened to her. I think she feels Ma's pain. I do not.

'DID YOU HAVE LUNCH?'

'I am not hungry.' I never knew why she was never hungry. She goes outside onto the ground. She loves sitting there.

I serve myself, and since Rani is not hungry, I eat her share of roti. I eat two rotis. I am happy. I wish to have more such afternoons, the ones with my tummy full. Ma comes home.

'Ma, do you want to write a letter to mamu and ask if he can pay for my make-up course? I am not comfortable writing the letter on my own.' I immediately regretted asking her. She is in pain. Her eyes, cheeks, and eyebrows are red.

Ma walks to me and, as far as I remember, the very first time hugs me. Her eyes are full of water. I feel her chest going in and coming out as she whimpers. I feel her hot head on my shoulder and her hair on my face. She has soft hair. Her soft hands are tight on my back.

'Agha, I must tell you. Life is not what we think it is. It takes turns, and sometimes the bad ones. My life took a bad turn. But I do not want that to happen to you. You must accept sooner or later that no one can help you now for your Guwahati adventure, including mamu. But it can happen after your marriage. Trust me,' she says while she is crying.

How will someone react to such an emotional talk by her mother? I go blank. I have no clue. I want to run away from such a massive flood of emotions. *We are all human*-I remember the sentence from Chandan's chit. I am not sure what to say, so I keep quiet. Ma never really speaks her heart out, nor do I. No one at home does. She has been strict about going to school on time, studying. She has been strict about when to come home. But otherwise, she easily comes across as someone who hardly cares about her children. Today she tells me that she indeed thinks of me and not to expect anything from anyone. But I wonder how she knows that I can move to Guwahati after marriage. Does she know about me and Chandan? Does she know he has promised to take me to Guwahati after marriage? If yes, how? Does Dimi auntie know about us? Has Chandan told Dimi auntie about us? Has Dimi auntie told Ma? I have so many questions. My head will explode. Of all that Ma has said to me, I am going to remember just one thing: that I can move to Guwahati after marriage.

I see possibilities; I see some hope. Even though it does not happen now, it happens in the future. It does. I feel confident in myself. I look into Ma's eyes. They are red. When had I seen her eyes dry and beautiful, the way they actually are? I guess a long time back. But I still smile at her.

'Remember, life can change at any time. We must be pre-pared,' she says and sits on the floor with her head resting on the wall and eyes closed.

I am not sure, but probably I want to talk. I want to tell Ma that she is beautiful. And that she should not cry. I am there for her. But I rethink. No, I am not there for her. I just want to have three times meals and do the makeup course.

The next minute, Ma screams and cries hard. I am not sure what is happening.

'Ma, are you alright?' I ask.

Ma does not answer.

I rush to the ground; I do not see Sajid. I see Rani. I take her hand and bring her home. She offers a glass of water to Ma, wipes her tears and hugs her. I could have done that, I think. But instead I went out asking for help. Dimi auntie has come too. She stands at the door looking at Ma.

'Be strong; you have to go through it,' she tells Ma from where she is standing. Her eyes are wet.

'I can't, Dimi, I can't,' Ma cries. Then screams.

Dimi auntie comes in and holds Ma close to her. Viju uncle stands at the door; Chandan stands by his side. They are all concerned. They are humans.

'What happened, Dimi auntie?' I ask.

'Your *baap* will come home soon, with a surprise for you,' she says with anger. Her eyes are so big. Her teeth are so uniform, just like Rani's. I wonder what surprise Baba was coming up with that Ma feels so helpless about. For a moment, I wished Dimi auntie to be my Ma. She would have fought with Baba so much that he would never have beaten her or insulted her. I have no courage to ask for any further details. I wish not to have any further sweaty *salwar* or *pyjamas*. Ma is still whimpering. Dimi auntie gestures to Chandan and Viju uncle to leave. Chandan does not look at me. But I know he is as clueless as I am. I smirk.

Ma lies on the floor, still crying. Rani lies by her side, holding Ma. Sajid comes in some time. He looks pale. He sits beside the stove. I look at the clock; it is four p.m. I want to have some *chai*.

'I will make *chai* for you, Ma,' I say. But it is for me. I do want to ask Sajid why he is upset, but instead decide to wait for the surprise that Baba is coming home with. I wonder if Baba has beaten someone in the paddy fields. Or if he is going to come home drunk and fight with neighbours. He has done this in the past; a few neighbours beat him in return. Ma cared for his bruises. They were stubborn and stayed for more than a month. So, he is less likely to repeat it. I wonder if he is going to beat everyone at home today. If that is the case, I should not go outside tomorrow. Why show the bruises to the world?

Chai is ready. I offer it to everyone. Sajid does not take it. I have his share. That day is unusual in many ways. Ma has her *chai*. Her eyes are not wet but swollen. I wonder where Rashid is! No one says anything. Dimi auntie comes home; she brings *Nimki* to Ma.

'Eat this; you haven't eaten anything all day,' she says.

Ma rejects it outright. Dimi auntie insists. Ma does not listen to her. Dimi auntie gives up, keeps the *Nimki* near the stove and leaves. I look at it. I want it. But I should wait for Sajid and Rani to go out. Ma never pays attention to what I am doing.

'Ma, they will be coming anytime,' Sajid says, looking at the clock.

'Who is coming?' I ask.

Sajid looks at me with anger or sympathy or pity. I do not know what it is. But it is not his normal look. 'What happened?' I ask again.

'Do you ever understand anything that goes around? Don't say anything; I know you don't. But at least you can show some sympathy for Ma, right? All you do is eat and sleep. I know now you want to eat *Nimki*. Here, eat it.' He is angry. His eyes are red. And his hands are shivering. I take it from him and eat. He looks at Ma and Rani in surprise. They say nothing. He leaves the house. I think whether what he says is right or not. He clearly does not like me. When I finish eating, I wash the bowl. I see Sajid sitting outside, looking at the sky. Dimi auntie's door is locked. I do not see Chandan's cycle parked outside.

I wonder why the evening is so beautiful. The sun is so mild, and the wind is pleasant. I wonder why Ma would cry in such pleasant weather. She is not hungry, and even if she is, I have eaten the snacks given by Dimi auntie. I see Sajid staring at the narrow lane. He stands up and walks to the house. I look down that lane and see Rashid, Baba, and someone else. I rush inside.

Rashid comes in and keeps the box of the sweet beside the stove.

'They are here, Ma,' says Rashid.

Ma is looking at the wall. Her eyes do not move. Baba is at the door and a girl. She is wearing a shiny green saree. Baba is wearing a sherwani. I have seen grooms who get married in the mosque wearing such a dress. She is holding Baba's hand, his palm. Both are standing at the door.

'Get up and welcome her!' Baba screams at Ma.

Ma does not move.

'Get up, you *harami*!' he screams again.

I am shaking. Rani is staring at Baba and the new girl. Sajid is staring at the ground.

Rashid hugs the new girl and brings her in by holding her hand. I realize what is happening. I know who the new girl is. She is the same girl I had seen in my dreams. No, in reality, I had seen her on the farm with Baba twice. They were holding hands. They were kissing. For a moment, it is inexplicable that Rashid is giggling and saying,

'Welcome home, Ma!'

MAHESH

29 May 1980

*E*veryone is interpreting the chaos in Assam the way they want, but the Group has made it clear long ago that the movement is against foreigners, not against any religion or language. I read in the Assam tribune that the Group has warned the State and the Centre that if no action is taken, then they will evict the illegal foreigners on their own. I think, sometimes, the Group gets desperate to take action. Either a few members of the Group are flying to Delhi, or the Lady at the Centre and her deputy are flying to Guwahati. Discussions are happening and they are going in the circles because of the cut-off year.

Mother and I had a fever last week. I kept the shop closed for one week. I lost around a hundred rupees.

AGHA

MID 1980

Ma is cooking dinner. I am helping. The new girl is sitting in the corner, looking at Ma and chatting with Rashid. Sajid and Rani are outside. Baba bought fish and then went out. I do not remember having eaten fish for a long time. I look at the box of sweets, which is unopened. Surprisingly, I do not want to eat those. They are for Baba's second marriage. He cannot manage one; I am not sure why he would have married for the second time. I think he does not know that he failed in the first marriage. That he could not provide us with food. Or enough clothes. Or money to do the makeup course. Ma is never happy with him. This is Ma's golden chance to walk away. Not to live with him in this house. She can go to mamu. I am sure he will take care of her, of us. I can even do a makeup course there if Ma goes to Guwahati to mamu. I drag myself back to reality before I dream about my unattainable future plans.

We are making puris, potato curry, fried fish, daal and rice to welcome Rumi, the new girl. Baba's new wife. Ma has not spoken to Rumi yet.

Dinner is delicious. I thought Ma would not eat, but she does. Rumi eats the most. After the dinner, I wash the dishes. Chandan is sitting on a chair on the veranda and staring at me. He does not wink at me, but continues staring. I do not blush today. Rashid and Sajid go to the school veranda to sleep. They had gone to the school veranda to sleep when there had been heavy rain, and the water had come inside the house-the entire floor was muddy. Baba had disappeared and returned only in the morning when the water had receded, and Ma had cleaned the house. Ma, Rani and I slept at Dimi auntie's house. It was four years back. Rashid and Sajid carry their bedsheets and a blanket with them. I lock the door and take my place. Rumi and Baba sleep under the same sheet. A mosquito net hangs over their small place, and Baba is covering the net with another sheet. It looks like a small plateau, like those surrounding Kopili. Rumi goes inside first and closes the cover. Baba turns the lights off and then enters the plateau. Ma is weeping again. Rani is sleeping on her side, not looking at Ma. Everyone sleeps in time. But there are strange sounds.

Rani snores. Ma wails. Baba grunts and Rumi moans. I lick the soil on the wall.

MAHESH

28 December 1980

*I*t took me an hour to find my diary. Mother had kept it in the suitcase and kept the suitcase beneath the bed. It's been about six months that I have written nothing. Even today, I was not very keen to write, but there is nothing to do here at the hospital. Mother is not well. She has pneumonia. Her situation is as critical as Assam's. Bhaijan told Mother that he had notified Agha's father through a letter about me. What about her mother? Mother asked. She is my sister; she knows my proposal is in her best interest. Do not worry about her–Bhaijan said. Ma found that strange. Ma is very judgmental; she just does not take people at face value. But she wants me to get married before long.

On Thursday, the Assam Tribune had many blanks in the newspaper, as reporters are angry at the new government for restricting their reporting of anything on agitation. President's rule has ended, and we now have a Chief Minister. Mother gets angry when I say this, but this is not *going in the right direction. The truth becomes inevitable if you try to suppress it.*

Another year is coming to an end, and Assam is as it was, chaotic.

AGHA

LATE 1980

Ma hardly speaks with anyone at home these days. She combs her hair once in two- three days. She does not change her saree after a bath and continues to wear the same saree for three –four days. I now know what sadness looks like. Like you have no energy in your eyes, in your face, or in your skin. You walk, talk, but you are not present. You are not alive. Baba's new marriage was to blame for Ma's situation.

Rumi, my new mother, is two years older than I am. I saw her at my school a few years back. Nobody knows when and where she met Baba. At home, she does not speak with Ma, me, and Rani. Rani always tries to speak with Rumi, but Rumi is not interested in speaking with Rani. Rumi speaks with Baba and Rashid. Even though Sajid does not talk with her, she tries to talk with him. Rumi does not cook, she does not clean the dishes, nor does she clean the floor after lunch or dinner. She just sits and sometimes goes out for a walk.

Baba allows her to go for a walk every day. I am not allowed. Rani nor Ma either. Rumi wears good sarees at home. New ones. Ma's sarees are old, and some of them are torn. Rumi always wears makeup. Ma never wears makeup. Rumi's hair is long and shiny, just like Ma's. Rumi is very thin, thinner than Ma. She is not beautiful. She giggles now and then.

Rani goes to school every day. I do not. Ma does not insist. She wraps her arms around herself and sobs. She stares at the walls and the sky. She cannot listen to what we say. She keeps doing the work at home, saying nothing to anyone.

I wonder if Chandan has dropped his plan to marry me or if he is contemplating his plan of moving to Guwahati. I write to him.

Dear Chandan,

How are you?

How is everything at your home? Did any new people come to get advice from Viju uncle? What's happening outside? Are the protests and chaos over? We have a lot of silent chaos going on at home. You must have already received the news. Everyone in Matiparbat is aware, and I see sympathy for Ma in their eyes. Already there are so many people at home; we have one more.

I dream of Kopou Phool every night. Should we meet at Kopili tomorrow afternoon?

Agha

I wait until Rani comes home from school. As soon as she is back, I hand over the chit to her to make the delivery. She does not deny my request. I decide to see how she gives the chit to Chandan. She goes to the ground and sits exactly in front of Chandan's door. It is closed, but his bicycle is parked outside. So, he is at home. Rani sits patiently in the mild sun, observing the trees around, the soil, the birds, and sometimes the people. The ribbons tied around her hair shine. The red ribbon. Rani's favourite colour. She looks at her palm and moves her hand over it. As if she is trying to read her destiny. This girl, my sister, I feel something for her. I want to go to her and hug her and tell her that she is different. Different from the rest of the world.

I go to the Kopili the next day afternoon to meet Chandan. He comes after me and parks his bicycle under the mango tree.

'Here,' he hands me a two rupees note.

'This is for our treasure,' he says and smiles. *Total four rupees.*

I take it. Hold it in my hands. Thoughts stir in my head-my dream is coming true. We will save money, get married, go to Guwahati and I will do my make-up course.

'How are you? How are the meetings on the ground coming up?'

'Here, have this,' he hands me *roti* and *sabji* wrapped in paper. I eat it even though I have had my lunch. Chandan is wearing a pink shirt today; it does not suit him. He is wearing blue pants, which he calls jeans. They suit him. I finish my food. Meanwhile, he is gazing at Kopili. I put the newspaper in the bushes around.

'How is Rumi?' he asks.

'Arrogant,' I answer.

'I am going to talk to my baba about our marriage,' he says.

'Our marriage? Isn't it too early?' I have no other reaction. I have agreed to marry him.

He takes my hand in his. I do not object. He looks into my eyes. 'Do you know your eyes are deep? Deeper than this Kopili water. I want to be lost in them all my life.'

I like him, even his face. I shift a little towards him. We both admire Kopili. I feel so good, so safe. Someone is holding my hand. *I am sure he would protect me;* I think. Protect from Baba, his violence. I will be free soon. Free from the crowd. 'You seem quiet today. How are you feeling?' I ask.

'I am okay,' he says. He is not.

'What are you thinking?' I ask.

'Some people burnt houses in Jorhat this morning. Baba has gone there to see the situation. I am not sure how long this is going to last. The situation in Guwahati is going to get worse with time.'

'How does that affect our plan to move to Guwahati after marriage?'

'We will. Even if Ma and Baba oppose. We will go.' He remarks.

I smile. He holds my hand tight. He's still lost in thought.

I put forward my opinion: 'I do not agree with keeping quiet. We have to fight back against outsiders.'

'I do not believe in violence,' he replies calmly, still looking at the Kopili. He is clearly hurt, and I do not know how to console him. I wonder whether I have inherited Baba's traits of not understanding others.

'Let's go,' he stands to leave. He pedals the cycle fast and does not look back. He does not wait for my response.

I tie the two rupees note tightly in my dupatta; I want to go too, but Kopili appears very inviting today. I walk towards it. I sense someone behind me. Someone sneaking. I turn back, and I see Sajid.

'It is late. Let's walk home,' he says.

I am not sure whether he was there all along. But I do not ask him. We walk side by side. He says nothing. I say nothing. When we reach home, he looks at Chandan's house. I quickly go inside. I do not want to have any awkward conversations or awkward glances. I slip the two rupees note into the yellow envelope in my bag. Sajid follows me inside. I cannot decipher what he is thinking. He drinks water and stares at me at the same time.

'Where were you, Sajid? Rashid was asking for you,' Rumi tries to make Sajid talk to her.

But he does not. He ignores her and goes outside. Rumi smirks. I wonder why she is so interested in talking to Sajid and Rashid. And she does not talk to any of the women at home. I wonder why. Ma is mopping the floor. She has grown old. Her skin is loose.

Rani is on the playground, sitting on the bench. I go there to chat with her and to see what Chandan is doing.

'Do you like the new Ma?' she asks me. 'New Ma gave breakfast only to Rashid and Sajid this morning; I and Ma got nothing.'

'ARE YOU HUNGRY NOW?' I ask.

'Yes', she says.

I hold her hand, and we go home. Rice and curry are ready. I take a plate and serve food to Rani and Ma. Rani eats as soon as I serve her.

'Ma, please eat.'

'I will have it with your Baba, Agha.' Ma, the loyal wife who would even die for her husband, says with no hesitation. I want to hold her by the shoulders, shake her, wake her up from a gloomy dream that she is going through every day. Tell her to run away. To find peace, and her own happiness. But my hunger takes precedence over these thoughts.

Food first, people later. I ate the food. I decided Rani and I will have dinner before everybody else going forward. Rumi stares at me, but I ignore her. I am hurt not because Rani is being ill-treated all the time, but because I am seen as a weak sister. Rumi just arrived and now dictates who eats. I cannot tell Ma what to do; she has blind love for Baba.

When Baba and my brothers come home, they all have dinner. Rashid and Baba speak with Rumi. Sajid and Ma are quiet. Rashid tells stories from the farm about how they plough for seeds and how they tie the livestock. He mentions appreciation from the farm owner for his work, and one rupee as a token of appreciation. I have not heard him talk so much to any of us. Ma has lowered her head and is eating her food. He laughs with Rumi and Baba. He gives Rumi a high-five. She pats him on his thigh. I see her saree drape loosening on her chest. Baba is busy eating his food. Rashid stares at her chest. She covers it up slowly while staring back at Rashid. He looks away and blushes. He asks her to serve him rice and holds her hand when she serves more than he wants. She immediately retracts herself, but is not uncomfortable. She is smiling, biting her lips. I notice. Sajid notices. The new Rashid is unfolding before us.

MAHESH

12 January 1981

I asked Bhaijan about Agha's daily routine. He said Agha helps her mother with cleaning jobs. She does not want to study further, but she wants to learn beauty parlour courses and to own a beauty parlour. That is difficult. Mother may have a different view. I do not know. And the beauty parlour fad does not have an excellent reputation. For a minute, I think that Agha is not the right choice for me. But somehow, I think she will manage my expectations. Maybe I will change and help her set up her own shop. Maybe she will change and leave this craze of doing makeup for other women. I still like her. I get lost in her eyes when I see her in the picture that Bhaijan has given me. She has long, curly brown hair, and her skin looks like a shining diamond. I am longing to see her for real and convey my love to her. I fear, will that ever happen?

When I talk about Agha, Mother looks at my face and says, 'Are you worried again?' with a strange expression. She does not wait for me to answer. 'The more you fear, the more you are going to attract problems,' she says. Her philosophy is true, but boring. So, I have decided not to worry about anything. Neither about the things going on outside, nor about my marriage.

AGHA

EARLY 1981

I sometimes wonder how rapidly things have changed. Rumi is sick for over ten days now. She fell pregnant and then, within a couple of months, her baby died in her womb. Ma takes care of her. Sajid and Rashid earn money. Sajid gives it to Ma. Rashid does not give it to anyone. Baba some days goes to work, some days does not. Sajid runs the house. Baba is free, like a bird. Rumi and he go out for walks or shopping. He never went out with Ma. Ma does not care, or at least she does not show it on her face. Rani and I eat together, sit on the ground, admire how confident Dimi auntie is, and discuss our favourite food in free time. Rani has a way of satisfying her craving. She closes her eyes and imagines eating. She feels the taste on her tastebuds. And then gulps it. She says that doesn't make her hungry. I do that these days. Not a bad idea. But I still feel hungry. She has control over her thoughts and behaviour. I don't think I have. She told me she wants to become a doctor. I looked at our house, our clothes and then told her that would never happen. She seemed upset. I did not feel bad. We should dream, but not fool ourselves.

I must see Chandan every day, otherwise I cannot focus on anything that I do. I see a supportive, nonviolent man in him. The one who will keep me happy. And I will keep him happy too. Why should only one person take effort? I have learned to cook. *Machher jhol, aloo pitika, patol torkari, roti, rice, daal.* Chandan likes all of these. I do not think his nose is a problem anymore. I somehow like it. I can easily hold it between two of my fingers when he comes close to me.

Baba talks about marrying me off frequently these days. Ma writes to mamu, unsure of what. But she says *you will go to Guwahati, Agha.* I have my *chai*, wash dishes and read Chandan's old letters. I have reserved a corner of our tiny abode. When I am home, I sit there. Only there. Rumi sometimes sits in my corner and does not move even when I ask her to. She thinks this is her house. She still looks at Rashid with narrow eyes and a slight smile on her face. I find that strange. Rashid and she go for a walk sometimes. I do not like her. She is the primary reason I want to leave this house as a priority. I go to Kopili every afternoon at three. Chandan comes there sometimes, and we chat for an hour. I come home before sunset and before Baba comes home. My only fear is that Baba should not see us together. Not before Chandan's family asks him for my hand.

The clock shows three in the afternoon. I wrap up my lunch, wash my plate, take my dupatta, and leave. No *burqa* today. Rumi is sleeping. Ma is at Dimi auntie's place. I reach the Kopili. Chandan is already sitting there.

He pulls my hand and makes me sit by his side. I sit. We do not talk. I know what is going to happen. He shifts close to me. He holds my hand in his hands, and we both take deep breaths. A shiver passes through my body every time he is this close to me. He moves his hand behind me and holds my waist tight. He is close to me. His lips are almost on my lips. I feel him breathing. Our eyes are locked. He kisses me gently on my lips. I shrink. I bite my lip. I move my hands and legs close to my chest. He kisses me again. Our tongues are engaged. My hands are on his shoulder. I feel his yellow check shirt. The collar is stiff; it is relatively new. I move my hands onto his cheeks. He is sweating. He is tired after working hard all day at the petrol pump. I shift my focus to his lips. They are soft. *Does he apply butter?* I ask myself. My tongue is still engaged with his. He is not letting me go. I pull myself out and take a deep breath. He laughs. I laugh. That is long.

'I spoke to Baba yesterday about us,' Chandan says.

'And?' I say and widen my eyes.

'He does not approve of our marriage. He says there is already chaos in the society; we will add fuel to it,' he remarks.

'And how will we add fuel to it?'

'It will be a Hindu–Muslim marriage. People see Baba as someone who supports and cares for Hindus. He may not be taken that seriously if we get married.'

'And what do you think about this?'

'I do not agree with him. But I am going to convince him.'

Isn't the Viju uncle the most literate and broad-minded person in Matiparbat? I ask myself. He is. I am disappointed in his approach-what does he mean by *adding fuel?*

Chandan and I both sit on the bank for a long time. I smell the wind. It is fresh. I see the *Kopou Phool* lying around us. I want to ask them-what do you think will happen to us? Do you know? Can you guess? I was confident until yesterday that I would marry Chandan and go to Guwahati. But today, I am not. I am not. I walk to the Kopili. I wet my feet in the Kopili's water. I bow down and take the water in my palm. I drink it. Why does it feel that I am saying goodbye to Kopili? I sit there on the sand. Chandan follows me.

'Chandan, don't you think Kopili is more than a river?'

'No,' he laughs.

'I think Kopili has a big agenda in her life. She seems quiet. But she is meant for bigger things.'

'Like?'

'Helping people.'

'She is already helping people with her water in transportation. With all these *naukas* that move from one end of the river to another,' he gave a practical answer.

'She is one of us. She feels our pain. She feels our struggle. When I die, I will die here. In Kopili,' I say.

'Are you crazy? Why will you die? We are going to get married and make babies.' He pulled me towards him and kissed my cheek.

'Babies?' I ask.

'Yes, at least five,' he says, and winks at me.

'Five? I will die giving them birth.'

I laugh. He laughs.

My Kopili, please take care of us. I need your help. Please let Viju uncle be convinced of our plan, our marriage. I need nothing else from you.

The water is enchanting. The mountains around, the trees, the wind-I hold everything close to me. As if someone is going to snatch them away from me. I know no one is. I know I will keep coming here to Kopili every day. But I still fear. *Fear is good. It shows that you care.* I tell myself.

'Let's go. It's late,' Chandan is ready to leave. He is upset.

I walk ahead; Chandan follows me. The day passes in the usual way. Nothing changes. Neither the routine nor the thoughts. Rumi, Baba, Sajid, Rani, Rashid, Ma. All are the same. I sleep thinking of Chandan and our days after marriage. I wonder how he or Viju uncle would tell Baba about us. Will Baba agree? Will Ma agree?

***

Sajid hands over a chit to me. He is one of us now.

Dear Agha

I am going to Guwahati to my chachu's place.

He is unwell. I will be back in a few days.

We will get married when I am back. It doesn't matter who approves our marriage and who does not. We will elope :-D

Yours

Chandan

I slip the chit into my bag; Rumi is staring at me. I do not fear her; I looked her in the eye. She does not lower her gaze. She married a man who is of her Baba's age-and my father has married a girl who is his daughter's age. *What a couple!* In my mind, I am boastful of the fact that I have a guy in my life who earns well and who is of my age and who is not someone's husband or father already.

I revisit all my previous conversations with Chandan in my mind. I take the earrings he gave me out of my bag. I see the envelopes. I remember keeping one two–rupee note in the yellow envelope and the other in the blue envelope. So, half of the saving is for building the house and the other half is for buying a motorcycle. The two rupees note in the yellow envelope has vanished. *Is it Rumi?* She is engrossed in folding her washed dresses.

Though deep down I know who stole the money from my bag, I decide to ask Rani first. She is outside. She is sitting on the bench, staring at the sky. She looks beautiful. She is waiting for one of her friends to join her. She has friends. She talks to them. Long talks. She is calm, irrespective of the situation. She is matured. I am not. People like her. They don't like me. I hold her hand and gesture for her to talk with me for a minute. She jumps off the swing. We go to the fence.

'DO YOU KNOW WHO TOUCHED MY BAG?'

'I did not,' the poor soul responds. Her innocence makes me laugh. I hold her close to me. She gives me a wide smile, straight from her heart.

'ALRIGHT, NOW LISTEN TO ME. I HAD FOUR RU-PEES IN MY BAG. NOW THERE IS JUST A TWO RUPEE NOTE. DO YOU KNOW WHO MIGHT HAVE TAKEN IT?'

'I saw Rashid opening your bag yesterday morning, when you were taking a bath.'

I kiss Rani on her cheeks. I hold her face in my hands and look at her. Guilt covers me yet again for ill-treating her in the past. I come home, thinking about how I can confront Rashid.

'Agha, go to Sajid and tell him to get vegetables on his way home,' Ma orders me.

Hearing that, Rumi gets up. 'I will go to the farm; I want to meet Rashid's Baba.'

Ma's face changes, but, as always, she does not respond to Rumi. Rumi wears her *burqa* and leaves home in a minute.

'Ma,' I say without thinking about what I want to say next.

'Why did Baba marry her? She is just two years older than me, and I have seen her at my school. It is so awkward to see her pregnant. I don't like what's happening.'

'I have told you this many times now. Life is not what you dream of, Agha; it is what you never expect.'

'Ma, we can make it how we want it. Why do we always behave as if situations are not in our control?'

Ma looks at me, and this time with anger in her eyes. 'Stop meeting Chandan, Agha. Your Baba does not like it. His father's reputation in the society is way too high for your father's.' I cry. Ma does not console me. She is stone-hearted. She is immersed in cooking. I do not know how my marriage to Chandan will happen. When Rashid and Rumi are back in the evening, Rashid has two bags in his hand. He hands the one with veggies to Ma.

'Baba has asked you to wear this dress, Agha,' says Rashid.

I look inside the bag. There is a new dress, pink, and a very nice *burqa*, the same as the one Rumi has. There are accessories along with the dress. I am unsure what for.

Before I can ask anything, Ma immediately gets up and goes out. She looks nervous.

'What is this for?' I ask Rashid.

'I do not know; Baba did not tell me,' Rashid says.

'Get ready, Agha, a family is coming to see you,' Rumi finally says.

'See me?' I am surprised.

'Yes, for Nikah.'

'I am NOT ready to get married. Baba should have asked me before inviting anyone here.' I feel helpless. 'And I will not wear this.'

'WEAR THIS OR GET READY TO DIE!' Baba screams from the door.

My throat is choked; I never had the courage to argue with Baba. I want to cry.

'DON'T CRY, THEY ARE GOING TO SEE YOUR FACE. IF YOU CRY, YOUR MOTHER WILL SEE YOUR FACE FOR THE LAST TIME TODAY,' he says. His eyes are red.

I get up from my place, lock the door from inside, and change into the dress Baba has bought for me. The gown is pink, and the pajamas are red. The dupatta is red, too. I wear the bangles and earrings. Rumi has done the shopping for me. Her eyes are constantly on me.

'You are looking beautiful, sister,' Rani says, but she is not smiling. I don't respond. She does not know what I am going through. Nobody knows. I miss Chandan every second and pray to *Allah* for Chandan's quick return.

Rumi opens the door and goes out to talk with Baba. Ma comes inside. She was speaking with Baba. I think she is glad that she gets to speak to Baba about something, even though it is about my forced marriage to a stranger.

'You knew about this family coming to see me, didn't you?' I interrogate Ma.

'I knew about this family. But not that they are coming to visit today. I have already told you, Agha, life is what you don't expect. Do not dream. Your Baba will take decisions for your life, not you,' Ma says. She lost the respect in a second. Baba has ruined her life, and she still gives him the respect that he does not deserve.

'I want to marry Chandan; I love him,' I say to Ma, gathering whatever courage I have left.

'That will never happen.'

'Why?'

'Because the world will not let you live peacefully if you take control of your life,' Ma says.

'I do not care about the world. Do you approve of my marrying him?' I ask.

'No. I do not approve of anything that your father does not approve.'

Even though she is my mother, I see her as my enemy at that moment. She is the one who does not understand what her daughter is going through, or maybe she does not want to understand.

'You already knew about Baba and Rumi, didn't you?' I asked Ma.

'And how do you feel about Rumi carrying your husband's baby?' I continue in my rage.

Ma slaps me hard.

'Everyone knows this as well, Ma. He has already ruined your life; now he is ruining mine, and you are assisting him with this even when I am your daughter. He will do the same to Rani. You only stay here and watch our lives getting damaged.' She does not respond. She deserves the treatment she receives from Baba. She deserves that no one at home cares for her. She deserves a Rumi in her life.

Exhausted, I sit by Rani. She keeps her head on my shoulder.

I am sad, upset, angry and scared at the same time. The only thing I can do is pray to *Allah*. I close my eyes and rest my head against the wall. And then there is a knock at the door.

MAHESH

3 February 1981

When Mother recovered from her illness, we moved to Nellie. Kamal uncle, Mother's elder brother, passed away and left his house and other belongings to her. Mother wanted to move there-away from the chaos in Guwahati. The house is enormous and is beside paddy fields. It is the only cement house surrounded by mud houses. I have set up a tiny shop here. I asked Bhaijan to use my shop in Guwahati as his. He could pay me whatever rent he thinks is correct. He agreed. Also, Guwahati is not safe anymore. The attacks have increased, be it on ministers or on foreigners. There are regular bomb-blasts and frequent panic. I had to close the shop on most days.

Today, Mother was showing me the photo-album of my childhood. Time flies. Father looked so much like me. I look so much like Father. Had he been alive today, he would have managed communication with Agha's family for my marriage. But Mother is an excellent communicator, too. When we received a response from Agha's father last week, Mother noticed the regards were from Agha's father-Amir-and Rumi. She stated, 'This man is married again. I wonder how women survive when their husbands marry someone else. Poor lady.' I did not comment. I already knew through Bhaijan. I just don't want Mother to think that I can get someone better than Agha, or a girl from a family that is better than Agha's. Also, they want to plan the wedding the very next day we go to their place. I pray to God that everything goes as planned.

I am going to continue working at the shop until the date I get married. I need more money now. Expenses will increase, and I want to provide all that I can for Agha. Or may I say, my Agha-she has already become mine in my head.

AGHA

EARLY 1981

'RANI, COME OUT!' Baba screams at her.

She immediately gets up and goes. Rumi, too, waits outside. Sajid and Rashid peep inside once and they disappear. I have a feeling as if my hands and legs are tied, and a piece of cotton is stuffed inside my mouth.

When everyone enters, Ma hurries towards me and covers my face with the *burqa*. It is new and fairly transparent. There are three people with Baba. An old woman, a man in his thirties, and mamu enter the house. Baba has a bag in his hand, which he gives to Ma. Rumi follows Baba inside and sits beside me.

There is *nimki* in the bag. I love *nimki*. Ma puts the pan on the stove and starts making *chai*. She has a wide smile on her face I have hardly seen before.

'How was your travel?' Baba asks them.

'Not bad. But it was difficult to find your house,' the old lady answers. Baba nods.

The lady looked everywhere in our tiny room for one minute. She has *tikhi nazar,* as Ma says sometimes, about Dimi auntie. Such people notice anything and everything around them. I was a fool to think nobody knows about me and Chandan. People are usually smart. I am dumb.

'Please sit down,' Baba says while laying down the *chatai* in front of me. They sit.

'Would you mind if we spoke with your daughter?' the woman continues. She has a sharp tongue, too. Baba nods. I wonder why they do not bring the groom to see me.

'What is your name?' the lady asks.

The other two men keep quiet. Mamu is looking at the floor, not at me. He has betrayed me. I do not answer. I am too busy to notice everyone in the room. Thoughts about Chandan are lost somewhere. I am seeing this setup for the first time.

'Tell your name, girl,' Rumi says softly and keeps her hand on my shoulder. I look at Baba; there is rage in his eyes.

'Agha,' I answer in a soft tone.

'Can you speak a little louder, Agha?' Rumi asks me again in a mild tone. My hand was itching to slap Rumi. She was *harami,* as Baba usually addressed all other women.

'Agha,' I repeated with a louder sound.

'What is your education, Agha?' the lady continues.

'I have completed my high school,' I answer. That is a lie. I did not go to school in tenth standard. None of us did, except Rani.

'What do you do in your spare time?' the lady continues.

'I cook, wash dishes,' I say and realise that I have no hobby.

'You don't want to go to college?' the lady asks.

'I want to do a beauty parlour course,' I blurt. They all share glances.

'She is a little naïve; she does not know what is right and what is wrong. But she is exceptionally good at housework. She is quick in cooking, she washes clothes, cleans dishes, cleans the floor,' Rumi says. I never clean the floor. Ma washes clothes. I know washing dishes and cooking — that's all.

'She is good-natured, loves everyone at home and is very kind,' Rumi continues with a smile on her face. She is lying to them. I imagined slapping Rumi across her face-once, twice, and thrice. The lady looks at Ma, maybe for her confirmation of what Rumi said. Ma smiles and nods. The lady looks back at me.

'Can you walk, Agha?' the lady asks me. That is an unexpected question.

'Umm, yes,' I reply.

'Can you show us how you walk?' the lady continues. The other two men who have come with her are all en-grossed in eating sweets that Baba had bought in a big bag.

'Get up, Agha, walk here. Walk four steps forward, turn and walk four steps back.' Ma tells me what to do.

I get up from my place and walk four steps forward, and then I have a thought in mind to take two more steps to the door and see whether Chandan is back. I realize how helpless I am. I pity myself. My throat chokes and I start shaking.

I do not want to go back, but I do. I go back and sit with my back to the wall. I cover the patch on the wall. My little secret. Or no. Everyone knows everything; nothing is a secret.

'Can you take your *burqa* off? We want to see your face,' the lady continues her demands. Ma immediately reaches for me and uncovers my face.

'Look up, Agha,' Ma says in a soft tone. I look up.

The man with a beard drops a sweet from his hand. Everyone laughs. He is embarrassed. He looks away. The lady has a wide smile on her face.

'You are very beautiful,' she says. The lady was beautiful, too. She sat with a straight spine. She had short hair that she had held in a tiny ponytail, and she looked confident, just like Dimi auntie or a little more sophisticated than Dimi auntie. I close my eyes; my cheeks are wet, and I am wishing for Chandan to come back as soon as possible. Ma covers her face quickly to hide her sorrow from the world. From my would-be in-laws.

'If you are done asking questions, we will go out and discuss further,' Baba suggests out of impatience. He wants to take everyone outside as soon as possible.

'Sure,' mamu says. The lady comes to me before moving out of the room. 'I can't wait until tomorrow when you will become my daughter-in-law, Agha. You are unbelievably beautiful. This is for you,' she says and puts a ten rupees note in my lap. She leaves.

Ma closes the door.

My anguish echoes through the air.

MAHESH

01 March 1981

We went to meet Agha and her whole family today. Her younger sister, Rani, seemed innocent. Her mother is quite timid. Both of her brothers came to see the Jeep that I had hired. Mother, as always, embarrassed me by asking Agha to walk around, talk, and answer her weird questions. Mother, Bhaijan, and Agha's father did most of the talking. Her father has already made the arrangements on their side. He wants to have a small wedding. We don't mind.

Her mother was quiet and a little worried, so I gave her a big smile when I left. Sometimes you just need someone to smile at you to get rid of your stress. I do not know if I can understand a mother's pain whose daughter is going to get married to a family she has met just once before, but I can make her mother trust me with the fact that I am going to keep Agha happy.

When Mother and Agha's father approved of the union, Bhaijan seemed the happiest. Laughing and hugging everyone around. Agha's house is smaller than our bathroom. I am sure she will find our house no less than a palace.

Talking about Agha, what do I say? Her beauty left me without words. The picture that I got from Bhaijan did not do justice. I liked everything about her. God has surely taken a lot of time to create a beauty like hers. Her hair is shiny, and her eyes are blue. Her lips are naturally pink, and I am sure she had applied no makeup. The green and red salwar kameez that she was wearing suited her so well. But deep down, I knew she had cried. Her eyes told me that. I had carried a bangle with me, but I had no courage to talk with her and give that to her. So, I handed that over to her little sister, Rani, who is as beautiful as Agha, just that her eyes were not swollen.

I have made all the arrangements for the wedding as I knew Mother would approve of the wedding as soon as she realised that Agha was not mute or deaf or handicapped. Tomorrow morning, I and Mother along with Bhaijan will travel to Matiparbat again.

While coming back, Mother, surprisingly, was talking about her plans for when Agha comes home, and a few people stopped my Jeep. They asked us to produce our ID cards, which we had with us. Even though the president's rule is extended in Assam, the Group continued its activities. Sometimes they are intimidating. I dislike the stop-and-ID approach, but Mother is supportive of it. She supports the Group. She even wished them good luck with a smile on her face, and then the next moment slapped me hard on my back and said, 'Why don't you do something like this?' That was beyond embarrassment. I started the Jeep and diverted my mind to the road. I had no energy to argue with her.

Anyway, the most important thing is that tonight is my last as a bachelor. And I may want a drink to celebrate this night and welcome tomorrow, the day that I have waited for so long. I shall ask Bhaijan to accompany me to the celebration.

AGHA

EARLY 1981

I see only a few neighbours attending my wedding. It lasts for ten minutes. It takes place on the ground in front of Chandan's house. His door is still locked. Baba has said that we would follow the Assamese tradition. But that is not true. We follow no traditions. We signed some papers. Then Mahesh put a necklace around my neck. Then we both put garlands around each other's necks. Everyone claps. I am wearing a *chador*, a *mekhla* and a blouse. The *chador* is soft, just like Ma's skin. Rumi has done my makeup. She gives me her handbag-a wedding gift. Pink handbag. I put Chandan's letters and his envelopes in the handbag. I do not like pink. I like Blue. Mahesh is wearing a blue shirt. Rani is wearing Rumi's dress-an old dress. Ma is wearing Rumi's saree-a new saree. Baba is in his sherwani that he had worn for his wedding with Rumi. Sajid and Rashid are in their new shirts with old trousers. I am also wearing the bangle Mahesh has given to me.

After the ceremony, everyone eats the food sitting on the ground. Mahesh and I are sitting in the chairs on the ground. Chandan enters with a bag in his hands. He stands looking at both of us. Mahesh looks at me; I have started crying. He looks at Chandan; Chandan is frozen. Viju uncle holds Chandan's hands behind his back and drags him inside their house. Dimi auntie looks at me and then follows Viju uncle. There is screaming. The sound of throwing things from one place to another and the sound of bashing a head against the wall from inside Chandan's house. There is crying. Chandan looks out the window after an hour. His eyes are red and swollen. My eyes are red and swollen. There are bruises on his face. We stare at each other. Our dreams are shattered. It is so easy to run to him, but I do not. It is easy for him to scream my name and say that he loves me. But he does not. Mahesh has seen everything and said nothing.

***

It is late in the afternoon. We have started our journey to Nellie, where Mahesh has a house. He is sitting in the front with the driver. Mahesh's mother and I are sitting in the back. There is no door on this vehicle. It is open on both sides and has a roof. People call it a Jeep. Everyone came. I think they wanted to see the Jeep. Mahesh is chatting with the driver, smiling, laughing, and catching glances at me when possible. Much of the road is empty, except for the trees and birds chirping around. The birds are going home. I used to go home at this time after meeting Chandan. My Chandan. I remember his face, his tears, his red eyes, and red nose while he was looking at the garlands around Mahesh's and my necks. His eyes said, *'What's happening, Agha? This is not what we dreamt of.'* I was craving for him to ruin my wedding. Push everyone aside and say that he loves me. He wants to marry me. He could have fought with Mahesh. Though it is impossible to win against Mahesh. Mahesh is tall, muscular, and appears strong. But Chandan could have tried. Mahesh would have left after feeling humiliated. I and Chandan would have run off to Guwahati. But he kept looking at me through the window, thinking — not sure of what! My Chandan! My love! Everything is ruined. Everything.

Wind and dust are hitting everyone in the Jeep. The men cover their faces with handkerchiefs. Mahesh's mother covers her face with her saree drape, unlike me. I feel the wind and dust on my face. We travel alongside the Kopili. I see my spot; I see Chandan's spot and I hear the cycle bell. I see the *Kopou Phool*. Wind carries the flower to me. It lands in my lap. I pick it up and kiss it. Mahesh sees me and smiles. I lower my gaze. I clasp the flower in my palm. It is dead anyway. I will keep it in the envelopes Chandan gave me. I am carrying them with me. They are my only power, my positive-bright window to see the world. I think of the newspapers that I have thrown in the bushes around Kopili while they still had the smell of the food cooked by Dimi auntie. Food. I am going to miss the food cooked by Ma. I am leaving all of this behind. I look up at the sky, which is clear. I wonder whether I can see *Allah* and tell him to take care of Chandan. To take care of Rani. To take care of Ma. I wonder where *Allah* lives, not in a mosque. Otherwise, there would be Chandan at Mahesh's place as my groom. I wonder if *Allah* at all exists. I wonder if such a superpower exists at all. Or was it created by humans? People can make up anything, anything that gives them peace. That satisfies their agenda. Any agenda. Good. Bad. God must be a man–made concept. It does not exist. I am convinced.

On our way, we see villagers. They have some placards in their hands. Same placards that Sajid and Rashid brought home some days back. '*Go foreigner, go!*'-the placards read. I wonder when the mess is going to stop. Take some decisions already. Make peace.

If only I had been a boy, life might have been easier. Stay out of the home as long as you want. Do whatever job you like, with no restrictions. No one would mock your desire to work at a petrol pump, on a farm, or for a coal company. Go out and smoke as and when you want, like Chandan did once. No need to wear a *burqa* and cover your face; instead, hold your chin up.

I am drawn back to the real world when Mahesh's mother covers my face with my saree drape.

'Your beautiful face will be spoilt,' she says and smiles. But I open it. I want to see out.

'Careful, driver. I will not pay for rash driving,' she scolds him.

'He is fine, mother,' Mahesh says, and he looks at me.

Why would he look at me now and then, even when he is talking to his mother? I look away. We have left Kopili far behind, along with the evening. It is dark now.

Mahesh's house is like a mansion for a girl who has lived in a small room with six other people. The house has a small area in the front where a bicycle is parked. We climb four stairs to reach the living room. Mahesh's mother rushes inside to get an *arati thali* to welcome me. She keeps the clay pot by the door. I push it to the floor, and it breaks, the grain inside spilling over the floor. I cross over it and enter the house.

'I dreamt of this day for a long time. Welcome home, my daughter,' she says, and applies *kumkum* on my forehead. I have never seen Ma wearing *kumkum*, but Dimi auntie does.

The living room is big, with a small bed and a chair in one corner and a TV in another. Mahesh's mother holds my hand and takes me inside. In the kitchen, she feeds me *laddoo*. The kitchen has a cabinet for keeping cups, plates, spoons and glasses. The house has two more rooms other than the living room and the kitchen, and they each have a bed. She takes me to a room with a big window. The walls of the room are coloured blue, and the window has yellow curtains. There is a wardrobe in the corner to keep clothes. It is the same as I have seen at Chandan's house. This thought makes me feel dizzy, and I cannot hear half of what Mahesh's mother tells me. What I gather is that there are some dresses for me inside the cupboard. I open it when she goes out. The dresses are neatly folded in the upper part of the cabinet. The lower part of the cabinet is empty; I put my handbag and small luggage there. The toilet and bathroom are inside the house. I like that. I like this big house. At this moment, I like marriage. I like this change. There is at least something good about it. I drag myself to my house in Matiparbat. I think of our small stove. I think of Ma fuelling it with kerosene and making *chai*. I wonder how happy Ma would be to have a kitchen like this.

Mahesh sits in the living room. Mahesh's mother has asked me to change and get ready for dinner; she is going to cook. The bed in our room is decorated with flowers. I wonder why. I open the window. I see a farm outside. The wind in Nellie is warm. The sky is clear and dark. I see a star. Alone. Like me.

Instead of wearing the salwar kameez kept in the wardrobe, I change into the yellow salwar kameez that Baba had brought for me, the one that Chandan liked. I cannot manage everything new. I need some knowns, some familiarity.

We are having dinner-Mahesh's mother has cooked puri and sabzi. I eat until my tummy says no. After I wash my hands, I notice that Mahesh and his mother are looking at me. I look at the pot in which puris are kept. I have eaten at least half of them. But I don't care. I am hungry, and I like puris, I tell myself. Mahesh's mother said she would wash the dishes. Good for me.

I go to the bedroom, and Mahesh's mother follows. She brings a bowl of fruit and a glass of milk. She smiles and leaves, closing the door behind her. I lie on the bed, looking out the window. I know what is coming my way. I recall Chandan's words about our first night together. I recall his promise to always make me happy, to cook chicken for me every Sunday while his parents were at the temple, and then to take a long walk and stay away for hours.

I think about Rani. *How would she live in that house where no one liked her?* I remember how hard she cried and how tightly she held me when I left. I wonder what she would have for dinner today. I think about Ma, who hugged me and cried. For a while, I had thought that she had understood my pain, knew what I was going through, but she would pretend not to understand all this. She would pretend that Baba was doing the right thing. It is complex – love. When people you love are around, you think nothing, just go with the flow. I think about Sajid. He had shaken hands with me. He had hugged me and said, *Take care, Didi.* I think about Rashid. He smiled. Said *Bye!* I think about Rumi, who waved goodbye to me with a wide smile. She was happy that I was leaving. She is the only person who angers me. I think of slapping her across her face. I think of how my finger marks would appear on her cheeks. I think of her crying, her sad face. I think of her leaving our house forever. An impossibility.

The door of the room opens, and Mahesh enters. I close the window and sit on the bed. Mahesh locks the door behind him and sits by my side on the bed. There is pin–drop silence in the room. In a minute, he keeps his hand on my thigh, and my heart beats twice as fast.

A powerful wave passes through me, and I stand by the bedside right up.

'I am your *shauhar*, Agha,' he says to me patiently.

'Come to me,' he says. He smiles. He spreads both his hands towards me. I notice something in his gaze. Warmth? Love? He does not even know me. My cheeks are wet. Everything in front of me is a blur, but I can see Mahesh has left the room already. I sit on the floor, my back against the wall and my head touching my knees. I cry. I let my emotions go. I had tried to hold them inside me for a long time. How happy would Baba and Rumi be to be free of me? Would Rani be missing me? Would everyone else treat her well? Would Sajid take care of her? Ma, would she spend at least one night without crying? I want to know. I want to know that they will be happy. I want to know that Chandan will be happy without me. I miss Matiparbat. I miss looking into people's houses. I miss seeing Rani sitting on the playground, thinking, contemplating, unsure of what.

But something good. Not bad. She is a good person. I have missed those moments when I could have become closer to them. Telling them what I think and why I think so. I miss everything about Matiparbat, including Ma. I want to go to her and hug her. I am dozing off here on the floor. And I see a dream. Mahesh is in the room. He opens the wardrobe and takes out my handbag. He opens it. He takes out the letters between me and Chandan, sits on the bed and reads each one of them. He puts them back in the handbag and the handbag back in the wardrobe. He leaves. It is a dream indeed.

MAHESH

30 June 1981

I married Agha on the 2nd of March 1981. How do I describe the experience? Are men supposed to cry? Can men be upset and show it on their faces? Well, I cried the night I got married. Agha did not let me touch her, and I respected her wishes.

The next day, Agha helped Mother cook and clean the house. Mother orders her relentlessly, but Agha does not get upset. She keeps working all day. As if she is keeping herself busy to forget something or someone. During our wedding, I did witness something disturbing. A boy. He was looking at Agha, and Agha was looking at him, both crying. He ran from one window to another to see her. I saw anger and sadness in his eyes. Agha's mother came close to turning her head in a different direction. But Agha persisted. I do not know what she saw in him, what had made her love him so much: he is not even half as good-looking as I am. But the love between them seemed real. My love for Agha *is real, too. However, I will not force myself on her when I know she does not love me.*

AGHA

LATE 1981

I like every corner of this house. This big house. I walk from one corner to another without touching my hand to anyone or anything. The ceilings are high too. I haven't dared to lick the cement on the walls yet. But I want to soon. The window to our room gives a clear view of the paddy field, the plateau, and a few houses. Mahesh says that the house is part of his inheritance. He could not afford to buy such a house or even the furniture. I think good things have happened in terms of where I live and what I eat. I eat everything that is served on my plate. I cook, and Mahesh's mother, Mother-in-law, serves everyone. She has an eye for detail. She notices everything. When I walk, when I sit on the ground with my legs folded, when I stare at the door, when I chat with other ladies, when I am upset after seeing Mahesh. She notices everything. But does not question me. Just like Ma. I imagine me and Chandan living in this house along with Rani, Ma, Sajid, Viju uncle and Dimi auntie. I imagine Ma cooking food every day and me eating with my tummy full. I imagine inviting Masha to my house and showing her how beautiful my house is and how normal my family is. Just like hers.

The bed in our room has a soft mattress and cushions. I enjoy sleeping there, especially in the afternoons when Mahesh is not around and there is no awkwardness. The wardrobe is half the size of our room in Matiparbat. Mahesh had bought enough clothes for me, even before we got married. I enjoy making puri and sabji. I have made it three times since our marriage six months back. Mahesh keeps track of all the money. He gives money to his mother for safekeeping. *Give it to your wife*, his mother scolded him once. But he never listened to her. His mother holds a special place in his heart. Though he does not like it when she blames foreigners entering Bharat's territory illegally. He does not like it when she talks about her husband, Mahesh's father, and complains that Mahesh is nothing like him. But he must see her and know her well-being as soon as he is back from his shop. He treats her like a child. She *is* a child. She screams, cries, talks uninterrupted, stares at the wall for hours. Everything was unannounced. She can be in any state-you have to acknowledge it and then try to calm her down. But when she is calm, she talks to me. She tells me about the tea estates that Mahesh's family worked on. She tells me about Mahesh's father, a god-like man-she says. She tells me about their house in Guwahati and about their move to Nellie just a month before our marriage. From here on, I take everything slowly. I wonder why they had to get this house as an inheritance just a month before the marriage. Was it my destiny not to take me to Guwahati? I do not know. I would have gotten into the makeup course

by now. Then I get up from the side of Mother-in-law
and make my way to my bedroom. To read. To read
those letters written by Chandan. The letters where we
discussed moving to Guwahati. The letters extensively
described the room that we would rent there. The letters
where we witnessed each other's love. I cry. I whimper. I
become quiet. I stare at the walls. I lie down on the bed.
I close my eyes. I dream. I dream of *Kopou Phool*.

Mahesh comes home in the evening. I open the door. I do
not look into his eyes. I take his bag from his shoulder. He
always complains about his bicycle not working properly
because it is old. I think of telling him to buy a motorcycle. The kind Chandan is going to buy. But I stop myself.
I do not know if he has enough money to buy one. Also,
why bother about someone else's problems? He brings with
him groceries-sugar, milk, tea-powder, veggies, grain. I cook
while Mahesh and his mother talk. We eat. After dinner,
Mother-in-law sleeps in her room if she is all right. If
she is troubled, she sits on the *veranda* blaming foreigners.
Many people in the village are not originally from Assam
or Bharat, for that matter. Hence, Mahesh worries that
someone might harm Mother-in-law. He tries to bring her
inside, but she does not listen. Once Mahesh lied to her about
me being pregnant, and if she kept causing trouble, I might
go to my mother's place forever. That was far-fetched. First,
I am not pregnant. And second, I will not go back to Matiparbat. I like some people there, not all. Especially, I do
not like that one-room house. But Mother-in-law took it
seriously and came in. She kissed my forehead and went
to sleep. The next morning, she had already forgotten about
the lie we told her. But I realised Mahesh wanted to be

a father. *Do I want to be a mother?* I asked myself. The answer is no. I do not.

Mahesh and his mother talk daily about the Lady at the Centre. His mother maintains that she likes her. I like her too. A lady – that too at the Centre; she runs the country. I had always heard from Chandan that Viju uncle says the Centre is not helping. I did not know that he actually talked about a lady, a Lady at the Centre. She controls everything. And Mother-in-law was her fan. I have become her fan, too. Who would not? She has reached where no other woman has. She shines among everyone around her, be they men or women. I wonder why men are powerful. Or why they are courageous. Why they are everywhere. And why women must struggle even to go out and do a makeup course. Who made the world like this? Who rules the world? Who gives men higher status than women? I wonder how this system came into existence. And I wonder whether it can be changed. Is the Lady at the Centre a beginning of this evolution? I wonder. Then I think of Rumi. There are so many ways to feel powerful. Some good, some bad.

But Mahesh says that the Lady has the power to change the situation. He is against violence, just like Chandan. He fears something ominous will happen if she does not take the Groups' demands seriously. This has not changed since my marriage. Discussions on this topic. It is everywhere. The tension in society is worsening. Everyone is talking about it.

I am sitting in the bedroom, on my bed. We are done with our dinner. Mahesh comes in. We sleep in the same bed. On two different sides. He sleeps on his side. He turns to my side. I look the other way. He is a gentleman. I think how good it would have been to forget what had happened in the past and move on with life. He has not touched me, as he thinks it would be against my will. For someone who had nothing as per wish, this feels like too much to receive. I am blessed. I wonder if I can ever accept Mahesh as my husband. And my mind says yes. Yes, definitely yes. He is a pure soul. One in a Million! But what about Chandan? He is one in a million, too! Will I ever be able to move on from his thoughts? Will I ever be able to stop loving him? My mind says no. Definitely, no.

SHABANA

LATE 1981

I had witnessed how Chandan and Agha reacted when they both saw each other. Agha was in bride's attire, but Chandan was not the groom. I witnessed Mahesh acting as if he had seen nothing. He cared for Agha, even though he suspected Agha and Chandan's involvement. I always liked Chandan. He was someone who would keep to himself, just like Agha. He, similar to Agha, harboured dreams. Wouldn't want to follow his father's footsteps, just like Agha. However, he seemed different since Agha's wedding. He attended all the meetings on the ground since that day. Put forward his opinions. Served tea to the people. Avoided gaze with me. But he maintained his friendship with Rani.

I would sometimes look at Rumi's face and sympathise with her. She was young, almost Agha's age, and I was sure she did not love Amir. She regretted not marrying someone of her age, or someone with less chaos in life. Rumi came from a good household. Three-room house. She was her parents' third child, preceded by two boys and followed by two girls. She once said that she never cooked at home. I did before I got married to Amir. Her parents were forcing her to study. But she liked Amir and married him. She had shared this with Rashid. Rashid told Sajid. And Sajid told me. We were united at least in sharing gossip. But Amir loved Rumi. He would speak with her at length, even when I was around. He would speak about his love for duck curry, about Meena Kumari-his favourite actress and Rashid. Rashid was Amir's most favourite. They both would then continue talking about Rashid-how he out-smart people double of his age, how quick he is in understanding trade, his ways of impressing the farm owner and getting the bonus which almost no other workers would get, and many other things-including his charming looks. I felt proud to hear some of these things.

'Will you cook today, Rumi? My hand is hurting,' I said to Rumi one day. She agreed. Amir had twisted my hand the day before, as I had called him haramkhor. He knew he was, and that's the only reason he got angry. He twisted my arm and screamed in my ear-'tu haramkhor, randi.' I did not cry. I laughed. I rarely got into any arguments, but I could not help myself sometimes. Fighting was against my nature, so when I fought with him, I took time to get back to normal. When Rumi served the food, she served the most to Rashid. I was served the least. Amir was drunk, so he ate what he was served. Rani shared her food with me, but I instead gave her some of mine.

That night he told her about his days in Goalpara. About his family. His many siblings. That he does not miss them. They would have asked him for money for their education and food and clothes. He was free from that additional responsibility, and away from them here in Bharat. He had beaten his own father with a stick. Pushed his mother into a well. As they both did not give him enough money, nor were they selling their land so that their kids, including Amir, could use that money. Amir was not sure whether his mother had survived. His brothers came after him with rocks in their hands. He ran away from Sylhet to Bharat. After hearing that, Rumi's face was pale. She looked at me. I looked out of the house. The moonlight was dim that night. It had taken me almost twenty years to know Amir's past.

If I want anything in this life, it's you, Rumi, my love! Amir said and pulled Rumi close to him. Kissed her on her lips while we were all watching. She shoved him away. He kept biting her lip. Sajid got up and left. Rani followed him. Rashid got up and hit Amir with a stick. I didn't feel bad, even though I should have. Not when he was kissing Rumi, nor when Rashid beat him.

AGHA

EARLY 1982

Mahesh has not touched me, even though it's been a year since our marriage. I sometimes want to talk to him, but he only talks about his tiffin, grocery shopping and asks where his clothes are kept. He brings me dresses and sarees. I do not tell him that I like them. He does not ask. I sometimes look at him when he is wearing his shirt, or when he is combing his hair. His arms are strong. And his palms are wide. His eyes are big. Ma used to say people with big eyes have a clean heart. I know Mahesh has a clean heart. He is getting ready to go to Guwahati.

'Any messages for Nadim Bhai?' he asks me.

'No,' I say. 'Can I accompany you? I want to see Guwahati. The roads, the university.'

He looks at me in surprise. 'I will take you next time. We must make prior arrangements to stay overnight.'

'We can stay at mamu's. I have never seen his house, his shop. Only heard of it.'

'Nadim Bhai is not in a good mental state.'

'What happened?'

'He fears someone will kick him out of Bharat anytime. He entered Bharat in 1958. I tell him he is safe. But he does not take me seriously.'

'What does mamu say about Ma?' I changed the topic. There are already enough talks about the surrounding tensions.

'That your mother is a very courageous woman. She married on her own terms. She fought to send you and Rani to school.'

'Yes, she did.' I accepted. Ma was different.

'But...', Mahesh continues.

'Say it,' I say, and keep my hand on Mahesh's hand. He withdraws it.

'I did not find her fierce, Agha. She seemed like someone who could be dominated. Your father married another woman. Your mother accepted it. She did not question him. She seems defeated, Agha. She is broken from the inside. She has lost hope. Such people are dangerous. Not to the world, but to themselves. You should write to her often. Give her hope. It is your job as a daughter,' he continued.

At this moment, I think about the things that I wanted to do, but I did not. Asking Masha to share the butter so that I can apply it to my cracked lips. Asking her for one more puri from her tiffin. Telling Rani that I love her. Telling Ma that I care for her. Asking Sajid to take care of Ma and Rani. Telling Chandan how much I love him. Slapping Rumi for making Ma's life worse. Telling Baba what an enormous failure he is.

I now want to tell Mahesh that I respect him. I see him as someone whose words I would never ignore. I look at him. I see his pure heart. I see his transparent soul. I want to kiss his hand. I want to move towards him on the bed and kiss his forehead. I want to tell him that having him in my life is a blessing. I move my hand towards his. But he withdraws his hand from the bed and starts rubbing the back of his head. He gets up and leaves the room. I wonder what he must be thinking about me. I wonder if we can spend our lives like that-without being close to each other. I go after him and pull him into the room. I closed the door. I push him onto the bed; I am lying in the bed beside him. I keep my hand on his chest. He slides my hand away from him. I repeat what I did. I enjoy teasing him. I then keep my head on his shoulder. He looks at me. We are close. Very close. We have never been this close before. I look at his lips. Pink. Thin. Long. His beard over his lips looks royal. I move my hand through his hair. And then to his hands. There is a bracelet on his wrist. It is too tight. I try to take it off.

'You cannot take it off. I wore it when I weighed forty kgs. I am seventy now,' he says and holds my hand tight.

The look in his eyes has changed. His eyes look narrow. He pulls me towards him with both his hands. I am on his chest now. He kisses my forehead, then turns over and kisses my cheek. The *pallu* of my saree is off my chest. He plants a kiss on my lips. A gentle kiss. To tell me that he loves me. He unbuttons my blouse. And takes off my saree. My knees are weak. But my eyes and lips are wide awake. I am smiling. Cuddling Mahesh. Kissing his lips, his chest, his hands. We move from one side of the bed to the other. Fall on the floor. Laugh. Make love.

***

I write a letter to Ma in the afternoon.

Dear Ma,

I hope this letter finds you in good health!

Mahesh has a big house and ample food. Mother-in-law treats me like her daughter. Does not scold me. Let me do what I want to do. Are all mothers-in-law like this? Rumi told me that mothers-in-law are rude, strict, and harsh towards daughters-in-law. My experience is different. I go for walks with her. She showed me the road that goes to Matiparbat. A road that goes to Guwahati. I know you never saw your mother-in-law. But what about your mother? Do you know whether she is well? Mahesh is a gentleman. He is very soft-spoken. He buys dresses for me very often. And brings sweets of my choice.

Is everyone at home well? Is Rani all right? What is she going to do after her school is completed? How is Sajid? ~~How is Chandan?~~

Keep me posted.

I miss you,

Agha

I keep the letter in the cupboard. I am going to ask Mahesh to post it for me later.

'How do I look, Agha?' Mother-in-law has come to my room.

My eyes and mouth are wide open. There is a surprise for Mahesh when he comes back from Guwahati. Mother-in-law has cut her hair shoulder length. She has done it at home in her room.

'Exquisite!' I was doubtful when I said that.

'Are you sure?' she asked.

'Yes, yes, I am sure. You look beautiful.' I get out of my bed and walk to her.

'You do not sound convincing,' Mother–in–law responded.

'I am just surprised by your skills. It is very difficult to cut
your own hair. I am sure Mahesh would love it,' I say, but
I do not mean a single word of it. Mother–in–law has also
applied *Mehendi* to all her grey hair except a thin layer at
the front. She looks like someone familiar.

'Do you know one thing, Agha?'

'Yes?'

'Your face tells what you think, not your tongue. So stop
lying. And make a cup of *chai* for me.' She leaves the room
with her chin up. Someone walks like that. I don't quite
remember who. She is also wearing a different saree. A
cotton saree. She usually wears silk sarees. She has draped
her *pallu* over her left shoulder and over her head. She had
never draped her *pallu* over her head before. Something has
changed.

I make *chai* for her. She is sitting on the veranda in a
chair. She has her glasses on. She is reading a newspaper.
I give her *chai*. She reads for a minute and then takes a
sip. Then, she pushes her glasses onto her nose and looks
around. Then she takes another sip. Pushes her glasses
back on her eyes and reads for a few minutes.

In the evening, Mother–in–law invites neighbours home.
Shobha, Malti and Heena come.

'Agha, make some *chai* for us all,' she orders me.

I am curious to see what will happen next. I put a pan on
the stove and stand in the kitchen entrance. Shobha, Malti
and Heena, who are older than me as they have a kid or two,
have taken seats near Mother–in–law's feet on her order.
She is sitting on the chair, like a boss. Her pallu on her head,
her chin up, her glasses pushed on her nose.

'I know you and your families have come from Bangladesh,' she starts the conversation.

The ladies do not like it.

'That is not true. Not sure who spreads these rumours,' Heena defended herself.

Shobha and Malti hang their heads. They make no eye-contact. Mother-in-law is making them uncomfortable.

'Okay, calm down! This is not why I asked you to come here. Agha, bring *chai*.'

I brought five cups on a tray to the living room. I sit beside Heena. We are the crowd. She is the Lady sitting on the chair. I now know who she looks like, and who she is imitating.

'I have called you here to tell you not to believe the rumors that are spreading outside. That foreigners are abducting locals and locals are abducting foreigners. That foreigners are raping local women and local people are raping foreign women. Locals are attacking foreigners, and foreigners are attacking locals. Do not believe them. Tell your family not to believe such news. They are only out to create chaos.' Mother-in-law is confident about her narrative. But I am not. I wonder if it has really happened, even though just once. Should we ignore it? It does not matter whether outsiders troubled insiders or insiders troubled outsiders. People are getting hurt irrespective of their citizenship, gender, ethnicity, and religion. This is what Mahesh has told me. Now, I agree with what he said.

Mother-in-law explains that the Group is trying hard to put forward its concerns. That the Lady at the Centre is not helping. She is a good-hearted woman, but she is confused about how to manage multiple sides, Mother-in-law adds.

Malti, Shobha and Heena leave with mixed emotions. I think Mother-in-law is offending people and complicating the situation. Malti, Shobha, and Heena moved to Nellie from outside. They are happy here. Their husbands get good money, and their family life is better than it was in their homeland. How that affects the locals, the ladies would not know. Even if they do, they cannot do anything about it. They certainly are not the decision-makers. They follow orders. Orders from their husbands, fathers, sons, fathers-in-law. I understand them, especially after witnessing Ma's life. Why does Mother-in-law bother these innocent ladies?

Mother-in-law is trying to imitate the Lady at the Centre. Her haircut, her saree style, her walk. But the Lady at the Centre has power and protection. Mother-in-law has none. I decide to tell Mahesh.

MAHESH

22 March 1982

A *person writes a diary only to get free of the thoughts that he or she can't share with anybody else. I did not write for long, because Agha is there for me. She shares my feelings and sometimes opinions, too. I have never been this close to anyone in my life. Agha is like my best friend but also someone who keeps me happy. Her skin is very soft, and her lips are very juicy. When I tell her this, she feels embarrassed. She does not like the word juicy for her lips. But they are. And her blue eyes. Their colour matches the envelope where she keeps the saved money.*

A minister has resigned. The Lady at the Centre has ordered the President's rule in Assam again. There is less chaos in Nellie compared to Guwahati. There are many people around to talk to when I do not go to the shop; in Guwahati, it was just me and Mother.

Reading the news every day is a task. You must be up to date in order to chat with customers, but I am tired now. I want to write a letter to the Lady at the Centre telling her how afraid a common man is to live in Assam. I am going to Guwahati next month to meet Bhaijan. I am sure he is worrying as always, and I need to be there to comfort him.

We celebrated our second wedding anniversary this month. Agha made Kheer for me. I gifted her a small purse made of green silk, her favourite colour. She was happy when she saw it. I was smart enough to hide the purse that I had bought for her from a second-hand shop. Next year I shall buy her a new purse from the big shops in Guwahati. There was more money in Guwahati, whereas here very few people come to buy a cup of chai. People come to buy bidi and gutkha. It is not fair to have such a shop close to a school, but I found no other place to set up the shop. And morals can wait-the most important thing is to earn money. Agha does not like this location for the shop, but I have told her that by the end of next year I shall have a big shop far from the school. Agha has made friends here, all good and all from Bangladesh. Some of them are from Hakimpur, where Agha's mother is from. She remains busy with her friends.

Agha reads the newspaper that neighbours bring to her and asks me questions about the agitation almost every day. She wants to know when all this will stop. I do not know. I do not want to tell her the severity, but she is a smart woman. She thinks her parents are in danger. The cutoff year remains the mystery. Moreover, no one will ask you the year you entered Assam if they can figure out you are an outsider. People from Bangladesh have a different dialect.

The newspaper only has news of deaths, protests, arrests, bomb blasts, and failed talks. But I trust the Group; they will *get the Centre to listen to them one day. I only wish that the day comes when nothing bad happens.*

AGHA

EARLY 1982

Mother-in-law talks with neighbours every day. Malti, Heena and Shobha come home each afternoon for *chai*. Sometimes they bring *chai* for us; sometimes, Mother-in-law orders me to make *chai* for everyone. Sometimes she takes her shawl like the Lady at the Centre and smiles, holding a cup of *chai* close to her face. *How do I look?* She would ask. Good, I would answer.

'*Just like?*' she would say.

'Just like?' I would ask.

'Who do I look like when I take the shawl like this and hold a cup of *chai* close to my face?'

'I do not know.'

'Guess, Agha. Guess. We see her on television every day.'

'Oh, the Lady at the Centre? YES. YES. You look like her.'

A broad grin would appear on her face, and then she would keep the cup down, without drinking even a sip.

Malti, Heena and Shobha would hide their smiles. I want to feel embarrassed, but I do not. I instead offer Mother-in-law biscuits and ask her to have some more *chai*. She denies and looks up at the ceiling and smiles. I eat my biscuit and avoid eye contact with Malti and Heena. Shobha would anyway always look at the floor. But her behavior doesn't offend them, even if she calls them outsiders.

Mahesh has told them she is not in a good mental state. That is true. And I think she is sometimes in a different world. A world where she thinks she is surrounded by politicians. She speaks to those imaginary characters about Assam, act that she is signing some papers and says-You have my approval. Only she knows what she approves every day. Then she says, we are all people. All are humans. All have legs, hands and heart. But most importantly, all of us have minds. We know if we are wrong. We know. Our conscience tells us. We must act accordingly. Let us listen to our mind. It will guide us. I sit in the kitchen, listening to this and thinking about what she means by it all.

Mother-in-law is now getting old. She forgets most things. Even the way to our house if she goes out for a walk. People around are generous and kind. They bring her home. Sometimes, they bring hot *chai* for her when she is sitting on the veranda. Even though she is not a fan of most of them, they respect her. She does not cry. She has a smile on her face. I wonder if Ma cries. I think of Ma. I wonder if she receives even half the care Mother-in-law receives. But who would take care of her? I should have. I did not.

Mother-in-law sometimes talks for hours while she is lying on the bed. She says she can't move her legs or hands. I massage her legs. I massage her hands. I massage her scalp, hoping that she will sleep instead of talking all day.

But she does not sleep. She talks. She talks about neighbours and their sarees. She talks about the government. She talks about a tea garden. She talks about her love for Assam and Assam silk. She talks about her favourite *mekhla* and *chador*. She talks about daal and rice. And fish. She talks about Bihu. She tells me she has danced to Bihu songs. My Mother-in-law. Most of the time, she does not eat meals with us. Mahesh takes a plate to her room and feeds her with his hands. He sobs quietly at her condition. When she knows he is crying, she wipes his tears. When she does not know, I wipe his tears. I feel fortunate to be a part of this family, where there is only love for each other.

MAHESH

15 August 1982

Yesterday while I was searching for my dhoti, I found a few papers in Agha's cupboard. They are the letters that Chandan had written to her. I wonder if she still reads them. I wanted to burn them once and for all. But it was indeed unfair of me to damage those letters or confront Agha about them. With a lot of courage, I put them back where they had been. Marriage is difficult. I guess loving someone is difficult. It changes you. Mother tested my patience, while Agha has deepened it.

It's been thirty-five years since Bharat achieved independence. I wish each problem in Assam was a person whom you can either convince or fight and make them leave your territory. People at the shop told me some stories about Hindus abducting and raping Muslim women in the north, and Muslims abducting and raping Hindu women in the south. I did not believe them. These are rumours created to further stress in the society.

I have seen the Group closely and I know how truthful they are to Assam. But sometimes, the Group has to be very clear about their communications. There are chances of misunderstanding or of people using this movement for their benefit. Rumors are that some local people supporting the Group are getting ready to attack villages. I prefer not to believe these rumors. I've told Agha to stay home; better safe than sorry. I have asked her to meet her friends at our place. Agha understands these things, and she listens to me.

We went to the Nellie Bazar this weekend. Agha looked beautiful, as always. All colours suit her. She told me how much she loves me, and I believed her. I know she does. Whenever the thought of Chandan's letters comes to my head, I just downplay it. As a man, I do not want any other man to love my wife. And more than that, I cannot tolerate my woman thinking about or liking any other man. Agha is a blessing to me. She loves me, and I want nothing else from God.

Agha is pregnant. I want a son. But I have no courage to tell Agha. She may think that I am like all those other men who prefer a son to a daughter. But that is not true. I always wanted to be a cricketer, but I never told Father about that. I still watch the students playing cricket, and I still have no courage to go join them. So, I want my son to become a cricketer. Easy. Make your children accomplish your dreams. It is unfair, but exciting.

MAHESH

19 January 1983

*L*ast month, we were blessed with a baby girl. Mother named her Indu. She is like a blessing to us. Her eyes are blue. Agha says they are green, but no, they are blue. I understand colours better than Agha. Indu's small, round, blue eyes keep me engaged all the time. Agha says that we should have enough money to admit her to a medical college; she must become a doctor. I nod. As I am the one who will pay the fees, I must work hard. We are not wealthy; Agha knows. But still, she dreams big, and I get the pressure of her expectations.

I haven't mentioned this to Agha, but I want to leave Assam soon. I don't want Indu to grow up in an unstable society. There is a lot of uncertainty about Assam's future.

The Lady at the Centre has scheduled elections in the next month. And she is also not going to revise the voter list. This comes despite having strong resistance from the Group and from the locals. Won't this upset the Group? The Group *says that there are many illegal entries on the voter list. Shouldn't that change before the election? I wonder if the Centre is to help us or to ruin us. I only dream of a world where I can breathe peacefully, and I am sure my dream won't come true soon. The election machinery is already rolled out.*

The Group-Centre talks failed again. When the Group Leaders reached Guwahati from Delhi, they were arrested.

SHABANA

EARLY 1983

I went through Nadim's letters that night. I re-read some of our old letters, including the one where Nadim had written to Amir about Mahesh. There was one unopened letter. Nadim had written it to me right after Agha's marriage. I opened it. It read -

My dear sister,

I know Agha did not want to marry Mahesh. But he is a kind-hearted man, you will see. Now that you have one less thing to worry about, I want to share something. I did try to share it earlier, but could not gather the courage to be open and honest about it. Our mother died the day Abbu and she were traveling back to Hakimpur. There was a stampede at the deportation camp. Abbu saved himself; he could not save her.

I am sure she had forgiven you. Abbu is healthy. I am in touch with him. I am planning to go see him soon. I shall

*keep you posted as and when I make arrangements. Would
you want to accompany me?*

I hope you forgive me for not sharing this earlier.

Your brother,

Nadim

Ammi was free. She was free of this world where
men ruled and women followed. Men made decisions, and
women followed. Men instructed women what to do, when
to do it, and how to do it; women followed. Women were
treated differently than men. Men had so much freedom.
They could marry multiple times, they beat people around
them, they could go outside be it day or night, they could
cross the border without asking their family, they could
dominate people around them. Society decided if a man was
a good man or a bad man. And similarly, if a woman was a
good woman or a bad woman. The character of a bad man
was hardly discussed. But the character of a bad woman
was the talk of the town. A bad man was accepted by the
society. A bad woman was not. A good woman must work
every day to impress the people around to keep proving
her worth. A good man was a good man all his life, with
minimal or no effort.

Nadim had once mentioned the next life. That we get another chance to correct our mistakes. I decided to ask *Allah*
to make me a man in the next life. I refused to live next life
as dictated by others. I was done blaming myself for my
wrong decisions. And I was done being timid. I wanted to
be brave in the next life. If I had to be born as a woman, I
would never get married in my next lifetime. I would not fall
in love. Even if I would, I would be like Dimi-talking over
my husband. Not a loser like me. I would not have any kids.
It's an emotional burden. I wanted to fish with the same

expertise as Abbu. Not sure if Abbu went fishing then. He must be very old. I should ask Nadim.

I was in the doorway-not looking at Viju and thinking someone would love me as much as he loves Dimi. I was looking at my nails. They have started looking pale. I pull the saree a little above my knee to observe my skin. It had cracks in it, not very noticeable, but they existed. I thought other than getting married if I had any dreams. I would have loved to sell fish in the market or just talk to people about their lives. I thought if I could do that, then? No, I couldn't. I was not as free as Rumi. Rumi was outside chatting with one of the neighbours. He was looking directly at her chest. She was smiling and looking at the ground. I think she was free. Good or bad was different. She was free to behave the way she wanted. Where did she get that courage from? I pushed my saree down to my toes and cover my chest properly with my *pallu*. Did I want to be Rumi for a day? No. I still had a desire to be different, but not Rumi different, Shabana different.

MAHESH

4 February 1983

*W*riting *my diary has become rare these days. But the times are such that I must write a few things down. As I can't tell Agha everything. That's not good for her. She may get paranoid about the situation outside, and I need at least one of us to maintain peace at home.*

The plea to postpone the elections is rejected. So, elections are happening this month. Protests are still happening, but police are also present everywhere in Guwahati. Bhaijan writes in his letter. There are bomb blasts happening in various places in Assam, protesting at the election. Multiple bridges are torched. Markets are burnt, and there are constant clashes between the mobs. There were police shootings in Mangaldoi, where a few people were killed. There was also firing on civilians who were protesting about the election in Bura. A few people were killed. The Group has announced non-cooperation in the general activities from tomorrow. *At some places, teachers are gathered to protest too.*

There are also rumors of attacks by tribes. I have even heard some tribes beating drums nearby. Someone said that drums gather people for meetings. And these meetings are to discuss the details of the attack. This is false, but scary. I have noticed some people from outside the village keeping watch on the villagers, though. Some villagers have complained that their road was blocked by strangers a few weeks back. I have never witnessed that.

Sometimes I think the Group is supporting these activities. Sometimes, I think that's not true. Any wrong action by the Group is only going to make their efforts go to waste. Everyone is suffering, insiders and outsiders. We need only God's intervention now to resolve this issue. Only she can help.

I tell Agha every day how much I love her and Indu. I have promised her that I will keep her and our daughter safe. They are my responsibility. And I know who is capable of what. My gut says that nothing more than a protest or stone pelting is going to happen. It is a blessing to see your daughter sleeping peacefully. Even though I tell Agha that Indu is as beautiful as her, Indu is more beautiful than Agha.

AGHA

EARLY 1983

When I fell pregnant, Mother–in–law started feeling better. And she did not forget about it as she would see my grown tummy every single day. She often made *puri-sabzi* for me. I asked her if she wanted a grandson or a granddaughter. She would say, a granddaughter. And that she would name her Indu. Mother–in–law's love for the Lady at the Centre surpassed all boundaries one day when she saw the picture that Mahesh had brought and started crying. She asked Mahesh to stick that picture on the wall in my room. I spent my pregnancy looking at that picture of the Lady at the Centre. When I delivered a baby girl, Mother–in–law danced with joy. Mother–in–law distributed *barfi* to every single household in the village. Ma did not come to see me. The situation outside was not favorable for travel. I knew Ma and Rani wanted to see Indu as much as I wanted to see them. But Mahesh said we would go to

Matiparbat when the situation outside was normal. I asked him what was normal. He did not answer.

***

Indu looks like me, Mother-in-law says. She has my hair. Curls. But she has Mahesh's eyes. Big and brown. She cries a lot. Just like Mother-in-law. When I saw Indu for the first time, I felt something inside my chest. To the left. Where the heart is. Love. Happiness. And that spread everywhere else. In our house. In the neighbourhood. In my and Mahesh's relationship. Every single nerve in my body cherished my daughter's first day. Her soft skin is a reminder that the world is beautiful and pleasant. I spent days looking at her innocent smile. Just like Mahesh's smile. They two are my world!

Mahesh plays with Indu when he comes home from the shop. But he also looks exhausted, old. He worries a lot about Assam. His land. He appears serious. Very serious. In fact, frightened. I have received an ultimatum not to leave the home. But I am going to. How long would he shield me from the danger? I have to face it – if not today, then tomorrow. Maybe he thinks that something terrible is going to happen. Should not people in power understand that? Bharat is so generous to outsiders, to the world. But does that mean the world should take advantage of Bharat? Mother-in-law says that Bharat is a dreamland. It is a treasure. Everyone may consume Bharat's possessions. But that has a limit. People sometimes cross it.

MAHESH

14 February 1983

*T*he fear that we had is real. The violence is unending. Several houses are set on fire. People are dead. Day after day, the clashes are increasing. Despite that, the Lady at the Centre speaks at the election rally. She has security. What about poor people like me? People who have lost their lives in protests, rallies, bandhs, fires? What about these people? What about people who do not belong to the Group, who are not taking part in marches, not going to vote, not supporting the Centre? Aren't they trapped? It is a shame that this beautiful land of tea gardens has to face such violence every day.

The polls opened today.

My daughter is just three months old, but she still under–stands when I talk. I asked her if she wanted to eat kheer; she nodded. When I tried to feed her kheer, Agha almost screamed. Babies of her age have only milk, nothing else, *especially not kheer with dry-fruits and coconut-Agha told me. I followed. Sometimes she knows more than I do.*

MAHESH

17 February 1983

When I was in Guwahati, I would dream about buying tea gardens. I would dream about my family and me working in tea gardens. The beauty of Assam has always surprised me. But the British ruined it. By starting immigration. Assam is a land of opportunities, and we Assamese are lazy people. So, other people make use of these opportunities. Why would farmers sell their land to outsiders? Why would that happen on such a large scale that you become Otithi in your own land? Why has God made this state so porous to come and go as and when you want? Why is the border so weak? Why is the Centre too adamant to support outsiders? Why have we never felt any connection with the Centre? Why do we feel neglected? Did they really neglect us? Why are we collectively called North-eastern states and not by our separate names? Mother said that the baby comes to this planet with his or her destiny. Do states also carry their destiny with them, or is it the *same as the destiny of the people residing there, or does it adopt the destiny of its Otithis? But who is Otithi in Assam? Hindu? Muslim? Bengali? Assamese? Nepalese? Tiwas? Bodos? Other tribal people? The Group? The Centre? Who is Otithi, I wonder. Everyone is suffering here, the insiders and the outsiders.*

Five children from the tribal families have been found dead near my village today. My heartbeat has increased, and my whole body is shivering. Who would kill innocents? And why? Something is going to happen. Such turmoil in this land of tea gardens! Can someone from the cabinet give some wisdom to the Lady at the Centre? She can stop the killings, bombings, kidnappings. I wonder how some people get a lot of power and some people get none.

The second stage of the elections happened today. Followed by many clashes and burning of houses around the state.

I must go out tomorrow and look at what's happening around here. Why are the drums beating every morning? What is everyone up to now that the election is done? Indu and her mother are sleeping. I hope they remain safe in this chaos. I am going to tell Agha to lock the door from the inside and not go out unless it is an emergency. She has to understand the seriousness of the situation. I am thinking of Mother today. She is full of energy. She speaks about this issue every minute. She tells people not to vote. She loves Assam as much as Father did. But Father was more practical than she is. She brings out emotion in everything she does. She supports the Group with no hesitation and sympathizes with foreigners.

I miss Father. I miss his talks describing Assam. Some people love their land, their birthplace, their origin as much as they love their kids, and Father was one of them. He had a special bond with Assam, his house surrounded by tea gardens. With the Rivers. With the ponds, beels, and lakes. With the fish. With the wind in Assam, with mountains in Assam. He was a true Assamese. Do we remain the same person after our parents are dead? I don't think so. They take a part of us with them. And we continue to witness the void.

SHABANA

EARLY 1983

Rumi was cooking food. She was murmuring some-thing, as she was angry that I was not helping her. Her behaviour was still mature beyond her age. She had lost three babies in the womb. Allah had a mysterious way of guiding our growth!

I was lying in the corner with a blanket over my face, my eyes closed. I had my phases. Some days, I would follow all she wanted me to do. Some days I would not. That day I did not. Amir was sitting at the door, staring at the sky. Mahesh had mentioned about Indu in his letter. And that Agha and Indu were both healthy and happy. My hands were craving to take Indu in my lap. There was tension outside, so no one encouraged me to travel to Nellie. I was sure Indu was as beautiful as my Agha. I had not seen Agha since she got married, but Nadim had mentioned that she was happier than ever. Nadim was to thank for finding a man like Mahesh for my daughter. There was a slight sound of the beatings of a drum from outside.

'Is anything happening today?' Rumi asked Amir.

'I do not know. Am I a *messiah* to know everything? Don't forget you are Assamese, and I am Assamese. We fear no one.'

'But my parents have come from Nepal,' Rumi said.

'Are we talking about your parents here?'

'No, I am Assamese,' Rumi said, telling Amir what Amir wanted to hear.

'What kind of government is this to schedule elections under such a strain?' Amir said.

'Are you afraid?' I interrupted and asked Amir. He kept staring at me. I knew I was being courageous. I was free of any kind of fear that day. 'Are you afraid, Amir?' I repeated my question. Rumi looked at the floor. She wasn't expecting me to address my *shauhar* by his name.

'You, *randi*, keep your mouth shut. You are a *panauti*. You brought me bad luck just like you did to your Abbu,' he fumed. I realized his reaction was the same whether I talked or didn't and that he was afraid of the situation. He wasn't an Assamese, just like me. But he had his name on the electoral list; I did not.

'Why do we hear drum rolls? I better go outside and check.' Rumi rushed outside.

Amir looked at me with anger. I looked back at him. His blue eyes were still attractive. I could still fall for them, but not when he opened his mouth. I was happy to see fear protruding from his eyes.

'What will happen, Amir? They will kidnap some women, and rape them-then the other side will do the same. Or insiders will kill some outsiders. Outsiders will kill some insiders. Then a politician will intervene and give a speech-supporting one side. Then, people will keep that anger inside them and use it to create more chaos. Don't you think this has been happening for the last four years?'

'SHUT UP, YOU *RANDI*. And how do you know this much? Who do you talk to? Your lover tells you this?'

'Why do you bother about my lover? You married another woman yourself.' For the first time in my life, I was confronting him about his second marriage. And I was relaxed. I was comfortable. No shaking of hands, legs, or voice. It felt so natural. But his face relaxes.

'You should be grateful I have not abandoned you. Otherwise, you will become a *randi* for a lifetime,' he laughed. I envied Amir with his cruel mind. He never felt guilt for whatever he did. He lived his life the way he wanted. He picked up his bag and went outside in a rush. I followed him, only to witness his silhouette. His tall neck and hair were as stubborn as he was. The hems of his long trousers were dipping in the mud on the road, but he was okay. He went to the fields one day like this and came home with Rumi. I could never have guessed what he was up to. I then looked at Dimi's house. She had been avoiding me for a month. We hardly spoke. I tried speaking with her, but she would say she was busy. She had work. She had to help her husband in his social work, she said. Why would she not talk to me? Why would she do that? If I were weak, she should help me become strong, so what was the point of abandoning me?

I could hear the drums loudly by then. I put the pan on the stove. The water started boiling. I added *chai* powder-a little extra that day-I liked strong *chai*. Then, I added sugar and ginger for a change. I think of the first morning after our marriage; Amir had made *chai* for me. That was a time when Amir was mine. The time when he said he loved me, when he was different, when he was better, when he wasn't himself. I liked that part of him. The one who didn't show his true self. The fake one. The masked one. That was better, far better than his original self.

The *chai* boiled, and I could see the grains of *chai* powder in the water and some grains of sugar that had not dissolved. The grated ginger showed itself along with *chai* powder. I smelled the *chai*. The fumes reminded me of the *chai* that I got on the day of our travel to Bharat. Rumi was sweating when she came back.

'What's happening, Rumi? Why do you look so pale?'

'As if you do not know,' she twisted her mouth.

'Rani,' I called. She looked at me with those almond-shaped eyes. And her enchanting smile. She showed me her teeth, all uniform.

'Yes, Ma.'

'Please come here for a moment.' I made her sit beside me, put my hand on her shoulder, and looked into her eyes. 'Are you alright?'

'Why do you ask, Ma?'

I looked at her ears. They had deceived her long ago. But she took good care of them by wearing earrings in them. Two earrings, one over the other. I held her close to me. She was uncomfortable, but she did not complain. With the beating of drums in the background, the *chai* boiling on the stove and Rani in my arms-I loved that moment.

'You are my favorite person in the world,' I whispered.

'Ma, please repeat what you said.' She was trying to squeeze onto my lap. I had wrapped both my arms around her. I kissed her ears and let her go.

'Don't go to Kopili today. Spend the day with me.'

Rumi smirked from the corner of the room, but rushed outside. Something was burning. Rani ran after her. I added milk to the pan and filtered the *chai* into two cups. I heard heavy footsteps outside. Everyone wanted to know where the smoke was coming from. I cleaned the stove. Rumi had made roti in the morning for Amir. The flour equivalent of one roti was lying on the floor. Instead of putting it back in the flour tin, I dusted it. My Agha was getting enough food, and Rani did not expect good food, or much food, for that matter. I was free of worries that day, and I gave credit to the beating of the drums. They gave me a sense of freedom.

I took a sip from my cup. I thought of Nadim. My *Bhai*. I remembered our talks in the front yard at Hakimpur. I remembered our mud house. I remembered our happy family. And most importantly, the green scarf. He never gave me that. I did not follow up, especially after my marriage. He got busy. I got busy. But his letters kept me alive in Bharat. They reminded me of Hakimpur and the peaceful life that we had there. His letters made me realize how important it is to have someone. Someone who loves you. I think of his thick joint eyebrows. That could be the reason he did not get a wife for himself. A smile appeared on my face.

The second sip took me back to the Brahmaputra. To the banks of that giant river. And she was smiling at me. Embracing me. And telling me that life was not that bad. I kept the cup down. I thought about Ammi, her smile, her beauty, her silence. I thought of Abbu, his posture, his talks, his beard. My parents. They loved me. Abbu and Ammi had cried when I chose Amir over them. I wondered whether words were more powerful or actions. Why did I expect them to talk with me and answer all my questions? Had

I misunderstood them? Judged them too? Why did I have too many expectations? Was Amir a punishment given to me by *Allah* because I did not respect Ammi and Abbu? Was Amir a reflection of my sins? I brushed off all those thoughts, got up, and stood at the door to look at Dimi's door. It was locked from the outside. The neighboring villages were burning. I could see that from my door, but my *chai* was waiting for me. I went back to my cup.

I took the third sip. I thought of Agha. I knew there was a stream of pure love for me, for Rani, beneath her selfish behaviour. She struggled to let Chandan go. She struggled to accept Mahesh. She struggled not to love me, not to think of me. She struggled to unsee Rani's sufferings. She loved us, after all. She was my daughter. My reflection. Rani came back home, panting.

'Ma, we have to leave. They are coming,' she said.

'Who?' I ask.

'Some angry people with axe in their hands,' she said.

'Come here, sit beside me. Have this *chai*.' I pulled her towards me.

'For me?'

'Yes.'

'Ma, we will have this after we come back. Come, let's go now.'

***

Rumi comes inside panting. 'WE HAVE TO RUN!' she screams. I hold Rani's hand and we leave the house. Dimi's door is still locked. *Where had she gone?* Rani is screaming behind me. People are screaming. Attackers are coming.

To do what? I do not know. But I see the first house in the row getting burnt. To burn the houses. My Rani is crying. We both hold our hands tight and start running. Running. Towards Kopili. Towards the daughter of Brahma. I stop beside a tree to tighten the drape around my waist. Rani is panting. She is already sweating. I see fear in her eyes as she witnesses the first arrow being shot at us. She hugs me tight. My Rani. I hold her hand and run through the rain of arrows to the Kopili. I want to cross the river and reach the other side. It is possible. I know swimming. I plan to take Rani on my back after reaching Kopili. People are running, howling. I cannot see Dimi and Chandan. I hope only that they are alright. I cannot see Rumi. I only hope Rumi is alright. Rani is delicate. The stones are hurting her, and her feet are bleeding. She is limping while running. Men and boys are crossing us. Some men are carrying babies and toddlers on their backs. They are running fast, faster than us. Attackers are running behind us with swords in their hands. I can see Kopili. I want to be there as quickly as possible. I am wondering if there is a *nauka* that Agha spoke about. I want to be there first, but I know men would beat me to it.

'Ma, I can't run anymore.'

'YOU HAVE TO!' I scold her. I see a man running behind us with a sword in his hand. I cover Rani behind me. He hit me on my hand. The blood spouts like a fountain. The man follows people who run inside the paddy fields and spares us. I hold the injury with another hand and Rani with the injured hand. I see my broken skin, my red flesh. Rumi wore the same-coloured dress when she came home as Amir's bride. But that scar is far deeper than this one.

The attackers are using slogans such as 'Long Live Assam'. They are even shouting, 'Outsiders have made insiders *Otithis* in their own land'. Did we? Did I? I wasn't sure. But I knew that Bharat had treated me well with a few friends like Dimi. When I see Kopili, I imagine my Agha sitting there thinking about Chandan. I regret not having made her marriage to Chandan happen. How could I? I am a failure in my choices. How could I decide for Agha? I could not. But she is happy now. The wind hits my face. The injury does not hurt anymore. Rani is running with me. We are close to Kopili.

There are speakers in the trees on the banks of the Kopili. Announcements. Women supporting attackers are declaring over a speaker-'We have time, don't come back'. These women have climbed the mango trees. Some of them are wearing *Kopou Phool* in their hair. I wonder how difficult it would be to climb this lovely tree. While I am descending the slope along with Rani to reach the water, I crush the already dead flowers. I feel bad. They are my favorites, even the dead ones. And the tree is modest. It bears such beautiful flowers but has no pride. The purple and white flowers, the green leaves, the grey bark, and the blue Kopili water in the background. This is a beauty that every *manush* should witness at least once in their lifetime. As soon as we enter Kopili, the blood from Rani's feet dissolves in the water. The water changes colour. I hold her close and kiss her cheek. 'We have time. Don't come back.' The voice. The voice is familiar. I turn around to see the faces of women in the trees. These women are supporting the attackers. I see the yellow saree and the blue chappal. Dimi.

'Dimi!' I scream. She looks at me and then looks away.

'What are you doing there?' I scream, my voice shaking. Attackers have started descending on Kopili.

'Ma, we have to go,' Rani begs me. I cannot stop looking at Dimi. Now she is looking at me. She has started crying, whimpering. She has joined her hands and says something. But I have to go. I take Rani on my back and dive in the water. I hear a splash of water behind me. Some men have jumped into the water to kill us. I am fast. I remember Nadim teaching me how to swim. I think of Sona. Her freedom. I think of Brahma. Her freedom. I reach the other side of the Kopili. I see Amir standing there with Rumi. She is crying inconsolably. I see a few men in the green uniform with them. I see my boys standing beside Amir. Sajid runs towards me, but Amir holds him back. Sajid is crying. He is thumping his foot on the ground. Rashid is crying, holding Rumi. I look back. Attackers are coming for us. Dimi has climbed down the tree and is standing on the other side of the Kopili, still crying with folded hands. That was my life. People who betrayed me are standing on both sides of this daughter of Brahma. Isn't that a coincidence that Brahma wants me to give in to her daughter? Am I not lucky that Brahma herself in the form of her daughter has come to pick me up? I wonder how my life will be from tomorrow. Living in the same house with Amir and Rumi. Seeing Dimi's face every day. Is that the life I want? I want to be in Hakimpur, in our little mud house. I want to go to my mother. My Ammi. I have a chance now to give in to Kopili. I walk to the water, towards the daughter of Brahma. The attackers are swimming towards me. But then they stop. They are probably not sure why I am getting in the river, staring at them. One of them puts his sword across my belly. The belly that has given birth to my kids. My beautiful

kids. And I hold the hand of one of those beautiful kids. I will
not let her go. I am not ready to leave her in the world. The
world is full of men in green uniforms — Amir, Dimi, and
Rumi. But what are the chances that Rani getting someone
like Mahesh? What are the chances that her Abbu, Amir,
would not beat her? Nil. She is safe only when she is with
me. I have not made any decisions since getting married, but
I am going to make a decision now. Rani will come with me.
There is another blow to my leg. I fall into the water; my
grip on Rani's hand is tighter than before. I will not let her
go. She is struggling, but I she must know that I am helping
her. I see someone running towards me with a stone in his
hand. To bash my head. Chandan. It is Chandan.

I close my eyes. I let my body feel the water, the Brahma. It
touches all my injuries. All my pain. I have sacrificed myself
to the river. To this water. The stone has fallen onto my
head. My tongue has come out. My legs, my belly, my hands,
and my head are cold. Rani has stopped moving, too. I sink
deep into the water. I still feel my grip on Rani's hand. I
touch the riverbed. Rani comes along with me. I lie down
peacefully. I wonder who will tell Nadim that I am dead
and that I am dead because I did not run away. That I am
different. That I am courageous. On the banks of Kopili, I
see the *Kopou Phool* bidding me goodbye. I am uninvited.
My time is over.

AGHA

EARLY 1983

It is 18th February today. Mother-in-law is on the veranda. Sitting in a chair in a cotton saree. Her *pallu* on her head. She is having *chai*. She sees Heena running. Mother-in-law screams as she sees the houses set on fire. And instead of running inside, she follows Heena. She runs after her. To stop her and tell her, *Don't worry! The Centre will take care of it.* Mahesh runs after her, but before going out, locks the door from the outside.

You will not come out at ANY COST! he says. I witness everything from the unopened window and a partially opened curtain. I see people running. I see people getting killed. Houses being set on fire. People screaming. Babies crying. Old people struggling. Men surpassing everyone else in the running race. From another window, I see paddy fields where people are giving up. They are getting killed-with axes, swords, arrows, stones. Everyone is unsafe. Men. Women. Kids. Mothers. Fathers. Sisters. Brothers. Grandmothers. grandfathers. I hear drums beating. Some people speak over the loud-speaker and encourage the attackers to be more aggressive. I am not in a position to say who is killing whom. That keeps me safe from the hurt that follows. I think of Mahesh and where he would be; I think of Mother-in-law. Should I cry out loud? Or should I assume they must be safe? I got up and kept the pan on the stove to make a cup of *chai* for myself.

***

After waiting for Mahesh and Mother-in-law for ten hours, I break the door using a pestle. Mahesh is not to be seen anywhere. There are camps set up to look after the injured. They are provided with tents and some basic groceries. Schools are used as hospitals. There are nurses and doctors running all around. There are announcements happening on the speaker to call a particular doctor or a nurse to a particular tent or a cot. Some women are whimpering. Some are crying. Some are just lying on the floor. Some men are smoking bidis. Some are complaining to the army and police about the attackers. The sky looks the same. The land is red. I see very few kids. I check for Mahesh and Mother-in-law in all the tents, all cots, and schools where the nursing services are operating. I turn the people around — injured, dead, missing limbs. I do not see him. I pick up the cut hands, legs, and heads. None of it belongs to him. *He is alive; I am sure.* I do not see Mother-in-law anywhere. She must be alive, too. Acting like a Lady at the Centre and helping people. Talking to them. Asking them *what happened and how it happened.*

I am walking, carrying Indu, who is crying. I did not feed her anything all day; I rush home to feed her. I walk towards the house. Again, crossing these tragic sights. The tents, the cots, the injured and the dead. My hands tremble; my legs shake. But I have to walk home, get my baby her food. I walk through the colony. Through the houses of Heena and Shobha. The houses are burnt. I see the utensils. I see the flour lying on the floor. I see the unfinished cups of *chai*, plates with *sabzi* and half-eaten roti. I see the *charpai*s inside the houses-broken and burnt. I see the paddy fields from where I am walking. People are still pulling bodies out of there. Most of them are without heads, hands, or legs. Most of them are women and kids. They could not run as fast as the men. I see now. I see why Mahesh was afraid. I see why Mother-in-law said she knows that something bad is coming our way.

My eyes are still searching for Mahesh and Mother-in-law. I will not cry. I have decided. They are just hiding somewhere. Or helping someone. I have reached home. Ours is intact. Touched by no one. I feed Indu. I bath her. I change into a better saree. I have to welcome Mahesh home. We are going to be a happy family again. A few drops of water come out of my eyes, but I wipe them away. No, no. No crying.

***

Does the world have more love or envy? I think it is actually like a pendulum. Some days envy, some days love. Love and envy cannot be together. I love Indu; I love Mahesh, and I love Mother-in-law. I envy the people who crossed the river, the bridge, and the paddy fields and saved their lives that day. But winning that race is going to haunt them forever.

Once, Mahesh told me he likes me in a saree and not in a salwar suit. I am wearing a new saree every day, thinking he will come home. But they do not. I cook food for both of them. I have come to the camps again to see the Lady at the Centre. She visits us after four days. She has come by airplane. I want to sit in the airplane, after I find Mahesh and Mother-in-law. The Lady at the Centre is wearing glasses. I like her glasses. She is touching the pallu of her saree to her cheeks. People are asking her questions. Some are touching her feet. Some are crying, whimpering. But I like Mother-in-law more than her in the similar getup. I know Mother-in-law would come to see her. But she does not. Mahesh comes neither. I wonder where they must be hiding and why they would be hiding. The winter is chilling, but it does not seem that cold in the camps. There are many people, and their body heat is making the surroundings comfortable. But their situation is worse. They are living in tents. Cooking their food on the *chullahs*. Most people are without families. The rest are dead. Unlike mine. My family is hiding, playing games with me. I am going to scold Mother-in-law when she is back. And I will not talk with Mahesh when he is back. I walk back. To my house. I have to cook dinner. It is difficult to look after a baby and cook together. Indu is missing Mother-in-law and Mahesh. Indu is sleepy. She is quiet. I walk in silence. I feel something on the ground. A bracelet. Mahesh's bracelet. I pick it up. It is covered in blood, dried blood now. *How did it come off? Someone cut across his wrist, and it fell.* I walk two steps further. I see Mother-in-law's glasses, broken, covered in blood. *Someone must have hit her on the head.* I cannot walk. My legs are heavy. Indu is sleeping. I sit on the ground, my legs crossed. I put Indu on my lap. I hold the bracelet and the glasses in my hands. *I have to stop fooling myself.* I feel my stomach, empty since Mahesh locked me in, contracting until it touches my back. I feel a big, heavy thing inside my chest. It is hurting. I have to get it out. I open my mouth wide. I close my eyes. I scream. I shriek. I cry. I cry until my head hurts. Indu wakes up and cries. We cry together. With hurting eyes, a hurting body, a hurting soul, I see the *Kopou Phool* and a blurred road. A road that goes to Guwahati!

FAMILY TREE

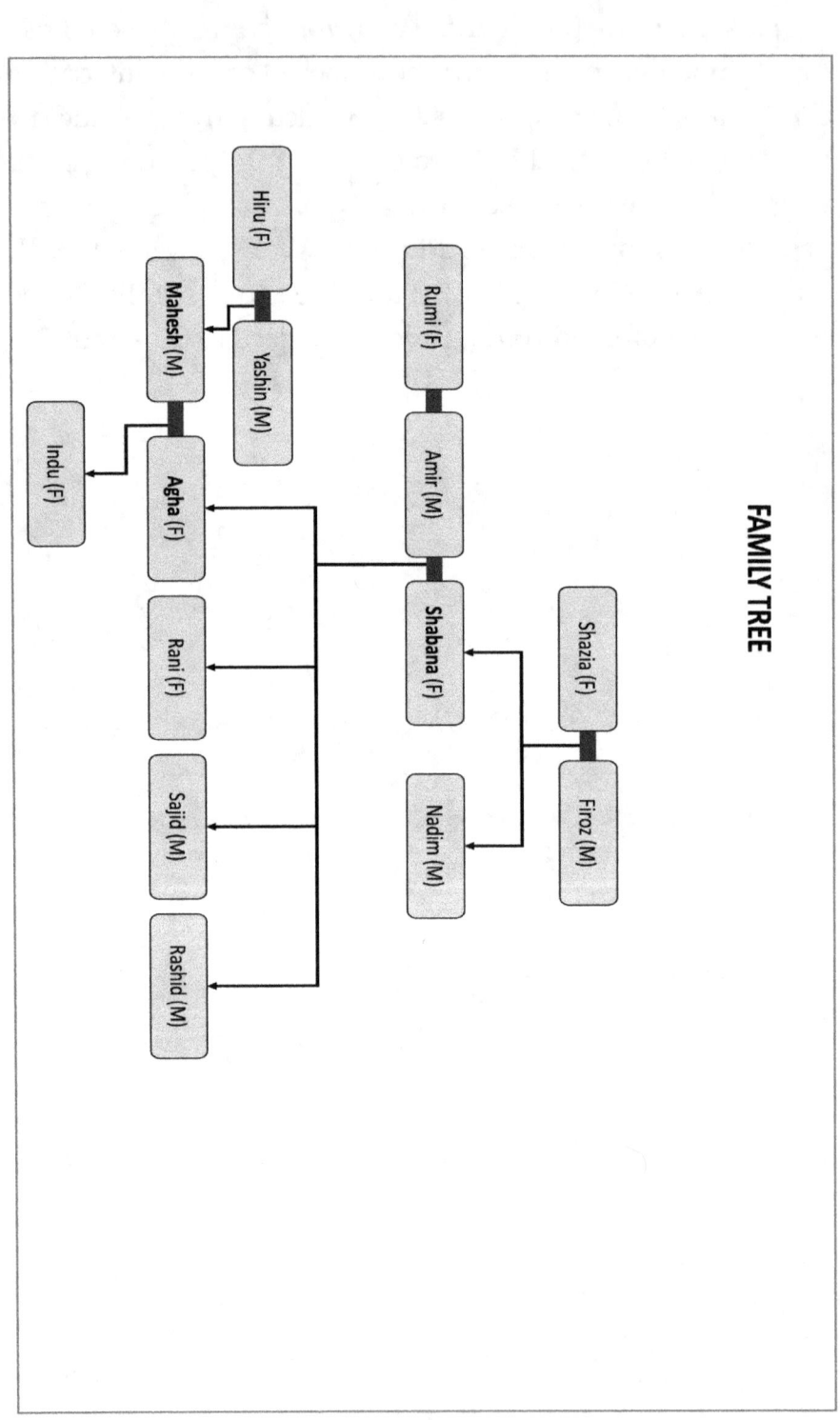

References

The Wildflower of Assam is shaped by extensive research (field as well as print/online resources) of certain events, places, and culture. This is a work of fiction; however, certain situations are shaped by real-world influences. Below are key references and inspirations:

The Nellie Massacre of 1983: Agency of Rioters by Makiko Kimura. Sage Publications, 2013.

India Against Itself: Assam and the Politics of Nationality by Sanjib Baruah. University of Pennsylvania Press, 1999.

Assam: The Accord, The Discord by Sangeeta Barooah Pisharoty. Context/Westland, 2019.

Rites of Passage: Border Crossings, Imagined Homelands, India's East and Bangladesh by Sanjoy Hazarika. Penguin Books India, 2000.

Numerous online resources, journal articles, and archived newspaper clippings from the 1980s and 1990s were also referred to during the research process. Interviews and conversations with residents of Assam were conducted between December 2022 and December 2024.

Credits

First and foremost, I offer my heartfelt gratitude to Lord Shiva. It is only by His grace that I had the strength, mentally and emotionally, to manage all that life demanded while working on this book. His presence has been a quiet source of peace, balance and clarity throughout. I feel His hand resting gently on my head, guiding me, and I pray I may always be able to say this for the rest of my life.

To my late father, who always believed in me. Your trust continues to guide me. Even in your absence, I feel your blessings every day. I hope you are proud!

To my mother, thank you for your constant support and silent strength. You have always stood by me without asking for anything in return, and that selfless love means everything.

To my father-in-law, I'm truly grateful for your openness and for the thoughtful conversations about my drafts. Your encouragement gave me confidence to keep going.

To my two sisters, thank you for always being there in your own special way: emotionally present, full of unsolicited advice, and always just a phone call away. Your love and humour kept me grounded, and I wouldn't have made it through without your perfectly timed distractions, endless banter, and wisdom far beyond your years.

And finally, to my husband for bravely enduring my mood swings, endless edits, daily complaints, and unfiltered, expert-level opinions. You handled it all with the patience of a monk, the survival instincts of a married man, and the grace of someone who knows escape is not an option. You truly deserve a lasting recognition! Most of all, thank you for not running away and for loving me through it all. I am fortunate to have you!

About the
Author

Gayatri Sarkar, a computer engineer, is based in Brisbane, Australia. Born and raised in Pune, Maharashtra, India, she has contributed short stories to several acclaimed anthologies, including *Perfect Vision* (2020), *Delete Log Off Shut Down Corruption* (2018), and *Soul's Sojourn* (2017).

In addition to her anthology work, she has maintained a couple of blogs and written for a number of journals and magazines, exploring themes of identity, social change, and personal resilience.

She is also an Oxford alumna, holding a Creative Writing diploma from Oxford University with merit (2023).

www.ingramcontent.com/pod-product-compliance
Lightning Source LLC
Chambersburg PA
CBHW060856250626
47159CB00008B/2763